THE CASTLE *of*

INDOLENCE

Thomas M. Disch: A Brief Bibliography

NOVELS

The Genocides (1965)
The Puppies of Terra (1966)
Echo Round His Bones (1967)
Black Alice (with John Sladek; 1968)
Camp Concentration (1968)
334 (1972)
Clara Reeve (as "Leonie Hargrave"; 1975)
On Wings of Song (1979)
Neighboring Lives (with Charles Naylor; 1981)
The Businessman: A Tale of Terror (1984)
The M.D.: A Horror Story (1991)
The Priest: A Gothic Romance (1994)

SHORT STORY COLLECTIONS

102 H-Bombs (1967)
Fun with Your New Head (1968)
Getting into Death (1976)
Fundamental Disch (1980)
The Man Who Had No Idea (1982)

POETRY

The Right Way to Figure Plumbing (1972)
ABCDEFG HIJKLM NOPQRST UVWXYZ (1981)
Burn This (1982)
Orders of the Retina (1982)
Here I Am, There You Are, Where Were We (1984)
Yes, Let's: New and Selected Poems (1989)
Dark Verses and Light (1991)

CRITICISM

The Castle of Indolence: On Poetry, Poets, and Poetasters

THE CASTLE *of*
INDOLENCE

On Poetry, Poets, and Poetasters

THOMAS M. DISCH

Picador USA
New York

For Robert McDowell,
who asked for it

Production Editor: David Stanford Burr

Design: Junie Lee

Library of Congress Cataloging-in-Publication Data

Disch, Thomas M.
        The castle of indolence : on poetry, poets, and
poetasters / Thomas M. Disch.
                p.   cm.
        ISBN 0-312-13448-7 (trade cloth)
        1. American poetry—20th century—History and
criticism.   2. English poetry—20th century—History
and criticism.   3. Poetics.   I. Title.
PS323.5.D57   1995
811'.502—dc20   95-22811
                                                   CIP

First Picador USA Edition: September 1995

10   9   8   7   6   5   4   3   2   1

CONTENTS

Their only labour was to kill the time;
And labour dire it is, and weary woe.
They sit, they loll, turn o'er some idle rhyme;
Then, rising sudden, to the glass they go,
Or saunter forth, with tottering step and slow.
This soon too rude an exercise they find;
Straight on the couch their limbs again they throw.
Where hours and hours they sighing lie reclined,
And court the vapoury god soft-breathing in the wind.

— James Thomson
The Castle of Indolence

ACKNOWLEDGMENTS

The essays in this book first appeared in the following publications:

Boulevard: Death and the Poet

Foundation [UK]: The New World

Hudson Review: The Castle of Indolence; Poetry Roundup

L.A. Times: Pompes Postmoderne; The High Priest of High Times

The Nation: Music That Can Deepest Reach; Barroom Buddy and Prom King; Products of the Workshop

New Criterion: Delectable Always, and Fresh and True

Parnassus: The Difference; Onegin's Children

Poetry: The Occasion of the Poem; Having an Oeuvre; Christopher Fry: An Appreciation

Times Literary Supplement [UK]: Sound of the Raine, Prophetic Word; A Nashional Institution

Washington Post Book World: Fearing, and Falling Out of Love; Sunlight, Coffee, and the Papers; History, the Home Movie; Snapped Prose in Slim Volumes; Poets as Friends and Neighbors; Poets of Exile; Out of the Murk Plectrum; The Last Word on Death; Light Verse

I

THE CASTLE OF INDOLENCE

FOR MOST READERS, from those of highest brow to out-and-out bib-
liobulimics, contemporary poetry might as well not exist. They don't
read it and are not curious about it. These same readers might well
have a fair amount of poetry on their bookshelves, ranging from
translations of Homer and Dante to the last generation of high mod-
ernists—Bishop, Berryman, Lowell. There might be a copy of the
City Lights edition of *Howl,* and something by Sylvia Plath. Poets
who have endorsed the public's estimate of their art by their own
suicides, after long threatening such a stroke of poetic justice in their
writing, generally seem to have made the most significant dent on
the Collective Consciousness.

That poetry has lost most of its audience and much of its cachet
is not an original observation. In 1988 Joseph Epstein published an
essay in *Commentary,* "Who Killed Poetry?," in which he expressed
his across-the-board dismay at the condition of the art he'd once loved,
but which seemed now esthetically impoverished and unworthy of
serious intellectual attention. He blamed the system of creative writing
programs for fostering a closed-shop mentality among poets. In 1991
Dana Gioia's "Can Poetry Matter?" appeared in *The Atlantic,* ruffling
many of the same feathers within the poetry subculture.

Gioia is a poet himself, who reads and reviews widely. As a critic, he has been a fervent champion of many of his peers. Poetry clearly does matter for him. Yet his essay was even more damning than Epstein's, being based on a real familiarity with the work that Epstein had dismissed, unread, as being unreadable. Gioia cites the 1985 *Morrow Anthology of Younger American Poets* as a symptomatic example of the system at work. "Running nearly 800 pages, the volume presents no fewer than 104 important young poets, virtually all of whom teach creative writing." A capable bibliographer might well ferret out 104 other recent anthologies published in the last two decades, all assembled on the same editorial principle that governs the Morrow anthology (according to Gioia): the need for authentifying publication, a need that the poets in universities now share with other academics if they are to win tenure.

That most poets should be anxious to publish their poems, and that mediocre poets should feel a special anxiety in this regard, is not to be wondered at. When not only one's reputation but one's salary is at stake, the ante is upped exponentially, and all the decorums of publishing, reviewing, and valorizing poetry reflect the wagon-circling wariness of poetry professionals. It is thought bad form to review one's peers other than applausively. Many poets, therefore, refuse the task of reviewing altogether, or else make it known beforehand that they will only review books they are certain they can praise.

Prize-giving and related perks are administered in the manner of children's birthday parties, so that no poet must leave the party empty-handed. In England, laureates are laureates for life. In America, there is a new laureate each year—not only nationally, but state by state. Laurels, after all, are cheap. Even so, it is a rare poet who doesn't glory in his garlands in public like a Ruritanian generalissimo. In a recent press release from the Academy of American Poets, the three judges of the Lenore Marshall Poetry Prize are to be seen sporting no less than twelve awards and fellowships among themselves, "including," the release notes of the jury's chair, "the Bernard F. Conners Award from *The Paris Review* and Melville Cane Award from the Poetry Society of America." I would wager that the juries for *those* awards, the enablers of their fellowships, and the poets who commended them to the university writing programs that employ them are all as liberally belaureled.

Theoretically—and, indeed, empirically—a case can be made that there ought to be more first-class poets at the present than in earlier centuries. There are, after all, many more people, and more of them receive an education that could expose them to the possibility of poetry. There are all those workshops, throughout the country, which every year award diplomas to a new cohort of MFAs, among whom some significant percentage should have what it takes.

Whether or not workshops are, in fact, the most fertile grounds for the breeding of good poetry, I think that the twentieth century has produced a bumper crop of excellent to world-class poets in America, and that if one were to compile an equivalent anthology of their best poems as judiciously comprehensive as that which John Hollander selected for the Library of America's anthology of nineteenth-century American poetry, it might well extend to seven or eight volumes as bulky as Hollander's pair. Not a few of this little multitude might be poets even now entering their prime. But—here I share Epstein's misgivings—I think the great preponderance of the best poetry of this century was written before our present laureate (Rita Dove, born in 1952) had indited her first poem to paper.

And for this simple reason—that the workshops, which have a monopoly on the training of poets, encourage indolence, incompetence, smugness, and—most perniciously—that sense of victimization and special entitlement that poets have now come to share with other artists who depend on government or institutional patronage to sustain their art, pay their salaries, and provide free vacations.

Let me deal with these in order. Laziness is, on the whole, not a bad thing for poets. Some of the best—Emerson, Whitman—have gloried in their indolence, from a Zenlike sense that good poems as often have their source in a chance encounter with a songbird as from the diligent pursuit of epic significance. Idle hands can be the Muse's workshop, as well as the Devil's. The pillowy borderland between our dreams and our daily routines can be a marvelously fertile soil for poetry.

James Thomson, who wrote the mock epic whose title I have here purloined for my own use, commends the "pleasing land of drowsyhead" both for its genial, noncompetitive ambience—

> Here naught but candour reigns, indulgent ease,
> Good-natured lounging, sauntering up and down:
> They who are pleased themselves must always please;
> On others' ways they never squint a frown.

and for its spiritual benefits—

> The best of men have ever loved repose:
> They hate to mingle in the filthy fray;
> Where the soul sours, and gradual rancour grows,
> Imbittered more from peevish day to day.

Thomson was being playful in these verses, but not sarcastic. His allegorical castle is a group portrait of his own circle of friends and fellow poets. In one stanza Thomson portrays himself as the arch-layabout:

> A bard here dwelt, more fat than bard beseems;
> Who, void of envy, guile, and lust of gain,
> On virtue still, and nature's pleasing themes,
> Poured forth his unpremeditated strain. . . .

Later, in another celebration of the spirit of Lazy Fair, Shelley echoes Thomson, in praising the blithe skylark that pours out his heart "In profuse strains of unpremeditated art." From Shelley it is but a stone's skip across the Atlantic to Emerson, with his lavish praise of the Aeolian Harp (celebrated in Thomson's poem, as well), that trope for the poet's responsive soul—and infallible first drafts.

And truly, there is no other form of writing that *feels* so good as a lyric poem as it gushes forth in a steady flow. If that metaphor rubs you the wrong way; if you would at once insist that poetry is

Hard Work and not a luxury product for intellectual sybarites; if poetry suggests to you rather the possibility of a Seriousness higher than prose rather than the possibility of sheer music—then nature did not intend you for a poet.

All this praise of laziness and going with the flow comes with one large proviso: the soil must have been prepared, the harp tuned, the fingers schooled. Then careless raptures may sound more like Liszt than listlessness. It should also be noted that the laziness of genius may seem, at lower altitudes, a great deal like exertion. George Eliot, for entertainment in her declining years, liked to read aloud from Dante. Auden vacationed in Iceland and learned the language in the spirit of an intellectual alpinist. It was there, so why not climb it? For such spirits, schools are superfluous.

This is not an argument for shutting down all poetry workshops and bankrupting the industry, since the object of those workshops—especially at an undergraduate level—has never been to produce a greater abundance of professional poets for the world to ignore. The workshops have a humbler mission, one not unlike university sports departments: they promote a sense of confidence and self-esteem. Playing football or basketball can be a source of great personal satisfaction, providing one is matched against players of comparable incompetence; so, too, with poetry. The workshops can't make Miltons out of the tin-eared, but they can instill those simple skills of impassioned self-expression that once were learned in classes of Rhetoric and Elocution—skills that should be cultivated by anyone with a sense that a gift of gab might be his or her meal ticket: teachers, ministers, salesmen, anchorwomen, and all other would-be retainers of the Castle of Indolence.

Beyond that, the workshops often allow students to get a high grade with minimum exertion. What better way to compensate for the demands of Organic Chemistry than to twang the lyre? Few teachers give grades lower than B's so long as one produces the negligible amount of work required. The reading burden is minimal, and there are no finals. Further, the actual classes tend to be entertaining, since most workshop instructors are skilled flaneurs, and many even possess the gifts of astrologers and tarot readers, who, from the evidences of a few cards on the table, can flatter their guileless customers into the delusion that they really might be poets.

With all this going for them, the poetry workshops can hold their own against most of the competing liberal arts departments and are in no grave danger of being disestablished, especially at a time when Theory has taken over graduate English departments, where it was once possible to study poetry in a serious way.

But what if one actually wants to learn to write poetry? There the workshops will offer little assistance. For the work that a neophyte poet must set his mind to is often tiresome and even demeaning. Most of the great English poets learned their craft in the course of studying Latin and Greek, and translating their hexameters and dithyrambs into a semblance of English verse. The object of their study was never to produce poetry but to subject impressionable minds to the most rigorous discipline then imaginable. A punishment as cruel then as now it is unusual—but it worked. At least, in those cases which we have record of, in the annals of English poetry, up to and including Auden.

Contrast to this what a workshop instructor is likely to encounter among today's students. No Latin, no Greek, and probably no other foreign language in working order. (I have only high-school Latin, crossword puzzle Greek, and my command of other modern languages is at hunt-and-peck level, so I don't speak from any loftier vantage point.) That is to say, no sense of language as an alien, mysterious, and yet systematic entity. No sense of grammar or syntax that is not sheer intuition. No sense of the history embedded in their own tongue. Even in their own language they will have read only a smattering of its classics, and they will have been taught to dismiss most of that as fusty, patristic, and irrelevant—postcards from Tintern Abbey.

Concerning "Tintern Abbey," the poem, an academic theorist named Marjorie Levinson has written (*South Atlantic Quarterly,* Volume 88, 1989) that "the literatures of the past, if left to themselves, confront us as despotic structures," which are best dealt with by reading them "tendentiously—for ourselves." Reading "Tintern Abbey" in this spirit, she faults Wordsworth for ignoring the beggars in the neighborhood of the ruined Abbey, whom she, with the hindsight of nearly two centuries, now rescues from Wordsworth's marginalization. In hypothesizing these ideal Victorian victims, homeless yet within the shadow of a great poem, Levinson uses a familiar ploy of theorists, setting against the actual body of literature the eloquent silences of various huddled masses whom history has scanted. The record of the past becomes a chorus of Baskerville hounds, significant for their not barking. Justice is done, while at the same time drastically simplifying the curriculum. Why bother with dead white males when there are so many living poets who share Levinson's more enlightened sense of the world they so systematically misrepresented?

In this devaluation of the past, academic theorists offer aid and comfort to the indolence of the workshops, where the poetry that is studied is, by and large, the poetry that is written there—by fellow students, by their instructors, and by those with whom their instructors network, poets visiting to give a reading. This is only natural, from a careerist point of view. Those who are not in the workshops just for an easy credit must soon acquire a sense of what is expected of a poet at entry level, and that is what the workshops teach. If that amounts to mediocrity, so much the better. Mediocrity is easier to emulate than excellence, which is usually, sad to say, inimitable.

So much for *laziness* and its twin brother, *incompetence,* along with it. The *smugness* of such poets, unschooled and unskilled, is the fruit of their parochial existence, where the talk is mostly of friends and family, the weather, and how one is feeling today. Unread by any but their friends and unchastened by any kind of criticism, the poets of the workshops can take themselves at their own, always high, estimation. When another estimation shatters their solitude, their astonishment is equal to their indignation. Being accredited poets, they know themselves to be above reproach: their hearts are pure, and they wear them on their sleeves. For if the workshops have taught them nothing else (which is usually the case), they do know that if they have written what they really, really feel, it's poetry and, as such, beyond odious comparisons.

Poetry workshops often serve as a kind of group therapy of the sort that promotes empowerment, with lots of hugs for those assembled and a chance to berate the group's enemies. The rhetorical strategy favored by the newly empowered is usually shouting, and its poetic equivalent, rant. Ginsberg's popularity among neophyte poets is due to his being an accomplished ranter, poetry's own Axl Rose, someone who is willing to let it all hang out.

Apprentice poets, once they've developed sufficient self-esteem, quickly graduate to self-reverence—a tendency that has its complement in the self-protective contempt that adolescents feel for the oppressive vistas of history and the intricate machineries of the world they never made.

The most benign form of smugness is that which dotes upon family snapshots. If there's nothing else happening in one's life, there are always births to be celebrated, deaths to be mourned, spouses to cherish, and skeletons to be exhumed from closets. Now, it would be a peculiar poet who *never* adverted to his or her Significant Others in his verse; who did not, indeed, often feel it incumbent to do so. But in the workshops (and not the poetry workshops alone) this theme has become all-pervasive. "Write what you know," the students are told, and what else do they know? Where else have they been, usually, except at home or at school? If their aim is to graduate directly into the professoriate and if they succeed, they may preserve their inexperience intact well into middle age or beyond, and they will write, as well or ill as their talents admit, about their domesticities.

A large life is by no means a guarantor of large poetry. Between the antipodes of a war correspondent-cum-poet like James Fenton and a recluse like Emily Dickinson the spectrum of first-rate poets is continuous, but even the quietest and most cloistered poet can, with Pegasus assisting, adventure over a broader imaginative terrain than the family chroniclers of the workshops. This being said, experience of the wider world does tend to affect poets like Miracle-Gro. Witness all the poems that get written on vacation—not necessarily because the poet has more leisure, but because he is being bombarded with new information. Poets ritually deplore the world being too much with us, the getting and the spending, the commuter trains, the crowd of workers flowing over London Bridge. But work is not necessarily stultifying. It may, indeed, be so stimulating that the poet neglects his Muse altogether. If Cromwell's Commonwealth had lasted longer and continued to employ Milton's services, *Paradise Lost* might never have been written. But this is not the received wisdom of the workshops with regard to other work than their own. Menial jobs may be admitted on a poet's CV as a token of what youth may have to suffer before it is granted tenure, but conspicuous success in another career than poetry is considered bad form, for smugness is the mother of envy.

And so we come to the lowest bolgia in the Dis of American poetry, where the damned are eternally tormented by their *sense of entitlement,* which whispers to the poets, even as it chews them up: "You deserve *better* than this. You are poets, descended from Homer and Shakespeare and Sylvia Plath, and as such superior to drudging novelists or the hacks of Hollywood. Yet do you enjoy an equivalent reward? The fame, the royalties, the readership? No! You have been *marginalized* by an Industry that respects nothing but the Bottom Line and the Almighty Dollar."

This is surely true, in part. Commercial publishing houses have realized that there is little to be gained, even of prestige, by accommodating the needs of poets. The books don't sell, and poets have become scruffier, so that their slim volumes have come to have less and less cachet in all but the academic marketplace, where an anthology edited by well-connected editors can still pay its way by being marketed as a required textbook. More and more, poets must rely on those publishing houses funded by nonprofit foundations and tax dollars, and this at a time when there are more and more poets, all of them acutely conscious of the injustice being done.

The dilemma may be faced in two ways. It may be lamented, and it is, often by those very poets who, by virtue of talent, luck, or social advantage, are still published by mainstream publishers. Or, like other irremediable misfortunes, it may be denied.

Usually, lamentation and denial operate in tandem, as they do in a review that recently appeared in *The Kenyon Review* (Volume

XVI, Number 3, 1994) of Florence Howe's anthology, *No More Masks!
An Anthology of Twentieth-Century American Woman Poets*. The reviewer, Adrian Oktenberg, begins on a triumphalist note:

> In the last twenty years, the feminist movement and
> the parallel emergence of feminist poetry, together with
> similar political movements and poetries of people of color
> and gays and lesbians, have utterly changed the landscape
> of American poetry. These movements have coalesced
> with such speed and force that mainstream critical and
> literary journals are still catching up with them, and re-
> main at the beginning in understanding the changes they
> have forced. What is considered "appropriate" for a poem,
> particularly one by a woman writer—the range of subject
> matter, language, the point of view allowed or expected—
> has changed to an extent almost unimaginable twenty
> years ago. We have new subject matters for poetry now,
> new languages to use in making poems. . . .

Oktenberg then provides a brief bibliography of the twenty years since
the first edition of *No More Masks!* appeared, cataloging at some
length not only the first publications of the anthology's more illustri-
ous contributors but the year in which they became important. Then,
still in a celebratory mode, she continues:

> . . . Women have begun to say more fully who we are,
> what we want, how we feel, and to publish it. And be-
> cause poetry has never been a luxury to women or to other
> marginalized or oppressed groups, women poets find
> numbers of willing and eager readers. The critical atten-
> tion that changes the canon has followed: some poets (Ad-
> rienne Rich, Audre Lorde, Rita Dove, Louise Glück,
> others) are being admitted to the canon, taught, antholo-
> gized, prized. Women's poetry has been and is a stunning
> success.

There is a *however,* and it constitutes most of the review, which, while accepting all Howe's selectees as meriting admission to the club, nevertheless is distressed at her admissions policy:

> . . . Howe does say in her introduction that, in order to be included, a poet had to have published at least two books. This rule is by itself a mistake. . . . It permits the omission of genius. . . . [T]he *feminist* anthology ought to recognize that the two-book rule would tend to penalize working class or poor writers, women of color, younger and older writers, lesbians, and so on. . . .

Is that classic, or what? Oktenberg goes on to list no less than thirty-six omitted geniuses unjustly excluded by the two-book rule. Feminists are, admittedly, under a disadvantage, having to bear a chip on their shoulders for over half of the human race. A gay or black or Mormon or Asian-American complainant might not have to cite so many contenders for the laurels of twentieth-century greatness.

But they might. For, in the absence of critical standards, all poets are equal. Oktenberg hasn't a bad word to say about anybody. They are women, they are poets, they are strong. In the poetry establishment, as presently constituted, everyone gets a hug, and expects to get a Guggenheim. One might take exception to poets of the wrong persuasion, as feminists do, categorically, to Ted Hughes, that fatal spouse, but on the whole it is impolitic to speak ill of poets, unless they are safely outside the pale.

In its ideal version, as reedited by Adrian Oktenberg, *No More Masks!* would probably bear a strong resemblance to the *Morrow Anthology of Younger American Poets,* except that there would be no men in it and there would have to be enough poems by poets of established reputation so that all the no-longer-omitted geniuses could bask in the reflected glory. Whether such a large proportion of the contributors would also be teachers of creative writing as in the Morrow anthology I have no way of knowing, but if there were such an imbalance, surely those presently lacking such employment would be speeded on their way to that happy condition by inclusion in any anthology that authenticated each of them as a "Twentieth-Century American Woman Poet." What other purpose, after all, is to be served by publishing anthologies?

It is a cruel dilemma. There are so many more poets than there are workshops to employ them, despite the best efforts of the industry. Unemployed poets might be heartened to know that they share this postindustrial fate with nuclear physicists, assembly line workers, actors, and cosmetologists. In all these fields the supply of contestants vastly exceeds the supply of prizes.

For education, like steel and music, is an industry, and the object of any industry must be to attract enough customers to keep the workforce occupied. The customers of the education industry are people needing jobs. Poetry has become one of the jobs.

Is there no remedy?

As well ask, Is there a problem?

To both questions I would answer, probably not.

Fame and fortune are capricious; resentment is forever, until the resentful fall silent and are forgotten (or are marginalized). Omitted geniuses either come into their own in the fullness of time or join the ranks of mute, inglorious Miltons. It's a crapshoot. And none of this has much relation to the *experience* of poetry. Keats was knocked out when he came upon (of all things) Chapman's Homer. I have a sincere regard for the antigenius of the Scottish bard MacGonaghal. We both might be wrong.

But I equivocate. For I do believe there is a remedy, and that is the disestablishment of poetry workshops as an academic institution. (Yes, I know, I said just the opposite above, but I was wrong.) The art of poetry is poorly served by its bureaucratization, and only the trade is advanced. I will even venture a prophecy (which is the prerogative of poets, if not of critics)—that they will, in my own lifetime, self-destruct. Not because Jesse Helms, or his like, mandates a holy war against the poets funded by the NEA, but because students, wiser than their teachers, choose other electives.

II

SOUND OF THE RAINE, PROPHETIC WORD

Collected Poems 1935–1980
by Kathleen Raine
GEORGE ALLEN & UNWIN £10.95 312 PP.

BEFORE A FULLY developed bicameral theory had politicized the brain into an antithetical left and right, poetry had long been living on the same uneasy terms of cohabitation with two hearts in its single breast. Corresponding to the left, language-dominant hemisphere of the brain is an Augustan rhetoric of lucidity and wit; opposed to it is a deep romantic chasm wherein Ossian sings inspired odes concerning his oceanic feelings. The two hemispheres must connect, the two hearts cohabit, for poetry (which is, willy-nilly, written in language) to result, but such is the lure of partisan politics that poets prefer to live (or to pretend they do) in a state of permanent insurrection and defiance, each lobe hurling its manifestoes and *j'accuses* at the other.

Thus Kathleen Raine writes, in a recent letter to the editor of *New Departures* (printed in its "Poetry Olympics" issue):

> ... I do believe, as you do, that the world can be saved— or that human beings can be saved from the world—only by Imagination, which ... is the expression of our true humanity.... But we live in a world of materialism.... What can poetry—the language of the immortal human

spirit, which Blake calls the Imagination and identifies with the Christian Logos itself . . . mean in a society which denies this spirit by its very definition? . . . Thus the very name of "poetry" has been usurped and manipulated, and the true essential of all the arts suppressed or merely lost sight of in a welter of so-called "self-expression" whether of the sentimental or nihilist kind.

Meanwhile, in the other hemisphere, other epithets are launched into the smoky air of battle:

> We cannot end like Dante on the stars
> Until we view them with the saintly gaze
> Of humble men acknowledging our knowledge
> Of nothing. Though we pretend to walk on Mars
> With its proposed canals, Platonic cities
> And supermen, while in the grip of art
> As Weltanschauung, we show that we have failed
> To cross the natural void. Secure on earth,
> The time of pure belief, its spirit spent,
> Tired, hysterical, diffuse, and vain,
> Beseeches such as Freud for sympathy
> And is rejected. . . .
>
> from *Essay on Rime*
> Karl Shapiro

Doubtless it is unfair to judge poets by their manifestoes and letters-to-editors. At such times they tend to look, like other ideologists, all too human and self-serving. A theory of poetry that yields clear demarcations between an upright Us and an opprobrious Them can easily evolve into a lonelier and less persuasive opposition of Me and All You Rabble. So it was with Laura Riding, and so (on the evidence, chiefly, of her three volumes of autobiography) it often threatens to become with Kathleen Raine. Yet Riding produced a body of poems that merits admiration, and Raine's oeuvre is, to my mind, even more considerable. One must consider it, however, apart from her own special pleading.

The most immediately appealing feature of her work, evident in even the earliest of her poems, is its sheer lyric loveliness. Loveliness does not stand high these days in the vocabulary of critical praise, but one only need stroll among spring flowers to be reminded that it does, verily, exist, and can't easily be called by any other name. Consider these lines from Raine's early collection, *The Pythoness* (1948):

> Primrose, anemone, bluebell, moss
> Grow in the kingdom of the cross
> And the ash-tree's purple bud
> Dresses the spear that sheds his blood
>
> from "Lenten Flowers"

Or this mini-theory of lyrical evolution, from the first poem in the collection:

> Stone into man must grow, the human word
> carved by our whispers in the passing air
> is the authentic utterance of cloud,
> the speech of flowing water, blowing wind,
> of silver moon and stunted juniper.
>
> from "Night in Martindale"

There is not a syllable in any of those lines that Christina Rossetti would not have coveted for her own Collected Poems. They have the impersonal, overdetermined, instantly memorable ring of one of Palgrave's redolent Golden Oldies, those poems that transcend mere prosody and issue directly into song. This is not the least of poetic ambitions, but in its nature it invites readerly much more than critical attention, since critics can do little more in such cases than to point out how the sounds are heaped up and sewn together, a process the ear has already perfectly assimilated.

This is not to say that Raine has no subject of greater moment than spring flowers or that one need not heed what "the speech of flowing water" is actually flowing on about. Raine has two grand themes, two bardic purposes, on which she discourses with a persistence that makes most other poets seem mere ramblers, motes in the breeze of any passing meaning. The first of these is the fusion, in the furnace of the "*Sophia Perennis*" of world and self into a transcendental unity, an ambition figured forth in the opening lines of what may be her noblest single poem, "The Hollow Hill":

> Outside, sun, frost, wind, rain,
> Lichen, grass-root, bird-claw, scoring thorn
> Wear away the stone that seals the tomb,
> Erode the labyrinth inscribed in the stone,
> Emblem of world and its unwinding
> And inwinding volutions of the brain.
> On the door out of the world the dead have left this sigh.

The second theme is a corollary and precondition to the first:

> A Gaelic bard they praise who in fourteen adjectives
> Named the one indivisible soul of his glen....
>
> from "Eileann Chanaidh"

One is grateful to that Gaelic bard for welcoming a rabble of adjectives to the one and indivisible, for without some spice of variety the loftiest wisdom will come to sound received rather than perennial. The chief occupational hazard of oracles is a tendency to stumble into hollows and to mumble riddles that can't be answered:

> Would not some essence pass, some chord
> Tremble into the harmony of the spheres,
> Lingering overtone of the remembered music that was
> ours?
>
> from *On a Deserted Shore*

> Beyond the looming dangerous end of night
> Beneath the vaults of fear do his bones lie,

> And does the maze of nightmare lead to the power
> within?
> The menacing nether waters cover the fish king?
>
> from "Isis Wanderer"

If this is the price a reader must pay for sublimity (and Raine is nothing if not sublime), so be it. Such spirit-trumpetings and wafting of the ectoplasm are rare, in any case, and the moments of Delphic authority vastly preponderate.

Whether, the oracle having been delivered, we are bound literally to believe it—there's the rub. Even Raine in a rare latitudinarian moment will allow that ". . . the song makes the singer wise, / But only while he sings." ("Eileann Chanaidh") The point of prophetic utterance—at least for those who do not attend to it as catechumens—is not so much truth as a condition of inward authority (call it "star quality") that commands unquestioning respect:

> To those who speak to the many deaf ears attend.
> To those who speak to one,
> In poet's song and voice of bird,
> Many listen; the voice that speaks to none
> By all is heard:
> Sound of the wind, music of the stars, prophetic word.
>
> from "Ten Italian Poems"

Intellectually I am inclined to dismiss much of Raine's paraphrasable discourse as theosophy, a branch of the tree of the perennial wisdom only a little loftier than astrology and rhabdomancy. Those who share such predilections will take her to their hearts as the best thing since Yeats, but it would be unfair to her genius to let her reputation be immolated in the Magicke Fyres of the Golden Dawn—even at her own vatic insistence.

For there is this redeeming paradox: Raine's authority as a prophet derives in good measure from a deeply integrated understanding of the very organon she professes to refute, modern materialistic science. Admittedly the science she knows best stops short of the latest wrinkles in cosmogony and particle physics. Quarks and black holes have no roles in the masques of her Imagination, but the loss is theirs. One may more reasonably regret that plate tectonics and the caduceus of the DNA molecule came to be formulated too late to have been apotheosized in her meditations, for it is in the mid-range of apprehensible reality (neither too macro- nor too micro-scopic) that her muse is most effective. In any case, the range of scientific knowledge she does command and transmute is quite wide enough to span the Two-Cultures gap, with room to spare. Only Ammons, among her peers, can move back and forth with as easy grace between the mist-haunted woodlands of the Sublime and the crystalline cognitions of the chemist, the patient observations of the field naturalist. What could be more Ammonslike than the lines open-ing the three stanzas of "Moving Image"?

> Inviolate spaces from infinite centre created at the opening
> of an eye. . . .

> Eighteen eider, three merganser, a jagged row of cor-
> morant. . . .

> Worlds within world each iridescent sphere of life re-
> volves. . . .

Not that Raine ever exerts herself along these lines; she has no ambition to play Lucretius to the nuclear age. Rather, that when she reaches for one of the fourteen glen-defining adjectives what comes to hand is resonant with knowledge of (in her own phrase quoted earlier) "the world and its unwinding." Unwinding in the sense both of its motions in space and of its entropic destiny. In another poet such a confluence of suggestions might be serendipitous; in one who was in her student years a friend and colleague of Empson and Bron-owski there can be no such suspicion.

Nothing so sustains a poet as an irresolvable dilemma. Through-out her career Raine's Aristotelian intellect has wrestled with the neo-Platonic angel of her soul ("My soul and I last night," one poem begins), and if no clear victor emerges from the battle, nor ever can, the ringside view is terrific.

Other irresolvable dilemmas of her life have not been so conducive to good poetry. In her long elegy for Gavin Maxwell, *On a Deserted Shore* (1973), sorrow and slight contest for primacy under the watchful eye of a merely theoretic serenity. Never does the poet allow herself to express what, despite her engrained reticence, becomes so clear in *The Lion's Mouth,* the third volume of her autobiography— that Raine, her love long unrequited, felt passionately injured by— and vindictive toward—the late Mr. Maxwell. In such circumstances elegy is not the best revenge, and, indeed, may backfire. The poem manages to be both facile and strained in its lyricism; in its discourse it is tendentious, repetitive, and dull; as confession it is disingenuous and self-protective. Heaven protect all poets from loves like this!

The question must be asked whether Raine is the best judge of her own work, whether she has not entrenched herself too determinedly in the role of prophet, forgetful or contemptuous of those poems she wrote when she was only human. From her first book, *Stone and Flower* (1943), she reprints only twelve poems; in her earlier *Collected Poems* of 1956 there were forty-seven. Some of the poems newly excluded were fustian, but others, such as "Invocation," "Cattle Dream," "Tiger Dream," and "Maternal Grief," have a kind of raging energy and extravagance of gesture that don't deserve oblivion. Consider the following exercise in the Martial arts (from her second (1946), even more ruthlessly winnowed book, *Living in Time*):

> Find your way now, blind Samson, with your fingers
> Feel at the latch. The door will open,
> And you will let the sky in, your wide sockets
> Open these blind temples to the sun!

One senses that the Pythoness (as her third book was titled), sedate upon her tripod, must wince to recall such outbursts of the old Delilah, but how much better a poem *On a Deserted Shore* would be with a small infusion of such honest, complex anger.

If only by right of seniority Kathleen Raine deserves to edit her lifework by whatever principle of selection she chooses, nor would it be seemly to look forward yet to a *Complete Poems* (though poetic justice requires it in the fullness of time). After the lapse of *On a Deserted Shore,* her more recent collections offer work as magistral as all but the loftiest poems in the three definitive books of her mid-career (represented here in almost their full amplitude). Poets of the sublime traditionally shine most brilliantly as twilight deepens about them. I look forward with something bordering on reverence to the *Collected Poems 1935–2000,* with whatever omissions its author, in her perennial wisdom, chooses to indulge. Meanwhile no serious reader can afford to ignore the present volume.

DELECTABLE ALWAYS, AND FRESH AND TRUE

Selected Poems 1950–1982
by Kenneth Koch
RANDOM HOUSE $17.95 249 PP.

AMONG THE DIMINISHING numbers of those who continue to read poetry after obligatory undergraduate bouts with the *Norton Anthology,* there has been a generally accepted sense that the object of poetry is perfect candor and its subject is the self. Poets in this view are expected to find their voices, a task equated with achieving personal authenticity, a one-to-one parity between the "I" or eye of the poet's poems and who he *is.* This consensus view is wide enough to include as many varieties of poetry as there are personas available for authentification, but it excludes a great deal of poetry in which the poet is either not personally present or, more problematically, is present in a playful, parodic, or otherwise "inauthentic" way.

For every consensus there is an opposite, if necessarily unequal, dissensus, and one of the most distinctive of dissenting antivoices in contempory poetry for the past thirty years has been Kenneth Koch. By the same dialectical logic that has made Allen Ginsberg a celebrity of the establishment he inveighs against, Koch has become the founding father of, and chief spokesman for, the one branch of the poetry business to prosper during the industry's years of decline—the business of teaching poetry. Teaching, that is, not the rigors and rigidities of the consensus style to academic apprentices, but rather instructing various captive audiences of the welfare state (schoolchildren, nursing home residents) in a more handicraftlike poetry whose organizing principle is Fun.

Koch's poetry may be a game everyone can play, but that is not to say it can't be played at various levels of skill. Indeed, if Fun is to be its measure, then no one's poetry is more successful than Koch's, for he is the funniest poet we've got. And yet, because he has sedulously avoided the jinglier forms of "light verse," he can't be dismissed as middlebrow or merely clever. Indeed, he is singularly secure against criticism, having devoted a significant portion of his poetry—as much as a third of these *Selected Poems*—to an *apologia pro arte sua,* poems in which he presents a moving target as hypnotically evasive, in its way, as that of his friend and coconspirator John Ashbery. Consider, in this passage from "Days and Nights" (the title poem of a 1982 collection, and one of many that are, ostensibly, essays in self-criticism), the flair with which he keeps changing the subject and staying that crucial conversational beat ahead of us the readers (of whose existence and needs Koch is, for a poet, uncommonly aware):

O wonderful silence of animals
It's among you that I best perhaps could write!
Yet one needs readers. Also other people to talk to
To be friends with and to love. To go about with. And
This takes time. And people make noise,
Talking, and playing the piano, and always running
     around.

Night falls on my desk. It's an unusual situation.
Usually I have stopped work by now. But this time I'm
     in the midst of a thrilling evasion,
Something I promised I wouldn't do—sneaking in a short
     poem
In the midst of my long one. Meanwhile you're patient,
     and the veal's cold.

Fresh spring evening breezes over the plates
We finish eating from and then go out.

Personal life is· everything personal life is nothing
Sometimes—click—one just feels isolated from personal
    life
Of course it's not public life I'm comparing it to, that's
    nonsense vanity—
So what's personal life?

Who could disagree with such *sententiae*, or fail to be delighted by the swerves from thudding obviousness to lyrical inconsequence with then a characteristic rebound to Koch's own accommodation to the poetry of the consensus, a version of the domestic sublime that is deflated and accident-prone but still full of the will to be thrilling in the grand remembered manner of *True Confessions;* and then, just as characteristically, the "personal" details become the occasion for turning the spotlight on the theory generating the details: "So what's personal life?"

Since Koch so ably sets forth the terms on which we are supposed to appreciate him, let me dispense with paraphrase and quote a key passage from "The Art of Poetry," his most exhaustive statement on the subject and a poem that should be anthologized forever, right besides Pope's:

. . . Just how good a poem should be
Before one releases it, either from one's own work or then
    into the purview of others,
May be decided by applying the following rules: ask 1) Is
    it astonishing?
Am I pleased each time I read it? Does it say something
    I was unaware of
Before I sat down to write it? and 2) Do I stand up from
    it a better man
Or a wiser, or both? or can the two not be separated? 3)
    Is it really by me
Or have I stolen it from somewhere else? (This sometimes
    happens,

Though it is comparatively rare.) 4) Does it reveal some-
    thing about me
I never want anyone to know? 5) Is it sufficiently "mod-
    ern"?
(More about this a little later) 6) Is it in my own "voice"?
Along with, of course, the more obvious questions, such
    as
7) Is there any unwanted awkwardness, cheap effects, ask-
    ing illegitimately for attention,
Show-offiness,   cuteness,   pseudo-profundity,   old   hat
    checks,
Unassimilated dream fragments, or other "literary," "kiss-
    me-I'm-poetical" junk?
Is my poem free of this? 8) Does it move smoothly and
    swiftly
From excitement to dream and then come flooding reason
With purity and soundness and joy? 9) Is this the kind of
    poem
I would envy in another if he could write? 10)
Would I be happy to go to Heaven with this pinned on
    to my
Angelic jacket as an entrance show? Oh, would I? And
    if you can answer to all these Yes
Except for the 4th one, to which the answer should be
    No,
Then you can release it, at least for the time being.
I would look at it again, though, perhaps in two hours,
    then after one or two weeks,
And then a month later, at which time you can probably
    be sure.

Now these criteria, for all their Polonian assurance, can't really
be said to be Koch's, but rather are those of a hypothetical "exigent
poet," whose response to the secret "quota system" of poetry (the
system that's been put in place to keep the universe from being
flooded with poetry at the awful rate of ten thousand poems per

annum per person) is "If I can write one good poem a year I am grateful." With such exigence Koch actually has little sympathy, and so all his counsels of perfection must be understood not as a loping and slightly loopy but *sincere* didacticism but as a grotesque impersonation of a comic character, one who, as comedy demands, is incapable of following his own rules, for what could be more "kiss-me-I'm poetical" than the stricture that comes immediately after that prohibition, that a poem should come "flooding reason / With purity and soundness and joy?"

This displacement of the poet's "voice" to somewhere always outside his own personality derives from a sense that the mind is a slippery thing and, like the children Koch has taught, a natural surrealist that can suppose a blue rose as readily as a red and that can only to its own self be true if it is free to deal in oxymorons. This programmatic need for quicksilver disjunctions has led Koch to some of the most pulverized poetry in the English language, and though the principle of selection for these *Selected Poems* deemphasizes the overt surrealism, and eliminates entirely work done in the vein of his infamously unreadable 2,400-lines-long *When the Sun Tries to Go On**, enough slippage remains, even in his discursive poems, to make a proofreader's life hell.

Almost to a poem Koch's selection corresponds to my own preferences, eliminating only some 20 percent of the material from his two meatiest collections, *Thank You* (1962) and *The Art of Love* (1975), and halving the bulk of his three other collections. He does not include excerpts from his two Ariosto-cum-Disney-inspired epics, *Ko* (1959) and *The Duplications* (1977), nor any of the playlets from the collection *Bertha,* and these omissions do a disservice to his oeuvre

---

*Whence this representative sampling:

> Scenic parachute. Column. Pear. Elevator
> Sent hair swans. Bam the students. Pillow
> Then Swedish underwear. Year-horse. Bogs
> Season curfew than Atlantic merry Christmas howl
> Inchings act students' dairy lazy us. Pegs!

that time and the decorums of reputation will have to remedy with a *Complete Works*. Meanwhile, this volume is *crème fraîche* and serves the essential purpose of canon fodder for those libraries, public and private, that have Koch-sized gaps between Kipling and Lowell.

Its appearance does, however, pose the question, which Koch himself keeps playing with like a sore tooth, of whether his genius has suffered a decline since the dazzlement of the poems in *Thank You* and its perceived renaissance in *The Art of Love*. "Is there some way," he worries,

> . . . to ride to old age and to fame and acceptance
> And pride in oneself and the knowledge society approves
>   one
> Without getting lousier and lousier and depleted of tal-
>   ent? . . .

And Again, also from "The Art of Poetry":

> . . . This fear [that one has "lost one's talent"]
> Is a perfectly logical fear for poets to have,
> And all of them, from time to time, have it. It is very rare
> For what one does best and that on which one's happiness
>   depends
> To so large an extent, to be itself dependent on factors
> Seemingly beyond one's control. For whence cometh In-
>   spiration?
> Will she stay in her Bower of Bliss or come to me this
>   evening?
> Have I gotten too old for her kisses? Will she like that
>   boy there rather than me?
> Am I a dried-up old hog? Is this then the end of it?
>   Haven't I
> Lost that sweet easy knack I had last week,
> Last month, last year, last decade, which pleased everyone
> And especially pleased me? I no longer can feel the
>   warmth of it—
> Oh, I have indeed lost it! Etcetera. . . .

His answer, in the first instance, is "Yes, / Yeats showed it could be. And Sophocles wrote poetry until he was a hundred and one ..." and in the second instance that "one does not lose one's talent, / Although one can misplace it...." But this does beg the question, which he raises earlier, of what went wrong with Wordsworth and Whitman that made their revisions of their early work "almost always terrible." He, however, needn't be so worried. Inspiration is surely still a regular visitor *chez* Koch, but she does come these days, as our old friends are wont, in clothes we've seen her in before. *The Duplications* duplicated, without improving, both the rhyme scheme and cartooning style of *Ko,* and many of the poems in the last two collections slip into sounding like the imitations of his own epigones, who have taken up Koch's campy tone and cartoon scenery strictly *pour épater* (and because it is so imitable). When Koch, in the fifties, began a poem "You were wearing your Edgar Allan Poe printed cotton blouse. / In each divided up square of the blouse was a picture of Edgar Allan Poe...." he was being as prophetic of the coming triumphs of consumerism as any Andy Warhol can of soup. But in many of the poems of the late seventies he slips into his earlier persona of the Inspired Maunderer—and then just maunders.

Yet these are venial sins, even in a *Selected Poems,* for the worst that can be said of Koch is that he is, like Picasso or Handel or Gertrude Stein, his own best imitator. As for Koch at his best he is simply too large and various in his accomplishment to be accounted for in the space of a review. For all his scorn of the "exigent poet," Koch's ratio of original invention to canny recension is respectably high, and there is no poet of our time who has lived up so consistently to his own exigent demands. I quote a last time from "The Art of Poetry":

> ... Remember your obligation is to write,
> And, in writing, to be serious without being solemn, fresh
>   without being cold,
> To be inclusive without being asinine, particular
> Without being picky, feminine without being effeminate,

Masculine without being brutish, human while keeping
     all the animal graces
You had inside the womb, and beast-like without being
     inhuman.
Let your language be delectable always, and fresh and
     true.
Don't be conceited. Let your compassion guide you
And your excitement. And always bring your endeavors
     to their end.

DEATH AND THE POET

OVER THE CENTURIES poetry has acquired some of the cachet of monarchy, and laurel wreaths have come to possess a more and more coronal aura. Shelley, a democrat but not without his own sense of grandeur, declared his fellow poets mankind's unacknowledged legislators, and poets subscribed to that idea en masse, though a few still opted for autarchy. Laura Riding, who has some claim to having been the supreme poetic megalomaniac of our time, was given to wearing a gold tiara across her brow that bore, like the name of a constellation across its component stars, the precious letters of her immortal name: LAURA.

Alas, for most poets, perhaps even for LAURA, immortality is usually a delusory hope. Most will be unread within their lifetimes, their books either unpublished or unsold; the happier few who secure some readership while they are alive will soon thereafter join the moiety, as their Selecteds and Collecteds are elbowed off the shelves of bookstores and libraries by younger, living aspirants, to be deaccessioned into Dumpsters or retired into the cryogenic twilight of the library's deepest stacks. There are simply too many poets and too little time to read them all.

That's why the canon has become an issue. The common reader

(whose vote finally settles these matters) samples the centuries gone by with a regard for their juiciest and most instructive moments, using poetry as one of the clearest windows onto an otherwise dusty prospect. What *are* the extant alternatives to Homer, Vergil, Dante, or Racine? One must make do with them, and with their current translators (who have a better purchase on fame than most other poets and can stay in print, if they're any good at all, for a couple of generations).

In determining the canon of more recent times, there can be some contention about who *must* be read, but not a lot. Browning's claim is surely greater than his wife's, Wordsworth's greater than his sister's. Multiculturalism has encouraged such novelties as the ninety-six pages of "American Indian Poetry" in the Library of America's anthology of nineteenth-century American poetry, but such token gestures have done little to disrupt the dim hush of the Pantheon where the dead white males still reign secure. Other languages have established their own priorities, no less inexorable. Until our own era, when poetry has mushroomed so wonderfully, there isn't a lot of argument as to what has to be read, only how it is to be interpreted. The battle over the canon begins in the welter of our own century, now.

Perhaps that has always been the case. One can envision inglorious Miltons who were not mute but only unlucky. But such hypotheticals don't alter the canon. The chances of slipping in after closing hours aren't good. Even John Clare was feted for a while, and Melville (though only as a novelist) had his moments on the bestseller list. How many have ever managed to become immortal without having first had at least a nibble of fame? Emily Dickinson. Anne Frank. Who else?

Poetry, like so much else that is beautiful, is ephemeral. A butterfly, a nightingale, a sip of wine. It slips away, the particular joining the general. How many marvelously apt haikus have been written—and lost before the sun came up? Several million at least. Any poet must be prepared to see his work arise and vanish in the same morning mists.

All this: preamble to some small guerdon of praise for the poetry of Peter Whigham. Do you recognize the name? If you're

American, probably not. If you're English, can you name a particular poem of his that you admire? That question undid me once, the one time I met May Swenson and told her how much I liked her work. She smiled politely and asked what poem I particularly admired. I failed the test, but so, in a way, did she. If the answer to that question isn't ready to hand, both parties must blush.

Peter Whigham was born in Oxford in in 1925, taught Latin at a private school in his early twenties, lived awhile in rural Sussex and briefly in Italy. In 1954 he served as one of Ezra Pound's unliveried attendants at St. Elizabeth's asylum, and in 1966, sponsored by Pound's arch-acolyte, Hugh Kenner, he took up a teaching job in Santa Barbara. These few facts courtesy of *The Oxford Companion to Twentieth-Century Poetry* and a memoir by Whigham's friend and fellow poet, Peter Russell.

I met Whigham once, as he passed through New York in 1980. At the behest of Peter Jay, his sometime collaborator and our common publisher in England, I'd agreed to advance him some money (which Peter Jay promptly repaid me). Whigham appeared at my doorstep to take the money; we went to the bank, and then he said good-bye. But he made a vivid impression in the course of that brief exchange. He would have been in his early sixties, and he looked like . . . well, Bardolph would be close to the mark. The roseate complexion; the rubicund, veined nose; the clothes—as though the last tweed jacket in the world had just received its last elbow patch. I sensed I'd best not ask after the cause of his distress, and he volunteered no information.

In 1987 I read his obituary in *The New York Times* (he died in a car crash), and was impressed, not by the sparse vita but by the very fact that he was there and had been accorded so many column inches. I'd never read his poetry till then, though I had the latest book in my bookcase: *Things Common, Properly: Selected Poems 1942–1980.* It had lingered awhile beside the toaster on the dinner table's recent acquisitions stack, and then, like so many others, got shelved, unread, among other alphabetically ordered poets.

I have read it now, and I can offer Peter Whigham my posthumous tribute, though it cannot be as fulsome as he might wish.

Perhaps I'm wrong in that, though, for there's nothing in the poetry, nor in the man I met, to suggest he had an overinflated view of his accomplishments. Like most poets of the middle rank, he wrote a few fine poems that deserve remembering and many that are agreeable but slight. I would say, to his credit, pointedly slight.

What most recommends the book (and the poet) to a lover of poetry is *his* love of poetry. Poetry mattered to Peter Whigham as it ought to matter to all poets. It is not his central concern (love is, along with sex), but it is his main Muse, the inspirer of his best moments, lyrically. One senses, from poem to poem, that poetry is the neighborhood he has lived in all his life, where he's worked and where he's partied. He knows its history and its latest gossip. When he travels it is only to enclaves that have been colonized by his old neighbors.

His surest claim to poetic fame will probably be his work as a translator. Penguin published his *Poems of Catullus* to much acclaim. He also produced book-length translations of Martial and Meleager; many of the later are included, with other work, in the Penguin *Greek Anthology* selection edited by Peter Jay. Whigham's translations, like Kenneth Rexroth's renderings from Chinese and Japanese, convey a flavor of foreignness while seeming diffident and contemporary as Levi's. Here is Whigham's spin on an epigram by Apollonides, a poet writing circa A.D. 1:

> The cup clinks out, my friend,
> Diodorus, 'Sleep apes but Death'.
> Wine! Here is wine. No water add,
> But drink till your knees sag.
> Soon, too soon, will come the day
> When we no more shall drink
> Together. Rouse up, Diodorus!
> Age, sobriety, have touched our brows.

In his own poems Whigham sounds much the same. He favors the codified topoi of classical elegy—nature's changing weathers and the heart's. In his single most ambitious poem, "The Ingathering of Love," the two are in sync:

> Despite the persistent dew soaking my bedroom slippers
> and the trees limp from too much summer
> like women, love over
> putting their soiled clothes off
> thankful to be alone with their own nakedness . . .
> despite all signs of a final departure
> autumn has caught us unawares.
>
> —And our love? . . .
> Will it pass in some cloud of euthanasia?
> Or like the birds?
> Or will you, undressing one day
> resignedly placing slip bra stockings over the chair
> turn
>   stripped of my desire
> sheathed
>   as in childhood again
> in your own nakedness?

Like Catullus—like most poets who are not the laureates of their own immiseration—he loves. He is of that breed of lovers—you can see them smooching in the park—who glory in public display. It doesn't come across as braggadocio but rather as the blithe insistence of one smitten that you should see all the snapshots in his album. He's the same about his kids, for whom he has written a delicious suite of nursery rhymes—of all poetic forms the most audacious because the likeliest to fail. Which his does, too, finally, from an excess of fatherly doting and protectiveness.

The love that steads Whigham best, poetically, is the love of other poets. He excels at metamorphosing fragments of long-ago verse into equivalent, telling wisps of English. He lets us have a scent of Sappho. His versions of the sixth Dalai Lama—a remarkable reprobate of the late seventeenth century, much loved in Tibet but not otherwise much noted—are decorously lubricious. The lama comes across not as another Omar Khayyám but as an alternative Peter Whigham whose ancient, libidinous utterances have been preserved by the accident of having fallen into a glacier or a tar pit from which Whigham has extracted coils of poetic DNA, miraculously intact. He breathes again with Whigham's breath.

In this connection it is germane to know that Whigham was, like many poets of his time, in fealty to Ezra Pound. He was, indeed, one of the poet's official epigones in the years of his incarceration and disgrace, for which service he has earned two citations in the index of Humphrey Carpenter's biography of Pound.

From the little I know of Peter Whigham, and the vivid memory of his brief visit, I think of him as embodying a type: the Poundian poet, in its ideal form. Not the poet as academic (yet more learned than most tenured professors now); nor yet the poet as beatnik (rather, a gentleman-wastrel). The Poundian poet was a pioneer of the Riviera and, eventually, of the entire North Mediterranean littoral, where the vine and olive twined, and the pound and the dollar would stretch the farthest. In this warmer bohemia of *dolce far niente* the practice of art in one form or another was more often than not a polite imposture. The milieu has been chronicled by Norman Douglas in *South Wind* (Capri), by Cyril Connolly in *The Rock Pool* (the French Riviera), and by many others. But among the remittance men, the whores, the hustlers, and the hangers-on, there were real writers who thrived in such environs: Lawrence Durrell in the Greek Islands, Robert Graves on Majorca, and Ezra Pound at Rapallo. What seems to have made the difference was a love of, and hunger for, classical civilization.

Whigham probably represents the last generation of that type of genteelly poor classicist for whom a jug of wine, a loaf of bread, and a volume of the Loeb Classics was paradise enow—a paradise that would be lost in his own lifetime, as the tour buses from all of Northern Europe descended on the shores of the Mediterranean and took possession. At that juncture another land of vine and olives beckoned, and Whigham went off to Santa Barbara to teach the art of translation in a landscape whose only ruins were younger than himself.

Whigham is a Poundian poet in the additional and more essential sense that for him, as for the Pound of *Personae,* poetry was an act of communion with the past that entailed conflation of his own ephemeral self with the equivalent selves who had preceded him in his art and led the way into oblivion.

In "Homage to Ezra Pound" Whigham says everything I've tried to say here and says it (which is the prerogative of poets) more briskly and poignantly, with the further poignance that now Peter Whigham's name must be added to his "roll-call of Dead Lords":

Since 2,800 years, Homer is dead;
His mouth more often filled with verses than with bread.
A-squat on the sun-hot stone, in the glare,
Blind to the lyrical sun,
And a blind man's fingers light on the sensitive lute.
Still, still the polysyllabled sea-rush rolls to our shores;
The singing voice is mute.

Lo! Ferlies befalleth where is love-gladness,
'Neath moon-sleight in orchard when pierceth love's mad-
                                                        ness.
Silken the song, spun of air, in the dew,
Tense with the immanent muse,
And coins & castles, heaulmes & politics their song.
Where now are the stones? Where is the bright hair of
                                            those women?
Gone, all, the long-gone dead along.

Dante Alighieri! Impelled by Love & led
By Wizardry, his death-mask hangs above my bed.
Pre-Raphaelite the work, the laurel leaves
Parnassian, smutched with gilt.
Pale eyes burned in the ivory stillness of that face;

Clothed in a white geometric vision, he stalked
Unsoiled through the market-place.

Dan Chaucer next, our 'fount of English undefiled'.
And would he, from his customs house, have smiled
At such a laurel, so bestowed?
Here there is no aroma
Of Dutch cloth, or coarse-grained bags of spice,
But an air as of conversations with Boccace,
And memory of Provence.

Ravens by starshine, by sunlight, in wind, in rain,
Have pecked poor Francis Villon skin & bone again.
Shrivelled the restless tongue, the nicked lip;
Empty the mock-lit eye.
Sunlight spills pattern of rose on cathedral floor;
Seine breaks under bridges; dark firelight & laughter
Leap from the tavern door.

The names fall now as in the roll-call of Dead Lords:
Douglas, Golding, Pope, each of glittering word-hoards.
Savage Landor, then ancient Roman,
Wrote for seventy years in stone.
The recent laureate, Browning happily shares
With Hardy, who endowed puppets with nobility,
And Yeats, that pursuer of arcane hares.

And old Ez, folding his blankets in Pisan meadows,
Unlocked his word-hoard, as of this troop of shadows.
You who have walked by Cahors, by Chaluz,
Made Odyssean landfall,
Your voice is as old as the first dead in my song,
And would you might perceive herein, such strength in
                                        gentilesse,
Such subtlety, as tips your tongue.

Each emblematic figure in this latter-day lament for the makers
is an aspect of Pound: a poet once blind and now mute; the champion

of troubadours; a modernist albeit smitten with the flummery of the Pre-Raphaelites; the paranoid theorist stalking "unsoiled" (and deracinated) through the marketplace; but even so a realist who could connive and scoff at laurels; the convict rotting in the cathedral's shadow (but in Pisa, not in Paris). It is a portrait as cruel and just as it is loving, and, in striking that fine balance, a truer portrait of the poet Whigham knew than is to be found in all the fragmented fretfulness of the later *Cantos*. Disciples, like translators, have a singular advantage: the last word.

FEARING, AND FALLING
OUT OF LOVE

WRITERS WHO DIE before they've made a reputation for themselves have little prospect of gaining posterity's attention, but writers like Kenneth Fearing who witness the evanescence of once healthy reputations must feel an even keener posthumous chagrin. They were contenders. Now their works are out of print, and their memory lingers on only in those century-wide anthologies kind enough to set a place at the table for the lesser dead.

Fearing is undoubtedly best known as the author of a single thriller, *The Big Clock,* published in 1946 and twice adapted to the screen, first in 1948 and again, under the title *No Way Out,* in 1987. Received wisdom would have it that *The Big Clock* is the best of Fearing's novels, and few readers now can easily controvert that judgment, since *The Big Clock* is the only Fearing title to have remained in print. The rest of his work, both prose and poetry, is now to be had only by making a special effort and/or paying a stiff price.

When I first became an enthusiast for Fearing, in the early sixties, it was still possible to find his thrillers on paperback racks, in used bookstores, and at the library. My own preference was for *The Generous Heart,* a suspense novel set in the tawdry milieu of charity scams. As a rule, each of Fearing's novels was centered around a particular institution: a hospital in *The Hospital;* a Luce-like magazine empire in *The Big Clock;* an arts colony in *Dagger of the Mind.* In this shift of focus away from the country house setting of British murder mysteries and the mean streets of the Fordist hard-boiled detective story, Fearing was an early prophet of the dawning age of the Organization Man and the Information Society. Family trees are of less import than corporate ladders. Fearing's most memorable characters, his villains, speak in the still imperfect Newspeak of white-collar Machiavellians.

I doubt that Fearing's novels can escape the usual fate of genre fiction. Indeed, of most things written. Shakespeare's boast, that his ink might outlast monuments, has become an article of faith for all the scribbling tribe, but the plain truth is that time deals with most books as it does with all writers. They become dust.

Poetry, traditionally, has been the best hope. Because it is condensed; because it deals, platonically, with essentials; because it asks only a few minutes, a poem, a single perfect poem, has a good shot at forever. Admittedly, it may be only the small forever of a minor poet—a Smart, a Gay, a Lovelace, a Clough, or a cummings—but even that is a forever a thousand other dead poets might envy.

Fearing, though now at the nadir of his fame, has a legitimate claim on being remembered as a poet who spoke for an era that would be, without his distinctive voice, less resonant. There is no other poet of his time who might have written lines like these, which constitute the first half of "Sunday to Sunday":

> Unknown to Mabel, who works as cook for the rich and
> snobbish Aldergates,
> The insured, by subway suicide, provides for a widow and
> three sons;
> Picked from the tracks, scraped from the wheels, identi-
> fied, this happy ending restores the nation to its heri-
> tage: A Hearst cartoon.
>
> Meanwhile it is infant welfare week, milk prices up, child
> clinics closed, relief curtailed,

The Atlantic and Pacific fleets in full support of Vera
     Cruz,
In court, sentence suspended, Rose Raphael dispossessed
     of a Flatbush packingbox,
Jim Aldergate in love with Mabel, but unaware she has
     been married to Zorrocco the gangster.

In the concluding two stanzas, we learn that the triangle of Jim,
Mabel, and Zorrocco is only a Hollywood movie, while the masses—
"hundreds, thousands, millions"—scrape along in their immemorial
way:

Unknown to the beautiful, beautiful, beautiful Mabel; to
     the deathray smile of politician or priest; unknown to
     Zorrocco, Jim, or the unknown soldier; unknown to
     WGN and the bronze, bronze bells of Sunday noon.

In an agitprop way this may be crude stuff, but as poetry it
actually has something going for it. The Mabel of the first line may
be a fiction in a movie "directed by Frederick Hammersmith and
produced by National," while the suicide of line two seems to have
come to us from a newspaper headline. In this conflation of the movies and the news Fearing presages our own era of information over-
load in which images, fictional and otherwise, contest for our
attention, asserting the equally dubious demands of "beautiful, beautiful, beautiful Mabel" and "bronze, bronze bells." The crude repetitions and the "deathray" smile insist upon the cartoonish qualities
of the poem in a manner respectful of the emotional truth that can
underline the Goshes and Wows of an Alexander Bumstead.

Before Frank O'Hara thought to say "Hooray for Hollywood,"
Kenneth Fearing was saluting the silver screen and the rest of pop
culture. Not with quite the same insouciant bravado, for Fearing
wrote in the thirties, when the movies were still infra dig and camp
uncodified. But he did understand, with a poet's special feel for the
Zeitgeist, that a paradigm shift was under way. Fearing's poems have
some of the proto–Pop Art fizz of Stuart Davis paintings. Himself

an employee of Time, Inc., and a cognizant cog in the big machine
of Modern Times, Fearing struck a new balance between deploring
and relishing Jazz Age America, while his modernist coevals—Pound
and Eliot, especially—only knew how to scold.

What his poems lack that might better recommend them to
contemporary taste is a persona—an account of himself, his feelings,
his poetic CV. Pound, Williams, Frost, even Stevens let us know
rather a lot about themselves, and the next generation—Lowell, Berryman, Plath, Sexton—let us know almost nothing else. Kenneth
Fearing is simply not to be found in his own poems. Indeed, he seems
to have a low regard for the first person singular; witness the way he
uses it throughout the early poem, "JACK KNUCKLES FALTERS: (*But
Reads Own Statement at His Execution While Wardens Watch*)":

HAS LITTLE TO SAY
Gentlemen, I
Feel there is little I
Care to say at this moment, but the reporters have urged
                                                    that I
Express a few appropriate remarks.

As the poem moves along, headlines alternate with Jack Knuckles's
                gallows-inspired protestations of innocence:

As innocent as any of you now standing before me, and
                            the final sworn word I

POSITIVE IDENTIFICATION CLINCHED KNUCKLES VER-
                                                    DICT
Publish to the world is that I was framed. I
Never saw the dead man in all my life, did not know
                            about the killing until
BODY PLUNGES AS CURRENT KILLS
My arrest, and I
Swear to you with my last breath that I

Was not on the corner of Lexington and Fifty-ninth Street
                                                    at eight o'clock.
    SEE U.S. INVOLVED IN FISHERY DISPUTE
    EARTHQUAKE REPORTED IN PERU

That recurring appearance of "I" as a line break is like the *ting* of
the bell on an old typewriter, alerting us to the presence of, and the
source of, the bad faith and denial that Jack shares with "any of you
now standing before me." Fearing eschews "I" because he distrusts it
and uses the word only as a ventriloquist. (The same is true of his
novels, in which each chapter is narrated by a different character, so
that there are soliloquys for all the cast—Hamlet and Horatio, Gertrude and Guildenstern.) In consequence, he need never be sincere,
or confiding, or friendly. Between each poem and its audience stands
a proscenium arch of irony.

   That irony, and a related ambivalence toward the headlines his
poems so often footnote, has kept Fearing from being adopted as a
totem of the diehard left, after the fashion of Muriel Rukeyser or
Langston Hughes, poets forgiven their lack of modernist credentials
by virtue of their unequivocal proletarian sympathies. While Fearing
often begins a poem in the righteous accents of a fellow traveler, as
at the start of "No Credit"—

      Whether dinner was pleasant, with the windows lit by
          gunfire, and no one disagreed; or whether, later, we
          argued in the park, and there was a touch of vomit-gas
          in the evening air;
      Whether we found a greater, deeper, more perfect love,
          by courtesy of Camels, over NBC; whether the comics
          amused us, or the newspapers carried a hunger death
          and a White House prayer for mother's day; . . .

—he characteristically segues to misgivings that are either darkly rel-
ativistic ("Whether the truth was then, or later, or whether the best
had already gone—"), or even honestly dismayed at the prospect of
a dictatorship of the proletariat. At the end of "No Credit":

> Only Steve, the side-show robot, knows content; only
>   Steve, the mechanical man in love with a photo-electric
>   beam remains aloof; only Steve, who sits and smokes
>   or stands in salute, is secure;
>
> Steve, whose shoebutton eyes are blind to terror, whose
>   painted ears are deaf to appeal, whose welded breast
>   will never be slashed by bullets, whose armature soul
>   can hold no fear.

The fear that Fearing can feel and Steve cannot is the same that inspired Karel Čapek's *R.U.R.* and Fritz Lang's *Metropolis*—a fear that the Common Man, freed of his chains, may become some berserk monster, a King Kong, a Godzilla, or just another mug on the street with a mug's eternal alibi:

> Robbery, yes, but you never meant to kill that crazy fool,
>   yes, robbery,
> But who knows how you needed money?—
>
> You've got to have what you've got to have, you're going
>   to do what you've got to do,
> And you are innocent of what has to happen. . . .
>   from "Winner Take All"

This tabloid-accented fatalism can induce a sense of affective and esthetic monotony when one reads more than a few poems at a time. Fearing returns to the same scenes, at the same hours, and paints them with the same palette of colors. Painters can repeat themselves with impunity, because their work will be dispersed. "Untitled No. 1" is not likely to wind up hanging alongside "Untitled No. 2." Only when they are given a retrospective do painters have to face that question that poets pose with each new collection: What does it all add up to?

For Fearing the verdict, even among friendly critics, has not been very favorable. "After a while," Leonard Nathan wrote in *Poetry* (August 1957), "the impression is that you have read the same poem

over and over until discriminations blur and curiosity is put to sleep."
More cruelly still, J. M. Brinnen in *The Yale Review* (Spring 1957):
"The general lack of distinction tends to remind one of the faults
that have inevitably dogged verse that teeters on the brink of horta-
tory prose."

To defend Fearing's claims one must shift ground and ask
whether all poets are best represented by entire books. Doesn't Donne
become much of a muchness at book length? Didn't Hardy incessantly repeat his own best effects? The difference is not between
major and minor, but rather between different ways of envisioning
the task of poetry. Is it a continuous process, so that a collection of
poems should have at least as much coherence as a diary, and, ideally,
should seem a spiritual journal? Or is each poem to be read by itself,
a bolt from the blue that (again, ideally) may strike the reader as it
did the poet with the force of an ambush? Obviously, poems get
written in both ways, and deserve to be read with appropriate expec-
tations.

In returning to Fearing's work after an interval of some three
decades, I found myself recapitulating the history of his critical reception. An initial Eureka! of (re)discovery, followed by a gradual
disenchantment, and arriving at a qualified admiration tinged with a
knowing and Fearinglike sadness for all the books that are bound to
end up on death's great remainder table. His are among them, and
there will probably be no Fearing revival, no *Portable Fearing,* no
Complete Poems.

Anyone wishing to arrive at an independent decision in this
regard will find it easier to access the critical consensus on Fearing
(there is a generous selection in Volume 51 of Gale's *Contemporary
Literary Criticism*) than to track down the work. Few libraries have
the poetry, and the novels have become true rarities. I paid fifty dollars for the *Collected Poems* of 1940, but I balked at shelling out
seventy-five dollars for what was once my favorite among his thrillers,
The Generous Heart. A poet's relation to the marketplace is full of
ironies, none crueler than the fact that the less one is read, the higher
the prices one's books may command. Perhaps in the computer age
now dawning that cruelty can be diminished, for with the technology

already existing it should be easy to create a central data bank of out-of-print poetry, thereby liberating the art from its present subjection to antiquarian booksellers and literary estates that possess copyright whose value is comparable to Confederate money.

[A happy postscript: even as I was writing the above essay, the National Poetry Foundation of Orono, Maine, was bringing out an edition of Fearing's *Complete Poems,* edited with an introduction by Robert M. Ryley. Ryley does much to explain Fearing's erratic art and waning reputation: he drank. Actually, the proximate cause of death was lung cancer (he also smoked), but the booze had been corroding his talent for decades. But that only means Fearing belongs to the company of Hart Crane, Dylan Thomas, and Anne Sexton—poets who drank too much for their own greatness. The book (lxiii & 310 pp.) is available from the National Poetry Foundation, University of Maine, 5752 Neville Hall, Orono, Maine 04469-5752 for $35 in a cloth binding, $19.95 in paperback.]

Of course, there can be beauty, and truth, and all sorts of autumnal poetry in the spectacle of obsolescence. That is one of the lessons of living in a modern metropolis, and one of the lessons imparted by what may prove to be Fearing's most enduring poem, "Green Light," which ends:

> Bought at the drug store down the street
> Where the wind blows and the motors go by and it is
> always night or day;
> Bought to use as a last resort,
> Bought to impress the statuary in the park.
> Bought at a cut rate, at the green light, at nine o'clock.
> Borrowed or bought. To look well. To ennoble. To prevent disease. To entertain. To have.
> Broken or sold. Or given away. Or used and forgotten.
> Or lost.

MUSIC THAT CAN
DEEPEST REACH

RALPH WALDO EMERSON: Collected Poems and Translations
Edited by Harold Bloom and Paul Kane
THE LIBRARY OF AMERICA $30 637 PP.

AMERICAN POETRY: The Nineteenth Century. Vol. I:
Freneau to Whitman. Vol. II: Melville to Stickney;
American Indian Poems; Folk Songs and Spirituals
Edited by John Hollander
1,099 PP. AND 1,050 PP.
THE LIBRARY OF AMERICA $35 PER VOLUME

UP TO NOW, the art of poetry has not been very well served by The Library of America. Only Walt Whitman had made a full one-volume niche for himself in that pantheon. While he surely deserves his place there, most of Whitman's readers would already have been supplied with *Leaves of Grass,* so the Library of America edition filled a ceremonial place on the bookshelf rather than a readerly need. It is quite otherwise with the three volumes reviewed here. Emerson's poetry, despite the sustained applause of agenda-setting critics, has been virtually unavailable for years, except the little that could be found in anthologies. A tour of New York bookstores before the appearance of this *Collected Poems* yielded, at best, the *Vintage Portable Emerson,* with thirty-eight pages of poetry (twenty-two poems)—as against 630 pages of essays. The two-volume *American Poetry* anthology of nineteenth-century verse edited by John Hollander offers a much more generous selection of Emerson—so generous, indeed, that it includes fully 40 percent of the essential oeuvre (not counting the rejectamenta and critical apparatus that bulk out the page count of the *Collected Poems*). So, if you are in any doubt (as I was) whether your appetite for Emerson will settle for nothing less than all of him, let Hollander be your guide.

There is probably no well-approved classic that cannot be accused of some kind of fustiness; no vein of poetry antique as this, with its chiming rhymes and metronomic meter, that won't strike many contemporary readers as antiquated; nor is there any poet of comparable stature so unremittingly preachy as Emerson. There were evenings when I thought Emerson himself had written the last and cruelest word on his own ever-fluent, never-failing, still-reverberating creative process:

> Many are the thoughts that come to me
> In my lonely musing;
> And they drift so strange and swift,
> There's no time for choosing
> Which to follow, for to leave
> Any, seems a losing.
>
> "My Thoughts"

There are five more lackluster stanzas, all tending to the fuzzy conclusion that, though the poet has many moods and his ideas are disconnected and even self-contradictory, yet, somehow, their predestined drift is heavenward. A conclusion with which only the most besotted Emersonian would concur.

Yet if we allow that even Homer nods, Emerson's batting average in the art of vatic utterance and raptured incantation—the specialty of nineteenth-century poets—surely equals or exceeds such contemporary rivals as Poe or Longfellow or even Whitman, who has a different *way* of producing *longueurs*, when that's what he's about, but one that's no less lethal.

That being said, what great poetry most of it is. Like the perfect hypnotic subject, Emerson gives the impression of being able to enter trance state at the drop of his high hat, whereupon the liquid measures flow, alternating the praise of nature, in true romantic style, with praise for the poet's large soul that can mirror so wide a view. Long before Ammons became the amanuensis of mountains, Emerson spoke up for Mount Monadnoc (and Monadnoc for Emerson), so:

> In his own loom's garment dressed,
> By his own bounty blessed,
> Fast abides this constant giver,
> Pouring many a cheerful river;
> To far eyes, an aerial isle
> Unploughed, which finer spirits pile,
> Which morn and crimson evening paint
> For bard, for lover, and for saint;
> The country's core,
> Inspirer, prophet evermore;
> Pillar which God aloft had set
> So that men might it not forget.
>
> "Monadnoc"

For many contemporary readers, even this brief sample will seem all too lullingly mellifluous and lush—and the poet has just got into gear. Although Emerson provided the prosodic theory for Whitman's free verse ("He [the bard] shall not his brain encumber / With the coil of rhythm and number," he advises in "Merlin I"), his own practice more closely resembles that of the Pre-Raphaelites across the ocean. When they are not sheer doggerel, his tetrameter couplets can be as lacily overdetermined as Swinburne's verse, or as frictionlessly smooth as William Morris's.

For those who can go with the Emersonian flow and still be alert to what the man is actually saying, there are some nontranscendental surprises. The boon companion of mountains was not much of a democrat. As "Monadnoc" continues, Emerson recoils at the sight of the mountaineer who lives there—"a churl, / With heart of cat and eyes of bug, / Dull victim of his pipe and mug." He is disillusioned, for: "I thought to find the patriots / In whom the stock of freedom roots." And finally he is outraged:

But if the brave old mould is broke,
And end in churls the mountain folk,
In tavern cheer and tavern joke,
Sink, O mountain, in the swamp!
Hide in thy skies, O sovereign lamp!
Perish like leaves, the highland breed!
No sire survive, no son succeed!

One would give several gross of the false starts, missteps, and
doodles that plump the volume to have a proper, gossipy account of
Emerson's contretemps with the churls of Monadnoc, but the book's
critical apparatus is, as with other Library of America volumes, skel-
etally spare. Indeed, the textual notes offered by Harold Bloom and
Paul Kane are almost exclusively of bibliographic or scholarly interest.
Hollander will at least give a quick gloss for poems such as "Xe-
nophanes," telling us which pre-Socratic fancy he invented that Emerson will filigree; Bloom and Kane have better things to do.

Still, Emerson is rarely all that recondite. He knew his audience,
which was, then as now, that part of the middle class that believed
upward mobility was not incompatible with spiritual aspirations; that
looked to poetry for affirmations not to be found in church, even
affirmations as broad as this:

One thing is forever good;
That one thing is Success,—
Dear to the Eumenides,
And to all the heavenly brood.
Who bides at home, nor looks abroad,
Carries the eagles, and masters the sword.

At such moments, Emerson's grandiloquence verges on that of
Sousa or Streisand, and one must be susceptible to both veins of
populist sentiment to enjoy him properly. Much the same can be said
for the poems that John Hollander has assembled for his anthology
of nineteenth-century American poetry. Poetry was a popular art in
the nineteenth century, and Hollander has shown a generous, un-

snobbish appreciation of that fact. The sixth poet on the contents page is Clement (" 'Twas the night before Christmas") Moore, and the seventh is Francis ("O! say can you see") Scott Key. Among the many old chestnuts to be found here, which a purer, more academic taste would have debarred, are "The [Old, Oaken] Bucket," "Home, Sweet Home!", "Dixie's Land," "[We] Three Kings of Orient," four song lyrics by Stephen Foster, four poems by James Whitcomb Riley (including "Little Orphant Annie") and two by Eugene Field. Hollander's rule would seem to be that if a poem has won a secure place in Bartlett's, it deserves a place in his pages.

And he's right, in practice as well as principle. The book has much of the fascination of a large museum, where a new curator has rehung familiar pictures alongside work that has spent decades in the deepest subbasement. Not every resurrection is an aesthetic triumph, but what a larger past they all add up to! Here is "Judith," a protofeminist effusion by Adah Isaacs Menken, the first woman to be a disciple of Whitman:

> Stand back!
> I am no Magdalene waiting to kiss the hem of your garment.
> It is mid-day.
> See ye not what is written on my forehead?
> I am Judith!
> I wait for the head of my Holofernes!
> Ere the last tremble of the conscious death-agony shall have shuddered, I will show it to ye with the long black hair clinging to the glazed eyes, and the great mouth opened in search of voice, and the strong throat all hot and reeking with blood, that will thrill me with wild unspeakable joy as it courses down my bare body and dabbles my cold feet!

There is only a single specimen of La Menken, but it's more than she's had for a century, and the same is true for some dozen of Hollander's resurrectees—hymn-writers and topographers of the newly opened continent, patriotic balladeers and Jamesian expatriates cooing sonnets over statues in the Vatican.

And then there are the roomsful and galleries of Old Masters: Emily Dickinson is accorded 90 pages, William Cullen Bryant 52, Melville 86, Whitman 220, Longfellow 80, Emerson 96, and Whittier 56. And given Hollander's perfect pitch in these matters, all of them are as good as one remembers, or better.

Does one remember? I am fifty-four and went to a parochial grade school in rural Minnesota, where beginning in fifth grade we were required to read and commit to memory good-sized chunks of "Snow-Bound" and "Evangeline," all of "Barbara Frietchie," "Paul Revere's Ride," "The Children's Hour," etc. For me the Hollander anthology was a nostalgia trip such as those Generation Xers might experience only when they see reruns of *The Brady Bunch.* Contemporary educational theory, abetted by multicultural aesthetics, has cleansed modern classrooms of much of the poetry of these dead white males and their few dead white lady friends, to the impoverishment of our general culture but with this silver lining: that younger readers with an ear tuned to traditional poetry will be able to approach all these golden oldies with something of the freshness of the audience that first read and treasured them.

One of the novel features of the second volume is the concluding diptych of independent mini-anthologies, the first devoted to "19th-Century Versions of American Indian Poetry," the second (and more conventional) to "Folk Songs and Spirituals." Some of the Indian songs are terser than anything by the Imagists or W. C. Williams, such as this specimen song of the Miamis: "I will kill—I will kill—the Big Knives, I will kill." How is one to read this? Is reading, indeed, the right approach to what were not so much poems as ritual incantations, presented here shorn of context, like so many display cases full of annotated arrowheads? Still, here's the case—what's to be made of its contents? Should we be vibrating sympathetically, taking the bare words into some mental wood and testing them out on our own Iron John tom-toms? Or, with more scholarly reserve, should our concern be limited to whether the translators have been faithful to the originals?

If so, the supporting materials do not so much elucidate or enhance as add their own ironic overlay. The notes quote at length from nineteenth-century ethnographers who transcribed and translated these "specimens," and one gets the sense that, as in Nabokov's *Pale Fire,* the editors and the edited are at daggers drawn. The Miamis have it in for the Big Knives, but the compliment is returned. For instance, Edwin James glosses the Ojibwa verse "I cause to look like the dead, a man I did," as follows: "The lines drawn across the face of this figure, indicate poverty, distress, and sickness; the person is supposed to have suffered from the displeasure of the medicine man. Such is the religion of the Indians! Its boast is to put into the hands of the devout, supernatural means, by which he may wreak vengeance on his enemies. . . . "

The American Indian selections are no doubt meant as a tip of the hat to multiculturalism and equal poetic opportunity, but their effect, in conjunction with the ethnographic notes, is not a little like a Wild West Show boasting a troop of "red-skins" with painted faces shouting war whoops and simulating carnage, alternating with a female chorus in beaded moccasins miming such gentler moments as the "Song of the washpálaks-fox," which is "Long and slim I am, long and slim I am." I can't think that today's Native Americans, many of whom eschew even the label "American Indian," will be entirely pleased at their representation here, but I may be wrong. Perhaps for some readers these pages will register as the anthology's high point, if only because they aren't burdened with the artifices of rhyme and meter and so more closely resemble the poems currently being written and studied in academia.

Buy both volumes of the Hollander anthology and they come boxed. This is the Library of America's proudest achievement to date, an anthology that can be expected to root itself as firmly in our literature as Palgrave's *Golden Treasury.* For anyone whose love of poetry is more than a decade deep, it is essential reading.

Postscript: A Parsing of Emerson's "Mithridates"

I cannot spare water or wine,
   Tobacco-leaf, or poppy, or rose;

From the earth-poles to the line,
  All between that works or grows,
Every thing is kin of mine.

Give me agates for my meat;
Give me cantharids to eat;
From air and ocean bring me foods,
From all zones and altitudes;—

From all natures, sharp and slimy,
  Salt and basalt, wild and tame:
Tree and lichen, ape, sea-lion,
  Bird, and reptile, be my game.

Ivy for my fillet band;
Blinding dog-wood in my hand;
Hemlock for my sherbet cull me,
And the prussic juice to lull me;
Swing me in the upas boughs,
Vampyre-fanned, when I carouse.

Too long shut in strait and few,
Thinly dieted on dew,
I will use the world and sift it,
To a thousand humors shift it,
As you spin a cherry.
O doleful ghosts, and goblins merry!
O all you virtues, methods, mights,
Means, appliances, delights,
Reputed wrongs and braggart rights,
Smug routine, and things allowed,
Minorities, things under cloud!
Hither! take me, use me, fill me,
Vein and artery, though ye kill me!
God! I will not be an owl,
But sun me in the Capitol.

This morning, early in October, the groundhog whose burrow abuts my backyard was out there, under the apple tree, munching on windfalls in just the spirit of voracious contentment that Emerson summons in "Mithridates." At such moments the whole world is edible, a kitchen steamy with invitations.

Emerson, as a New Englander, a Transcendentalist, and an Eminent Victorian, generally isn't thought of as an advocate of glorious excess, of mellow fruitfulness, *luxe, calme,* and *volupté.* But "Mithridates" is typically Emersonian in its celebration of unbounded and transgressive appetites. He was, after all, the man who gave Whitman his first, authenticating blurb and became by that act the godfather of the Beats. Of course, there is the *other* Emerson, who reneged on that blurb, from a canny sense of what the traffic would bear. He might commend the poppy; there was poetic precedent for that in Keats and Coleridge. But drug abuse, in so many words? Or sex?

Emerson's poems of voluptuary delight—and there are many— are like the poems of those Sufis who commend the wine their religion forbids them to taste and who insist (disingenuously, one always supposes) that the wine of their verse is a metaphor for Wisdom, or some such unassailable abstraction.

There is, in that very denial, a spice whose savor our tongues, schooled on the candors of a nouvelle cuisine, have difficulty savoring—the spice of hypocrisy; of disguising our meaning, even from ourselves; the tang of that hemlock in Emerson's sherbet.

But suppose that instead of Emerson's name being attached to the poem it were ascribed to Baudelaire. Wouldn't the author of *Les Fleurs du Mal* have been delighted with such a couplet as "Swing me in the upas boughs, / Vampyre-fanned, when I carouse"? It is pure Theda Bara. Campy, certainly; but isn't any middle-class evocation of Oriental delight a camp? Fitzgerald's Omar Khayyám? Matisse's odalisques? Emerson should certainly be alowed equal license.

And then there is simply the sound of it, and the syntax; the man's knack for giving a freshness to the stalest words in the language. That "works" in the fourth line has the modern valence of "If it works, then use it." His forcing "few," at the start of the last stanza, to do service as a noun signifying scarcity. And, best of all, the extraordinary catalogue in that same stanza that summons, in a single ecstatic breath, "virtues, methods, mights, means, appliances, delights, reputed wrongs and braggart rights, smug routine, and things allowed, minorities, things under cloud."

At such moments, the moralizing Emerson of the essays and the rhapsodic Emerson of the poems fuse into a single, distinctive rhetoric that entitles the man to have his own copyright adjective: Emersonian. At its fullest stretch, as in the last four lines, the Emersonian moment sails out beyond sight of the shores of didacticism and common sense and utters the ineffable. He is then closer kin to the Sybil, Dickinson, than to Longfellow; more likely, therefore, to satisfy contemporary appetites.

If, despite this, his books gather dust, the reason may well be political rather than esthetic, for when one takes the trouble to puzzle out the last vatic couplet of "Mithridates," the poem can be construed not as a simple hymn of praise to large appetites but rather as one more strophe in a national anthem celebrating the course of the American empire—" from the earth-poles to the line ... from all zones and altitudes." For what other bird would sun itself in the Capitol unless it is the eagle—the same emblematic bird—both Roman and American—that appears in the finale of another of the author's Heldentenor arias, "Fate":

> One thing is forever good;
> That one thing is Success,—
> Dear to the Eumenides,
> And to all the heavenly brood.
> Who bides at home, nor looks abroad,
> Carries the eagles, and masters the sword.

We are unaccustomed to poetry celebrating nationalistic or martial sentiments. Most readers of serious poetry would even find them reprehensible. Yet Emerson's popularity in his own time undoubtedly owed much to the underlying triumphalist vision of an America ever expanding and assimilating, along the way, everything and everyone in its path, including "minorities, things under cloud," and doing so, like Mithridates, harmlessly and without indigestion. In this regard, Emerson was the first prophet of the Pax Americana. Even those who don't approve such an ambition must credit his prophetic acumen.

If one doesn't squint too closely at his patriot raptures (and they are seldom overt; more like the marches threaded through an Ives or Mahler symphony), Emerson can be read unproblematically as America's most accomplished Romantic poet, in lively dialogue with Coleridge and Shelley. And possibly with Hegel, for it may be that philosopher's owl, living belatedly at the end of European civilization, that Emerson has in mind in "Mithridates"—"The owl of Minerva [that] spreads its wings only with the falling of the dusk." Emerson wrote in the springtime of America. We read him in the fall, and so his sweetness seems to us to have a tang more of cider than of apple juice.

III

THE DIFFERENCE

"Do novelists owe shit to poetry?"
—Marilyn Hacker, "Riposte"

ELEVEN YEARS AGO today, on July 14, 1983, I wrote a poem, "Working on a Tan," the third stanza of which contains this parenthetical remark: "I never could / Figure how anyone can justify poetry / As a full-time job. How do they get through / The day at MacDowell— filling out / Applications for the next free lunch?" These lines so incensed my friend Marilyn Hacker that she was inspired, when she encountered the poem a year later, in *Poetry,* to use them as the starting point and epigraph for a poem of her own, "Riposte," which appears in her collection *Going Back to the River* and will appear again soon in her *Selected Poems.*

Already in my own poem I'd anticipated Marilyn's possible response, in the stanza that immediately follows the lines she quotes:

"Do I smell sour grapes?" jeers
My imaginary friend at the colony
(Whose every summer has been subsidized
For lo these many years). Her nose
Is accurate, and in this matter of a tan,
As well, it may be I am moved mainly
By envy of those whose copper tones

Betoken subsidies that need not be
Applied for—the social lions,
The skiers, the climbers, and wealth's other scions.

The poem goes on to pick at the scabs of my guilt with regard to the capital sin of envy, and along the way it makes an effort to offer hedged compliments to the suntanned leisure classes who are the objects of that envy.

Marilyn, however, did not concern herself, in her riposte, with that side of the poem. Her attention was devoted to two matters only: first, to what she imagined to be the superior vacations that I, as a representative novelist, might enjoy "in the right Hampton," and then to my assertion that poetry is not a full-time job.

In the Hampton stanzas Marilyn depicts a hypothetical novelist's deluxe holiday in colors that rival the work of Judith Krantz: their shopping is done by *au pairs,* while they take their computers to Yaddo (and/or France), where (wickedly, I gather) "their royalties or last advance / [do not] cause the *per diem* rate to rise pro rata." When I first read this, I wanted to protest to Marilyn that I'd written my poem in a very redneck part of the Poconos, that I had no knowledge of Yaddo and employed no *au pair.* But to this she might well answer that other novelists are commonly guilty of such things, and that, in any case, the major thrust of her riposte was in the matter of whether or not poetry is (or should be) a full-time occupation. In that regard the later stanzas of "Riposte" note that many poets have had to supplement their income by driving taxis, teaching, translating, and waiting tables, and that they would be denied American Express cards if they listed their occupation as "poet" on the application form. She puts these words in my mouth: "And you see no excuse for poets' lives / *because* we're paid so mingily; that's it?" This leads her to "think of 'unemployed' mothers, housewives / whose work was judged equivalent to shit shoveling on Frank Perdue's chicken farm. . . ." She rounds off her riposte so:

SF writer snipes poets on the pages
of *Poetry:* that's also aiming low,

though nowhere near as low as poets' wages.
At fifty cents a line, where would *you* go?

And fifty cents a line's exemplary!
Measure it to your last *Playboy* short-short
and you might find an artists' colony
a perfectly respectable resort.

I gather from this that an SF writer, as a lower breed of novelist, has no business being disrespectful of his betters in *Poetry* (which then paid, by the way, a dollar a line, and now pays two). As to stories appearing in *Playboy,* they have been all too rare—two short-shorts in thirty years of submissions—and represent a fraction of the bulk of the work, in prose and poetry, that I've published in *Poetry.* Still, it better suits the expressive purpose of "Riposte" to suppose that my nonexistent sojourns in the right Hampton are funded by *Playboy,* that powerful metonymy for a materialist and patriarchal society with which lovers of poetry ought not consort.

I think it is safe to assume, as the poet does, that the sense of heartfelt grievance that informs "Riposte" is one that would be shared by most poets—and even a good many novelists in this era of the shrinking midlist, when writers of fiction are as likely as poets to depend upon academia and foundations for their livelihood. Similar invectives against the writers of best-selling fiction often appear in such venues of the counterculture as the *PEN Bulletin* and the *American Book Review.* Popular novelists are assumed to be purveyors of tawdry goods, which are hawked by venal publishers in airports and supermarkets stocked with nothing but trash, while novelists of the better sort are published by small presses, are read (like poets) chiefly by the captive audiences of their students and those with whom they network, and share with poets the conviction that they are being "marginalized" by a culture that values them no more than it does the minions of Frank Perdue.

This is still a minority view among nonacademic novelists, however, since most of them know their chief motive in writing is no different from that which impels TV scriptwriters or admen or Dr.

Johnson—to make money. Accordingly, they have studied the market with an eye to making the right accommodation between their own talents and the market's demands. Although only a few will earn the six- or seven-figure advances that are a ticket to the right Hampton, it is still possible for the more adaptable and industrious to make a middle-class living by their writing—and thereby garner an exit visa from the world of nine-to-five wage slavery. That possibility is a potent motivator, which guarantees a constant flood of manuscripts over the transoms of those who publish fiction.

Poets are less naive in the ways they seek to be published. Even the rankest novices know they must network. The networking is carried on in the workshops, at readings, in summer schools, and at the various Yaddos where poets go to rub shoulders. Perhaps the chief irksomeness of my remark in "Working on a Tan" was to refer to the MacDowell system as a "free lunch," when the practical reality is that such summer camps are where the real job of poetry gets done. Time at Yaddo is as little to be accounted a holiday as auditions should be accounted recreation for an actor. So, Marilyn, you have my apologies for my insensitivity in that regard.

As to whether poetry is or isn't a full-time job, whether it should be thought of as an occupation at all—in that I must go on being a grinch. I will even claim the authority of a Tiresias, with personal experience on both sides of the existential divide, having published over twenty volumes of fiction and eight of poetry; having, as well, noted the working habits of hundreds of poets and novelists.

Novelists put more hours in. They have to. It's simple arithmetic. My latest novel, *The Priest,* is 310 pages in its English edition; 500 manuscript pages; 114,000 words. It took me a year and a half to write, a rate of production that translates to a meager page of manuscript per day, or 250 words. Usually, I write at least two pages once I get going; on a good day four or five pages. That the book took as long as it did reflects the fact that it was often interrupted by time taken off to write reviews, short stories, and poetry. There are many novelists whose rate of productivity puts mine to shame, from the most mandarin, John Barth, to Tolkien clones of lowest brow who must churn out a new trilogy each year just to make ends meet. Not surprisingly, those novelists who command the largest advances—a John Grisham or a Danielle Steele—are usually exceptionally productive. Indeed, it's part of the job description: their publishers rely on them for a new book each year.

Novelists who produce a new book every year or two are probably spending fifteen to thirty hours a week at the typewriter, writing. And poets? High-productivity poets were once not that uncommon. One can imagine Tennyson, Browning, or Longfellow spending as much time at their desks as Honoré de Balzac or Ouida, but nowadays workaholic poets are rarer, and regarded with suspicion by their less hardworking peers. Still, some are incontestably first-rate. Albert Goldbarth manages to produce abundantly without slacking off; John Hollander, ditto. It's doubtful that their *Collected Poems* could be accommodated in a single wieldy volume without having recourse to India paper and microscopic print. But for most poets a thin volume every two or three years seems to be the norm.

I have one here, by a well-approved poet, who observes that norm. There are thirty-six poems, covering eighty pages (not counting pages that are blank). That would represent one poem, or some sixty lines of verse, every three weeks, if the poet were to publish a book biennially; or, three lines of verse a day. Poems, however, do not get written in such a fashion. Once the poet attains liftoff a first draft tends to get written in a day or two (especially poems less than a page long, which constitute a third of the poems in the collection at hand) with varying degrees of excision and revision thereafter. My rough estimate would be that the poet may have worked on these poems for some 125 days in the course of two years; or, one out of every six days. Even then, I doubt that many stints of poetic labor exceeded a couple of hours.

What I conclude from this is not that poets are, as a breed, lazy, but that their art is one that requires a peculiar intensity of energy, which often cannot be summoned at will on a day-to-day basis. (Poets who have schooled themselves to write narrative or other kinds of book-length poems are an exception to this rule, and their diligence must approach that of novelists, or exceed it. Often such poets are high-productivity novelists, as well: Robert Penn Warren, Vikram Seth, D. M. Thomas.)

Poets may object that the work of poetry is not one that time clocks can measure, that they live with their poems twenty-four hours a day; that their poems are collations of a thousand fleeting impressions, insights, puns, and epiphanies, from which nectar the poet will produce the honey of his poems. This is true, and just as true for novelists as for poets. Indeed, perhaps the hardest part of any novelist's job is keeping in mind all those elements of his work-in-progress that have already been written and that remain to be done, the latter a protean flux of possibilities that will not stop shape-shifting until it has been pinned down by the act of writing. So, in this respect, no less than with the matter of what the time clock registers, the novelist must make the larger exertion.

Marilyn's poem testifies to the de facto truth of my contention by noting how many poets have "exciting alternate careers." The range of jobs for poets that she cites is meant to underline the irony of "exciting," but it is surely the case that even a moderately interesting job outside the poetry workshop business is more likely to yield high poetic dividends than unlimited leisure or a work-life confined to cajoling guileless youths into believing they are our next Rimbauds. If Ezra Pound had had to work as a doctor in Paterson, New Jersey, the devils of fascism might not have made his hands their workshop. If Charles Olson had spent more than one summer doing the honest labor that provided him with his poetic persona for the rest of his life, he might not have wound up an alcoholic wreck and the king of sponges.

Good poets tend to be hard workers, because both good poetry and hard work are manifestations of high energy. They may complain about their work, as many hard workers do, but they enjoy its benefits—not simply their wages, but the accompanying Wordsworthian sense of resolution and independence.

My objection to a "free lunch" mentality—i.e., to the sense of entitlement that poets (and other Guggenheim and NEA applicants) have come to share with the homeless and other self-styled victims of the System—is that it is debilitating, demoralizing, and self-deluding. Self-deluding for the simple reason that the world doesn't owe us a living. If some novelists receive a great deal of money for their work, it is because there are people who will pay money to read what they have written. Their audiences can't be considered diddled, for they're not buying a pig in poke but rather a known quantity: another Anne Rice, another Tom Clancy, another James Michener.

I remember some years ago being part of a panel discussion at which another panelist expressed her passionate contempt for the crass commercialism of the publishing industry, which had time and again rejected her vampire novel. What set her vampire novel apart from all others was that it featured a black, lesbian vampire who was also handicapped. The author believed that handicapped black lesbians would flip for her work, and so they might—at least that portion of them who like vampire novels to begin with. It angered her to think that publishers were denying that potential audience the pleasure of reading her work.

Not to belabor the point: the amount of money any writer earns is directly proportional to the number of readers who want to read his/her work and will buy the books. Everything else is patronage, whether it takes the form of free vacations, university tenure at writing workshops, or Guggenheims and MacArthur awards. There is nothing inherently wrong with patronage. Patrons funded the work of all the great painters of the Renaissance, most of classical music, and some large percentage of all English poetry. Now that the system has been bureaucratized, it isn't even necessary for a poet to produce a servile dedication page; a mere acknowledgment will do.

It shouldn't matter. Nor does it. One has only to leave the cramped premises of the poetry establishment, and one realizes that no one cares. Contestants on "Jeopardy!" are good in most categories, but on a recent program no one could name the current poet laureate. Poets command little reviewing attention, and even such bastions of couth as *The New York Review of Books* accord poets less and less notice. Allen Ginsberg is the only living American poet who can still lay claim to celebrity status.

Poetry is not a route to money. As a career, it is still a clerical calling, a form of monasticism, with a wage ceiling, for all but the abbots, that guarantees little more than board and room—and, because they cost so little, laurels. However, for those who are made fretful by such limitations, poetry needn't, any more than religion, be considered a career. A spiritual life doesn't require taking Holy Orders, only a decision to submit to a lifelong discipline.

Poetry professionals, those who have been tonsured and anointed, may scoff, but look at the record. Among the nonprofessional poets who have created oeuvres that will surely outlast those of legions of today's poets of the workshops and networks are Wallace Stevens and W. C. Williams, Emily Dickinson and François Villon. Indeed, many poetry professionals of the past are now unfairly scanted: Longfellow and Millay and Jeffers all may legitimately claim some degree of neglect. But nowadays, by virtue of their positions at the center of the network, the professionals have a better-than-average chance of due recognition.

The cruel, Calvinist truth of the matter is that there is little relation between the effort exerted and the result achieved. This is true for novelists as well, of course. A writer may spend five years straining to produce a novel that is terminally dull, while Lawrence Durrell tosses off *Balthazar* in a mere six weeks. But the disparity is crueler for poets. A mediocre novelist may still find readers; a mediocre poet has only his chagrin and, if he's lucky, tenure.

All this can be accounted a blessing. Poetry, like salvation, is an absolute gift. When it is happening to the poet, when the Muse is there, what bliss. Whether the poem is any good, what bliss anyhow. One of the stock figures in the dramas of pop culture—in Altman's *Nashville,* in the TV series *Mary Hartman, Mary Hartman*—is the thoroughly self-deluded country-and-western singer, who believes in her gifts against every evidence that she has none, and who, in her apotheosis, is proven right. Yes, the Muse is with her, hallelujah. Every poet must make that same wager—a wager not unlike Pascal's, except that the poet's hypothetical divinity, his Muse, lives evanescently from poem to poem, quickens to a certain luster and then, like fireworks, fades.

Poetry is its own reward in a way that novels simply are not. I know of only one novelist over the age of sixty who persists in writing book after book in the virtual certainty he will not be published, and he is a reclusive alcoholic who sits down at his typewriter as though it were a pinball machine. That state of entranced self-absorption doubtless accounts for the works of many certainly quite sober high-production novelists, from John Jakes to Joyce Carol Oates. It is a condition that less productive novelists may envy, but it bears little resemblance to the experience of writing poetry.

Poets have one great advantage over novelists that is seldom noted: their artistic longevity. Novelists are much likelier to burn out in middle age, partly for the reasons cited above. They have to work harder, and those who write from their own experience will often exhaust the soil without judicious alternation of crops. Think only of the big shots and how they fizzled in their waning years: Fitzgerald, Hemingway, Steinbeck, Sinclair Lewis, Faulkner. There are hundreds of lesser figures who either fell silent or should have. Alcoholism is often a contributing factor, as it was for those five writers, all of whom used booze to fuel their imaginations and to meet an endless succession of self-imposed deadlines.

There have been, and are, many alcoholic poets, but in my experience poets tend to be a more sober lot, which is one reason they age so much better. It is not uncommon for poets to enjoy a final autumnal glory of creativity, for age brings with it a new menu of experiences. Friends die, the dark encroaches, the garden takes on a new significance. These are materials that lend themselves to lyric expression. Just because poems don't demand so much in the way of stamina and feats of memory, they are a suitable occupation for those who are older and wiser and shorter of breath.

Everything I've said here is easily controverted. Grand schematizations of polar opposites—as between men and women, rich and poor, east and west—either lead to vivid but obviously wonky ideologies, or ramify into thickets of qualifications and quibbles, where every rule has so many exceptions that finally one might just as well do without them and allow as how every poet and every novelist is a law unto him- or herself. There may be rich poets living far from academe, who beaver away at epic poems from nine to five and vote Republican. There may be novelists of lyric gifts and slender means whose entire reward is the consciousness of their lofty genius. Among thousands of writers every permutation is likely to occur some time or other.

Twenty-three years ago I wrote a poem, "For Marilyn," which, in the way poems often do, more satisfactorily addresses the matter of contention between us—the matter of contention, per se—than (I fear) my more overt disputation. Here it is:

> We are too fretful, you and I,
> For our own good, or for our art's.
>
> The heart is like a butterfly
> That flits about in fits and starts.
>
> The artist's task is patiently
> To stalk it, catch it, classify.
>
> He cannot take the time to ask
> The butterfly about his task.
>
> He craves its iridescent wings
> Too much to mark its sufferings.
>
> The heart surrenders him its facts
> But never, hopelessly, affection,
>
> And he must justify his acts
> By the scope of his collection.

ONEGIN'S CHILDREN:
POEMS IN THE FORM
OF A NOVEL

Judevine: The Complete Poems 1970–1990
by David Budbill CHELSEA GREEN 1991 $14.95 (PAPER) 310 PP.

Iris
by Mark Jarman
STORY LINE PRESS 1992 $23.95, $16.95 (PAPER) 124 PP.

The Marriages of Jacob: A Poem-Novella
by Charlotte Mandel
MICAH PUBLICATIONS 1991 (PAPER) 110 PP.

The Boys Who Stole the Funeral: A Novel Sequence
by Les Murray FARRAR, STRAUS & GIROUX 1991 $20.00 71 PP.

The Adventure
by Frederick Pollack
STORY LINE PRESS 1986 $15.00, $8.00 (PAPER) 182 PP.

THE LONG NARRATIVE poem is an art form that has come very close
to extinction in this century. Indeed, it was already an endangered
species in the Victorian era, as readers more and more came to prefer
stories that weren't tricked out in rhyme and meter, artifices at odds
with the main esthetic program of the novel, which was an ever-more-
perfect psychological and dramatic illusion of life that enabled skilled

readers vicariously to negotiate the novel's fictive terrains. Perhaps the most crucial figure in this process was Sir Walter Scott, who won a large audience with his long narrative poems but earned a fortune with his novels. It is hard not to infer from Scott's example that if one has a gift for storytelling it may more profitably be put to use in writing novels than in writing poems. Few writers have aspired to set a contrary example, and none have succeeded. Who now bothers to read George Eliot's *The Spanish Gypsy,* Thomas Hardy's *The Dynasts,* or William Morris's synthetic epics? And when contemporary poets have undertaken to write narratives of any length, they also invariably have written in serviceable, novelistic prose—Robert Graves, Sylvia Plath, James Dickey, D. M. Thomas.

However, the last decade has witnessed a small renaissance of narrative poetry, some of which—notably Vikram Seth's *The Golden Gate* and James Merrill's *The Changing Light at Sandover*—has met with a modicum of critical and popular success. More commonly, such book-length poems are ignored or dismissed out of hand by critics whose criteria for lengthy (i.e., more ambitious) poems derive entirely from modernist models that were created in defiance of the narrative impulse. Frederick Turner's remarkable epic, *The New World* (Princeton, 1985), was reviewed dismissively, despite florid tributes on its cover from Amy Clampitt and James Merrill, and it was chiefly reprobated for the vein of prose narrative it sought to emulate, nothing less déclassé than science fiction.

Why then do some few poets persist in invoking a muse generally supposed to be dead? For the best and most disinterested of motives, because they love her. The verse novel offers pleasures that even the most "poetic" of prose novels cannot (indeed, that epithet has come to be a euphemism for bombastic, overwritten, and florid, and most readers wisely regard it as pejorative), concinnity, playfulness, a longer breath, and, paradoxically, a quicker pace. But perhaps its most potent, if covert, appeal is to the capable reader's conscious connoisseurship. Such are its readerly dividends; it offers equivalent writerly advantages. Chief of them and most obvious is simply the chance to work on a larger scale than that of lyric meditation or confessional anecdote, the reigning poetic forms of our time.

There has been in this century a countertradition for long poems, as exemplified in such modernist texts as Ezra Pound's *Cantos,* with all its many emulators, John Berryman's *Dream Songs,* and A. R. Ammons's *Sphere: The Form of a Motion.* The plural titles of the first two books point to the mosaic character of most long poems in this tradition, while Ammons's *Sphere* is inspirited by the Emersonian afflatus of those long poems that depart from an autobiographical or diaristic format—e.g., Berryman, Robert Lowell's *History,* Marilyn Hacker's *Love, Death, and the Changing of the Seasons.* This countertradition tends to value poetry in proportion as it requires, like admission to Gramercy Park, a key that is reserved for a happy few. Elitist pleasures can be real, but they are not the only pleasures poetry has to offer, nor even its headiest. For all that criticism can do to establish a consensus, it cannot efface the record of the past, and while it is still possible to read Dante and Milton and Byron, et al., it will be impossible for a certain kind of poet to resist their challenge. It may be that there are rock faces in the Poconos that present greater technical difficulties to a climber than the Matterhorn or Mont Blanc, but they just aren't the same thing. Scale commands its own kind of respect.

Then why has there been such a long drought of narrative poetry, and why does it now seem to be back with us? For the same reason that it earlier withered away—because the marketplace has changed. It has become almost as quixotic an undertaking, financially, to write a certain kind of novel as to write poetry. Such has been the lament for many years of the "midlist" novelist, whose publishers, when they publish such work at all, pay advances that even extreme frugality cannot translate into a living wage. Now most novelists must do what poets are long accustomed to: they must look on their writing as an avocation and write for love. And poets, witnessing this, not without a certain grim satisfaction, must feel less temptation to turn novelist. If one must write for love, well then, why not go whole hog? Why not write a verse novel and say to hell with the marketplace?

Here are the results of five such quixotic ventures, and they are heartening. Three of the five authors—David Budbill, Mark Jarman, and Les Murray—have written their verse novels in the regnant narrative form of minimalist realism, with lower-class characters experiencing normative stress in dismal surroundings heightened by occasional lightning flashes of violence as well as by moments of resplendent beauty. This esthetic actually works better for these poets than it does for their peers in prose, with the single exception of Raymond Carver, who has the advantage of being a poet himself. This similarity disguises a radical difference, however, for while the minimalists of prose fiction appeal to a socially upscale, if not highbrow, audience that does not experience cognitive dissonance reading such work side by side with ads for Steuben Glass and Courvoisier, David Budbill's appeal is more like that of Carl Sandburg or Stephen Vincent Benet. His poetry is as accessible as a parking lot and plain as a pair of Levi's. He has no truck with rhyme and meter but writes in a syntactically uncomplicated free verse that accommodates itself comfortably to the tasks set for it—exposition, description, dialogue, and an understated advocacy for his underdog characters. Imagine a free verse version of *Tortilla Flat* or *Cannery Row* set in rural Vermont, somewhat less ribald and more politically correct than Steinbeck, but with the same benign Family of Man flavor. Indeed, that photographic exhibit is one of the author's touchstones:

> Doug's better than six feet,
> weighs more than two hundred and fifty pounds.
> He has a couple of teeth missing up front and his voice
> is high and pinched. It doesn't belong to his body.
> When Doug laughs he sticks his enormous stomach out,
> throws his head and shoulders back and laughs loud,
> with his mouth open, like a picture I saw once
> of a Russian peasant in *The Family of Man.*

Clearly, Budbill is determined that we shall like Doug, and he introduces most of the characters in his book with the same undisguised advocacy. For some readers this will register as old-fashioned; for others it will have the virtue of directness, as though one were being led round the room, handshake by handshake, to all the author's particular friends at a church supper. Budbill has good reason for liking his characters—who, he more than once hints, are based on real-life acquaintances—and it is the burden of his book to set forth those reasons. (This quality of open warmth and emotional forthrightness is just as characteristic of the poems by Jarman and Murray, and one could theorize that it may be a trait common to most poets turned storyteller, a habit of candor carried over from the confessional lyric.)

For all its imposing bulk, *Judevine* is not a novel in verse but rather a collection of tales, like Sherwood Anderson's *Winesburg, Ohio* or a series of character sketches, like the *Spoon River Anthology,* all set in the same locale, with some characters overlapping from one tale to the next. The book has been growing, poem by poem, for over two decades, and this latest gathering assimilates not only Budbill's earlier collections of poems about Judevine but, as well, the verse play *Pulp Cutters' Nativity,* while, to complicate matters, there is a dramatic version of the poems, *Judevine: The Play,* that has been widely produced at regional theaters.

Many writers, when saddled with the designation of "regionalist," at once protest their universality, but I can't imagine Budbill would be so disloyal to his Vermonter Muse. He is a regionalist to that degree he comes across in some poems as a Vermont jingoist, jeering at any state with fewer maples, milder weather, citizens less hardened by austerity than those of Judevine. So persuasive are the poems, and so circumstantial in their account of the rigors of the village's daily life, that that is a point most out-of-state readers would be willing to concede. If "regionalism" is abstracted to "rural," Budbill once again can be grouped with Jarman and Murray, whose poems similarly declare their allegiance to the Great Outdoors and a kind of Jeffersonian disdain for those who don't live as freeholders. Can it be that there is an intrinsic, causal connection between long poems and wide open spaces?

The example of Vikram Seth notwithstanding, I think it more than likely. Country living promotes longer thoughts and patient, sustained achievement, such as gardeners undertake. City life is noted for its speed, excitement, and variety, and while these virtues are not antithetical to a long poem (Ashbery's *Flow Chart* is a quintessential

long poem in the urban manner), they may well make it harder for
the urban poet to pursue the sober, steadfast pace that a long narrative
poem requires. This difference is likely to be exacerbated by the different reading habits associated with the city, with its flow of new
magazines, new faces, new lingos, and the country, where one may,
at last, settle down with the *Aeneid* in all its rival translations. As we
read, so may we aspire to write. Indeed, for someone harboring the
ambition of writing a long poem, I can think of no more practical
starting point than to change one's address to somewhere in RFD.

Of all the five books under consideration, Budbill's is surely the
most accessible, a book one could imagine suddenly connecting with
the same middlebrow audience that has made cult figures of Robert
Bly and Joseph Campbell. A book, which is a higher commendation,
that could be used as a text in high school English classes as a way
of proving that poetry isn't the exclusive province of those who must
worry whether or not they dare eat peaches. Budbill is a poet who
could appeal to readers of *Field and Stream* or *Popular Mechanics* as
much as to readers of *Harper's* (where a part of *Judevine* has appeared),
such as in this description of Roy McInnes's welding shop:

> The shop was built in stages.
> The tall center section with its steep pitched roof
> is sided with slabs from the local mill, whereas
> the lean-to shed on the left
> is particleboard, the one on the right is Homasote.
> Summer people says it's ugly, but what they can't, or
> won't
> understand is: the sidings write a history
> of its construction. Rome wasn't built in a day either.
>
> When Roy built the center section he needed an opening
> large enough to admit big trucks, like loggers' rigs,
> but couldn't afford the kind of rising, jointed,
> overhead doors gas stations and garages have,
> so he found a way to use salvaged storm doors,
> the kind with glass so he could get some light in there,

by hitching them with hinges side to side
and stacking them three high so that now he's got
two folding doors which make an opening fifteen feet
                                                    wide
and seventeen feet high: two doors of doors
made from eighteen smaller doors.

This is a place where—against the grinder's scream and
                                                    whine,
the moan of generators straining, the crackling spit of
                                                    metal
rent asunder—human speech is pointless, drowned
in a cacophony of unearthly voices. And when the ma-
                                                    chines
get still, it is a place to see through the smoky fog
something medieval, brooding, dark, fantastical.

It would be so easy to see this place as sinister,
to see the wizard-priest who rules this lair as evil,
that would be so easy if
you didn't know that he is Roy—
the one who lets the calm of his body flow into your arm
when you touch his hand.

Excerpting is always culpable, but especially so in the case of
long poems. Budbill lays the groundwork for Roy's apotheosis as a
saint of the welding shop by many touches not quoted here and
rounds out his account with a vignette of Roy at work repairing the
broken boom of a logging truck. Even to quote the six-page section
that concerns Roy McInness would be an insufficient sampling, for it
is only one in the series of portraits of Judevine's small businessmen
and business places that takes up much of the second of the book's
four sections, including: Beaudry's permanent lawn sale; Charlie Ket-
ter, who made and sold wishing wells and birdhouses; Jerry's garage
and general store; Conrad, the drunk who runs the garage for Jerry;
and the junk store run by the bull dyke Alice Twiss. To all of them,
Budbill accords a discriminating and respectful attention. Occasion-

ally, he lapses into sentimentality or lazy phrases, such as "Rome wasn't built in a day either" or that "cacophony of unearthly voices," but one can as easily read such locutions not as lapses but as devices establishing the narrator's homespun tone, an artifice no more objectionable here than in Garrison Keillor's monologues on "A Prairie Home Companion." *Judevine,* like Keillor's Lake Wobegon tales, is a labor of love not in the usual sense that the artist can be seen to love the labor he performs, but because he can be seen to love the place and the people he's writing about.

Mark Jarman's *Iris* is a labor of love in the usual (and entirely honorable) sense. Of the five books under review it comes closest to possessing the virtues one associates with a good novel. There is a continuous action, developed characters, and a narrative momentum with none of those speed bumps that poets introduce into their longer works on purpose to slow the reader down to the statelier gait of Dame Poetry. In both its plot and its prosody *Iris* is an homage to the most successful and critically neglected practitioner of narrative verse in this century, Robinson Jeffers. It uses the same long, loping lines, and agglutinative, semicolon-encrusted syntax that gives a poem like "Roan Stallion" its bookmark-defying momentum. Of all the poems under review, it is, despite its length, the one you'd be likeliest to read at a single sitting, the one in which the question of what will happen next has the same import it would in an ordinary novel.

What happens is this: The eponymous heroine, fleeing an abusive husband, returns with her toddler daughter, Ruth, to her home in rural Kentucky, and for a while enjoys a neo-hillbilly country 'n' western idyll with a family consisting of her boozing Mama, her brothers Hoy and Rice, who grow marijuana because it's the most profitable cash crop for subsistence farmers, and Mama's lover and drinking companion, Charles, a crossing guard at a shopping mall, whom Mama met in this wise:

> The day Mama found him he was like that, lackadaisical
>   as a nodding thistle.

A bad bearing on her cart made one wheel spin. Mama
had
   bought too much and tried to guide
The cart with her beer belly. Charles, ignoring her,
   motioned a car through. There was a wiry, soft
Collision. Mama's cart tipped sideways. Groceries sprayed
   across the asphalt. Charles cursed.
Mama grabbed his forearm like a wader caught by a current
   on shifting stones.
When somebody appeared—the manager?—he whirled
on Charles
   and Mama both and shouted.
He grabbed Charles's hat and said he would replace the
   groceries and Charles, too.
So, Charles had needed someone, just like Mama. Truck
   loaded, the poor boy stunned, Mama drove
To the state line and brought them both a beer or two, a
   few games of video poker.
Charles cheered up. You couldn't tell how old he was,
   like those boys on Lawrence Welk
Who dance at show's end with the grandmothers, smiling
   more tenderly than any son.

The idyll ends when Hoy, Rice, and Charlie are executed by other
drug dealers, whereupon Iris flees to California, with her daughter
and her now autistic Mama, there to marry the first man she asks
directions from. She spends the second of the poem's three sections
in a state of somnambulistic housewifery. Then, the moment her
daughter marries, she decamps for what had been, all this while, her
secret destination, the landmark-status seacliff home of Robinson Jeffers, whose poetry, first encountered in college, has been a talisman
for Iris through the years. As she explains, toward the end of the
book:

You'd think with
all the death in it, my life
Would be a tragedy. But I've kept my real life a secret—
    reading Jeffers
And trying to imagine him imagining someone like me.
                                                    It's
    when he says
He has been saved from human illusion and foolishness
    and passion and wants to be like a rock
That I miss something. I think I have been steadfast,
    but what does rock feel? I like him in bereavement—
When saying man can't last long, then admitting, since
    his wife's death, that he is short of patience.
Wanting to die, to lay his body down where he has found
    the wounded deer have done so,
In the hidden clearing on the cliff edge, then refusing
    to. That's when I like to read him.

That passage is a good self-reflexive critique of the book in hand
as well as of Jeffers, and it also serves to illustrate an essential difference
between the two narrative media, prose and poetry. In narrative poetry,
the characters tend, even when they speak in a plausible, demotic way,
to *think* in poetry and to share, as Iris does here, the core concerns of
both the writer and the (presumed) readers, to try, in her terms, "to
imagine him imagining someone like me." To put this another way, the
reader of a poem is always more conscious of the shaping intelligence of
the poet than the reader of the novel, whose art conceals art as best it
can. The poetic storyteller also relies on his readers' imaginative coop-
eration in filling out those blanks that novelists can spend pages in spell-
ing out. Imagine how long Mama's first encounter with Charles might
take in the hands of even so telegraphic a prose writer as Raymond
Carver. In this respect, *Iris* more resembles the punchy scene setting of
a screen treatment, with the poet counting on his readers to extrapolate
stage business and dialogue. The object of poetic narrative is to suggest
as much as possible with maximum compression, but without becoming gnarled or gnomic and losing the flow, as in "There was a wiry, soft

collision," which conveys the impact of a car on Mama and her shopping cart with an economy that can't be taken in without a mental notation of "That's neat." It is with poets as with the splashier sort of painters, Delacroix, Rembrandt, Manet, Johns—it's not enough that their pictures fascinate us, they insist on our admiring the brushwork.

Finally, one must ask of a narrative poem the same leveling questions one asks of novels: Is it a good story? Does it have a satisfying resolution? It is, and it does, though the kind of satisfaction it affords is one of Chekhovian quietness; yet not *so* quiet that one couldn't imagine the book serving as the basis for a good movie.

Charlotte Mandel's *The Marriages of Jacob* is subtitled a "Poem-Novella," but it is, of the five books under review, the one with the least resemblance to conventional fiction, taking the form of a series of lyric evocations of the biblical tale of Jacob's marriages to the daughters of Laban. A reader unfamiliar with the source of Mandel's story would be hard-pressed to figure out what was going on behind the gauzy scrim of her poesy. The effect, most often, is of a modern dance performance that mimes just enough of the story to let the audience know that they are witnessing Primal Events. For instance, here is the Marriage Night, Section VI of the poem, and one of the longest of ninety numbered sections, in its entirety:

Serpentine, the line of women
glides into morning, sandals
stir the waking village dust

Returning to the bridal tent, ritual
that echoes between thighs
like weeping too far to be heard

Women's hands pass like breezes
winnowing fronds of Leah's hair
still fragrant with oils of myrrh,
aloe, cinnamon

Left palm to the right of one,
right palm to the left of another,

circling the bride, voices
ullulating

Praise for the bridal cup
broken and mended
by marriage

Folded by the pattern of dance,
the wedding sheet will be burned,
ashes buried at the edge
of the wheat field—
her blood/his sperm

Ewers of sweet well water dissolve
traces of salt on Leah's cheeks,
dried flecks on her thighs

Now she is theirs
forever in the company of wives.

Without the obligation to review, a few pages in that vein would stop me in my tracks; nor did a dutiful perusal of the whole much modify my first impression that Mandel's poetry is thin, precious, and portentous. Even so, I gather that there may be a large audience for such poetry, to judge by the testimony of the book's back jacket. For Alicia Ostriker, "It feels sacred through and through, although with no sense of piety." For Colette Inez, it is "seamless, with authority in detail, and power in the musical surge of its rhythms." Sandra Gilbert, praising Mandel's earlier poem-novella, *The Life of Mary,* offered praise that I imagine she would accord *Marriages* as well: ". . . that Mandel is telling a story through a sequence of lyrics is fascinating, too . . . locating herself in a female—indeed, often consciously feminist—tradition of revisionary mythology."

And there's the rub. Mandel's lyrical modus operandi, even if one discounts its beaux arts prettinesses—"still fragrant with oils of myrrh, / aloe, cinnamon"—simply can't wrest a contrary mythic import from her inherited story, a story that ought to exercise a feminist imagination, since it deals with the rival property claims of father and son-in-law in both women and cattle. It also recounts the peculiar contest between two sisters in providing their spouse with male off-spring, a contest in which the two wives are assisted, in tag-team style, by their handmaidens, Bilhah bearing children on behalf of Rachel, and Zilpah serving as a surrogate for Leah. Readers of Margaret Atwood's riveting novel *The Handmaid's Tale* are already aware of what narrative excitement a feminist sensibility can generate from such themes. From these four women issue the twelve sons who will father the twelve tribes of Israel. A large story, but not very tractable, for the accessory detail to this foundation legend is some of the most unyielding mythic ore in Genesis, particularly the magical ruse in Chapter 30 by which Jacob obtains possession of a good part of La-ban's cattle and Rachel's bargain with Leah by which she allows her older sister spousal privileges in exchange for her son's mandrakes. Even Thomas Mann in his magistral retelling of the Jacob legends in the first volume of his Joseph tetralogy failed to extract living signif-icance from these materials. Mandel doesn't even try; her account is terser than that in Genesis:

> It is told their eldest brother finds love apples—
> now Leah may hire her husband back
> from her sister. Jacob accepts
> his bond, justice again—birthright
> purchased by a sister for something to eat.

This neither illuminates the original text nor offers anything vivid in its own right—"love apples" is currently defined as "tomato" and is an inappropriately archaic term for mandrake root—and in that it is representative of all those parts of the poem that must carry the expository burden. When the poet amplifies the original, it often sounds like a verse retelling of *Love's Tender Fury*, as in this account of Leah's wedding night:

> Her scent rises from his own sweat
> Virginal oils, blood and brine
> cloud his skin

("Rachel," he had groaned to her, "Rachel.")
He wants to dive into a desert dune
rake her sour-sweet dampness from his pores

and when she slips back into the tent
he lifts her by the waist

throws her to the carpet floor
thrusts into her
again and again
crying her name:
"Leah! Leah!"

The form Mandel has adopted is not necessarily unmanageable, though in her hands it gives that impression. The texts of Schubert's two great song cycles, *Winterreise* and *Die schöne Müllerin,* written by Wilhelm Müller, are splendid examples of how a sequence of lyrical poems can add up to a story that takes place, as it were, off the page. The difference between Müller's works and Mandel's is that the ninety component lyric fragments of her poem are not satisfying in themselves, as distinct poems, so there is no specifically poetic compensation for the loss of narrative continuity. The effect of reading the book straight through is not so much that of educing a story from a sequence of poems as of viewing a series of stills from a movie made by a feminist-minded Cecil B. DeMille.

The publicity accompanying Les Murray's *The Boys Who Stole the Funeral* declares that he is recognized as "Australia's greatest living poet," and, it follows, the premier poet of an entire continent, a distinction even poets laureate might envy. Without knowing Murray's competition, one couldn't begin to assess that claim, but on the basis of this long poem and the edition of his collected poems, *The Rabbiter's Bounty,* which Farrar, Straus & Giroux is releasing at the same time, he certainly registers as a poet of large and diverse gifts. Few of the poems in *The Rabbiter's Bounty* give a hint of the author's ambition to meet the challenge of narrative poetry, though many of the themes and settings of *The Boys Who Stole the Funeral* are prefigured in his shorter poems, particularly those that commemorate the hardier, earthier work ways of small farms, such as "The Milk Lorry" or "The Butter Factory," where

> . . . paddlewheels sailed the silvery vats where muscles
> of the one deep cream were exercised to a bullion
> to be blocked on paper. And between waves of delivery
> the men trod on water, hosing the rainbows of a shift.
> It was damp April even at Christmas round every
> margin of the factory. Also it opened the mouth
> to see tackles on glibbed gravel, and the mossed char lou-
> > vres
> of the ice-plant's timber tower streaming with
> heavy rain all day, above droughty paddocks
> of the totem cows round whom our lives were dancing.

Luscious stuff, yes? The verbal equivalent of double cream with lots of plump words for the tongue to fondle and a *density* of imagery that is the sine qua non of good narrative verse: just do the film montage in your mind that would correspond to the first four quoted lines.

I can't resist quoting another poem from *The Rabbiter's Bounty,* "Poetry and Religion," since it could serve as a manifesto for *Boys:*

> . . . A poem, compared with an arrayed religion,
> may be like a soldier's one short marriage night
> to die and live by. But that is a small religion.
>
> Full religion is the large poem in loving repetitions;
> like any poem, it must be inexhaustible and complete
> with turns where we ask Now why did the poet do that?
>
> You can't pray a lie, said Huckleberry Finn;
> you can't poe one either. It is the same mirror:
> mobile, glancing, we call it poetry,
>
> fixed centrally, we call it religion. . . .

Boys tells its story in a series of 140 fourteen-line stanzas, some in the form of rhyming sonnets, most in free verse, with a line length varying from the simple to the complex. An example of the former can be found in the tetrameter of the opening stanza:

> It is the story of the boy
> with his gift of laughing at deadly things
> who stole a Digger's funeral
> and took it on the country roads.

In contrast, Murray also employs lines twice as long, like these, in which Reeby, one of the two boys of the title, is confronted with the temptation to begin life over in the scrubby marshes between farm-land and desert:

> to spend your life here and further out in the desert min-
> ing camps
> among the evaders the maintenance dodgers and the lost
> men
> the grey-cropped ss men or to change your name re-
> enrolling
> remembering the new surname perfecting the new life
> history
> first comes the disaster then its allegance [*sic*] and the ev-
> idence

Of the five poems reviewed here, Murray's is surely the most beguiling and technically resourceful as poetry, but the narrative sometimes seems to fall captive to the poet's determination to carry out his oracular mission as stated in "Poetry and Religion." This is especially the case in a concluding visionary sequence when two ab-original spirits, Birrigan and Njimbin, perform ghostly circumcision rites on Kevin Forbutt, the other boy of the title, in a manner that devotees of Bly's *Iron John* would heartily applaud, but which I found a bit preachy: "Male tears, shouts the Njimbin, are a great taboo! / Women mustn't see them, or they will kill their children."

In its tendency to find the culmination of its tale in a moment of visionary afflatus rather than in dramatic action, *Boys* is representative of the trepidation most poets have when confronting the rival aesthetic of the novel. The trade-off, however, is considerable, for a poet's gifts can heighten otherwise humdrum parts of the story, as when Murray views a funeral at a country church from the point of view of an eagle circling above the church. The cars carrying the mourners become insects, and "dying, they open little wings, releasing humans." The eagle sums up the funeral so: "Human meat went into the pointed house / today, as a log with blinding silver crustings; / flesh, like she found once underneath a tractor."

In *Iris* Jarman views key moments from similar aerial perspectives: the moon contemplating an act of arson; Iris, in a dream, becoming a feeding gull. Frederick Pollack's hero-narrator similarly takes flight early in his poem: "out and over, following the stream, / the southern thermals, / the bits and specks / of high-flying food . . ." Perhaps because their Muses are winged creatures, poets are able to take such liberties; perhaps they are impelled to, by secret Orphic laws equivalent to the laws of copyright.

Murray's plot hinges on two points of honor. The book lifts off as Kevin Forbutt and Kevin's friend Cameron Reeby, "famous for an epic fight with women," abduct Clarence Dunn's corpse from a suburban funeral parlor. The boys transport the purloined uncle to his requested burial amid the hills of home, where they are at once assimilated and Cameron falls in love with Jenny Dunn, a romance that is doomed by the second point of honor, this time a revenge performed by a young harpy aggrieved by Cameron's "epic fight." There is an antifeminist subtext to this part of the story that the text itself never explicitly deals with, but to say more would be to spoil the plot's one unexpected twist. Feminist readers should be advised that they will wish to berate the author, but no more than they might berate most male poets of earlier centuries, whose higher wisdom it is the pastoral agenda of Murray's poem to celebrate. Indeed, *Boys* has a strong affinity with Vergil's *Eclogues,* a poem in which urban philosophers disguise themselves as shepherds, debate the meaning of Civilization, and assert a learned preference for whole-grain foods.

The difference is that while the *Eclogues* was written by a mostly absentee landowner, *The Boys Who Stole the Funeral* is the poem of someone who's actually done the dirty work of shepherding and still has something good to say about it.

Frederick Pollack's *The Adventure* was published in 1986, the same year as Vikram Seth's *The Golden Gate*. While Seth's book seems already to have won a secure place in the canon of contemporary poetry, Pollack's has been little remarked. Of the books reviewed here, it is my favorite, for the simple reason specific to narrative poetry that *The Adventure* was the most entertaining story. I realize that among a certain class of readers, entertainment is a suspect pleasure and that to commend anything as entertaining is tantamount to drooling over a cheeseburger. My sense of the matter is that those who deplore the virtues associated with entertainment—narrative suspense, the delight of bold strokes and bright colors, the satisfactions of dramatic closure—are the sort who think of art as an edifying ritual, like church attendance, more to be suffered in respectful silence than enjoyed with gusto. Lord knows that such readers have plenty of poets catering to their needs. And when a poet aspires to be entertaining, you can be sure he will receive a stony reception from that lot, as Pollack has.

The Adventure belongs to the distinct subgenre of fantasy tale that recounts the experience of the afterlife—not the heaven and hell mandated by conventional religion but a terrestrial afterlife where unpaid debts and missed chances can perhaps be rectified or, more usually, cannot. Earlier examples of this form are Conrad Aiken's story "Mr. Arcularis," Sutton Vane's play *Outward Bound,* and the recent film comedy *Defending Your Life.* Those who need authentication of a high order may hark back to Dante, though Kafka's novels would be a better touchstone for Pollack's poem.

The story begins with an awakening to a corpse's-eye view of the forest floor:

> ... I became
> superficial.
> I awoke. The forest was full of life.

Beetles and spiders, and that
part of a bird's life
spent on the ground. Ant columns

avoided me, worms twitched away.
Broad brown leaves, moist, softened twigs.
I was neither warm nor cold.

Sedate, wide-scattered
elms and maples
and an opossum

mother and young, moving among the weeds.
Ground mist.
Other animals stared. I was

playing for millennia
with the snooze-alarm ...

There follows an evolutionary series of metamorphoses as the
awakened sleeper assumes a succession of animal and avian forms
until, by an act of sheer will, he becomes a child's idea of a muscle-
man, and he acquires a steed designed on similar lines—

        ... It turned
to face me and I laughed:

no more a horse
than a man in a horse-suit. Not a cow
or a bear, though big and solid, a child's

drawing of an animal.
Absurd the huge sad eyes,
the wide hand-puppet mouth

dribbling greens. The legs crude pillars,
the hooves (—what?
elephant-stumps) hidden

in fur ...

I scratched its silly face
at which I could not stop smiling. It
stuck out a wide pink tongue

and rasped
my lean new bicep.
                          I mounted

gracelessly (had never done this). It
emitted a dying-fall sound
between a whoof and a whinney . . .

—and off he goes, on his Adventure, which takes him first to a shrine
and then, amid "pools, lawns, fountains, formal gardens," a palace,
where he encounters archetypal figures of Romance—a Countess, a
General, a Painter, a French Maid—all rendered with the same droll
too-muchness as his horse, Juggernaut, as if it were drawn by an
infantine Aubrey Beardsley.

This idyll is terminated abruptly somewhere before the halfway
point of the poem, and the narrator enters another, seedier precinct
of the afterlife, a grown-up world of taverns and highways, offices
and suburban amenities, where he has a second chance to make a go
of it with his old flame, Susan, who was a suicide on her first go-
round (as was he). This second part of the poem is a baleful parody
of various urban modes of Death-in-Life. Susan is a reader and goes
to a library from which

          . . . Even
     the rarest materials
     could be borrowed. I noticed

     on a small shelf
     the golden clasps
     of thick brown folios. A complete

     Sophocles. Aristotle's dialogues.
     The Q Document. And the radio, she said,
     played the lost music—

Schubert's lost Seventh,
a lovely, lilting
tomorrow-to-fresh-fields sort of tune

from the scherzo was
a local theme song.
The Bach cantatas

people had wrapped fish in . . .

Dead celebrities are sometimes visitable, as well. Picasso is still at work: "Wow," I said; "I had / forgotten Picasso." "What sort of stuff?" / "As per usual. What else?" The narrator interrupts a bus trip to the central city to stop at a windowless stone building occupied by a disappointed Kierkegaard, who professes to believe himself in hell. The narrator tries to jolly him out of it, and stumbles into a finer sense of his own despair.

Later, after a spell of cohabitation and nest-building with Susan, he absconds to Wolf's Tavern, a waterfront dive, where he hangs out with Gottfried Benn 1886–1956, doctor, poet, and suicide, who explains about the apparent absence of all the great men who can't be located through the Tracing Office—Shakespeare, Mozart, Pollock, Kafka. Later, in a scene both droll and chilling, the bartender, Wolf, screens a clandestine holographic film of a drinking session shared by Freud, Wittgenstein, and Marx. The brief coda that follows it, as the narrator departs the city and rides north, returning to a "Nature" now inhospitable and bare, is still chillier.

I hope that synopsis, even with its many omissions, gives some sense of the book's imaginative liveliness and of the verses' litheness. Of all the books, it offers the smoothest, i.e., most novellike, surface, and can be read straight through from start to finish in a single evening without having to come up for air. I first read *The Adventure* two years ago with no expectation of reviewing it and so can testify from my own experience that it is, as poems should be, as much a pleasure to reread as to read.

In the golden ages that are still the core of the literary curriculum, most poets of large ambition felt themselves compelled to test their mettle against the task set by epic poetry. The epic on the "*Arma virumque canto*" model is now pretty much a lost cause—most modern "epics," such as Derek Walcott's *Omeros,* being formally much closer to the novel as we know it. Few contemporary poets—unless those I've reviewed and cited here constitute significant and not rule-proving exceptions—think of narrative poetry even as an option, much less a challenge not to be shirked. That may be okay for the poets. But readers of poetry and aspirant poets, if that is not a redundancy, ought not on principle to exclude narrative poetry from their reading diet, from a mistaken sense that it is somehow a lesser breed. If any kind of poetry merits that standard accolade of blurb-writers' "risk-taking," it must be book-length narrative verse—the risk being the number of eggs in a single basket, the size of the basket, and the knowledge that almost everyone these days lives in fear of cholesterol.

THE NEW WORLD

The New World: an epic poem
by Frederick Turner
PRINCETON UNIVERSITY PRESS (1985) $ 9.95

THAT THERE EXISTS an innate correspondence between poetry and science fiction was an article of faith among the evangelists for the New Wave. The basis for such a belief was often no more than that both arts were products of the Imagination with a capital I, while stricter apologists urged that SF, like poetry, had a special relation to metaphor such that the "ideas" of SF were themselves "poetic" in a manner transcending their written form. This argument from metaphor was the theoretic basis for a few quasi-narrative poems by D. M. Thomas and George Macbeth published in *New Worlds,* in which these certified poets served up reheated recensions of such familiar SF stories as "The Cold Equations." But these seeds were either infertile in themselves, or fell on stony ground, for SF poetry, so-called, never made headway in a narrative mode. Instead, it has characteristically adopted a form common to much contemporary, non-confessional poetry (especially in the United States), that of a brief (less than one hundred lines), semisurrealistic vignette or expostulation. Within this lyric frame it deploys the familiar tropes of SF as a kind of allegorical shorthand. Reference to a common stock of images has the convenience that mythological or religious allusion once possessed: most readers will be able to extrapolate a coherent *mise-en-*

scène from a minimum of auctorial cues. SF shares this advantage with the other conventional (i.e., well-mapped) lands of Faerie, that having often been there before, it is easy to return.

Yet for twenty years or more, despite the theorists' claims and despite the single less-than-breathtaking instance of Harry Martinson's *Aniara* (the English translation appeared in 1963), there has not been a long narrative poem to put the theory to the test, a poem that tells an SF narrative in poetic form, an epic of science fiction. The reasons for this aren't far to seek. Most SF—indeed, most fiction—is written to meet the demands of a market (of editors, really) in which "poetry" exists only as an absolute prohibition. Any poet with the yen and the stamina to produce long narrative fictions would be a fool to do so in verse, and indeed both Thomas and Macbeth took to prose when they felt a narrative urge. So too did Frederick Turner, whose first long SF narrative, *A Double Shadow* (Putnam, 1978), took the prudent and prosaic form of a novel. But now Turner has had the courage to be a fool for art and has written the first genuine epic poem in the SF genre, and *The New World* wonderfully fulfills the hopes of the theorists. The form is not just frosting on the narrative cake; the story is genuinely richer and more resonant because of the specifically poetic gifts Turner brings to bear. The reciprocal benefit is no less remarkable: the task of writing an epic for a modern audience is made altogether smoother and more viable because the tale is set not in the mythopoeic past but in the science-fictional future.

Consider some of the difficulties. First, the sheer labor of writing six and a half thousand lines of verse, a good portion of which must, if the whole is to register as worthy the name of poetry, pass beyond mere prosodic acceptability and register as inspired—or why this fuss with invoking the Muse? The history of literature is strewn with the wrecks of would-be epics that died becalmed in Sargassos where the winds of Speriminh (as Turner names his Muse) would not blow. Turner adopts an unrhymed five-beat line of no particular meter, though with the language's natural tendency to iambic patterns and hence to blank verse. While in some hands so protean a meter might serve as an excuse for avoiding the rigors of strict form and doing pretty much whatever one wanted to, as Turner uses it, the five-beat line does the job nicely, allowing him to move among the various voices his narrative requires with flexibility and ease, achieving a high style (noble but not pompous) without the corsetings of compressed diction that strict blank verse encourages and which modern readers are unwilling or unable to negotiate at book length. Even Homer nods, of course, and Turner can produce a narrative patch as flat as this:

> The Tuscarawans must have decided to hold
> the crossing of the River Ahiah, and to wait for help
> from their eastern allies Mohican, Sandusky, and Wyan-
> dot
> but even with those reinforcements they are badly out-
> numbered. . . .

But Homer doesn't characteristically nod, and neither does Turner. Here he is at a representative moment, not at the top of his form by any means, but doing a good job at one of the tasks traditional to the epic, describing a battle scene at high speed in a series of telling but not too high-flown similes:

> . . . that moment the second wave strikes, cutting
> the line, choking the flow of reinforcements, and setting
> new panic among the Somerset men.
> The segment of enemy line, a cut worm, must turn
> in two directions at once, but they still outnumber
> the Ahians by three to one, did they but know it.
> Now the third platoon, strung out in a line,
> hears the order to charge, breaks into a gallop,
> thundering down the slope. Among them Rollo,
> his face very white, his eyes like coals in his head,
> lashes his sword from its scabbard, the hiss of a meteor,
> raises his voice in the family war cry: "Aoi!"
> They burst on the enemy line as surf on the breakwater

shatters in blossoms of phosphorescence and sweeps
in green tons over the wall. . . .

The next difficulty of the epic is less obvious but more formi-
dable: it must foreswear, or radically alter, a good part of the esthetic
resources available to the novel—not on grounds of generic purity
but because the looseness and diffuseness that give the novelist so
ample a canvas are death to poetry, whose glory is to suggest in three
or four lines what a novel would project onto as many pages of scene-
setting and dialogue. An epic is not a novel in verse; it does not aim
to create, as most novels do, a kind of hypnagogic movie on the screen
of the reader's half-dreaming mind, a movie usually enjoyed with a
naive, vicarious satisfaction. Epic is more akin to our experience of
another no longer living art, history painting, or the painting of mythological subjects. The object in both cases is to produce ideal human
figures on a scale larger than life, whose actions are conducted not at
the tempos of ordinary life but with the sacramental solemnity of (to
cite another lost art) *opera seria*. Done wrong, it is ludicrous, and
science fiction (and its sibling, heroic fantasy) has been doing it with
exemplary ineptitude for decades, as witness the creations of Robert
Howard, J. R. R. Tolkien, Frank Herbert, and their legions of imi-
tators, whose fustian fairy tales bear the same relation to the epic's
potential as do their illustrators' covers—the Frazettas and Vallejos—
to the standards set by the *Apollo Belvedere* and the Sistine Chapel.
The greatest risk, therefore, of undertaking an epic in our time is
that such a work will seem only the versified counterpart of these
devolved and déclassé descendants of the epic narrative.

Turner does not succeed unequivocally in evading the guilt of
this association. While he has invented a cunning rationale for a future
that accommodates both swordplay and microcircuitry in the conduct
of national wars, his motive in promoting such a union is surely as
much to meet the demands of his supposed audience (all admirers of
Star Wars) as those of his muse Speriminh. He does it well, but ought
it be done at all? That's to say, is the heroic ideal inalterably wedded
to images of a chivalric contest of arms? Or is it, rather, that knives,

swords, and armored horsemen are on file in everyone's visual memory? Putting aside this bone of contention (which can be urged equally against Tennyson and the Pre-Raphaelites), I have to applaud the imaginative vigor with which Turner pursues his martial artifice, however arrived at. His battle scenes are done with the catsup-spilling panache of a Kurosawa.

More to the point in grading *The New World* on the EAS (Epic Achievement Scale), where Homer is 10 and Jack Chalker −5, is an evaluation of the moral meaning of the plot. Do the figures of the tale engage in actions that have an import beyond the bogs of Romance, beyond even the uplands of domestic tragedy? That is, do their personal fates come to have an emblematic reference to the larger patterns of history? That's asking a lot of a poem, however long, but it is what the epic requires, and why they are so rare.

To answer this question with reference to *The New World* requires a synopsis of its plot at more length than is usually consistent with book-reviewing, and so here I will suggest that those readers who are willing, already, to take my recommendation on faith should read the poem before continuing with these reflections on its (considerable) merits. Any précis of the plot will inevitably spoil Turner's own narrative strategies and *coups de théâtre*. For those too impatient to follow these counsels of perfection, and to Turner, my apologies.

The Argument, then, as briefly as I can, is as follows: In the year 2376 America is divided in three parts: the utopian Free Counties of the Midwest, the fanatical fundamentalist theocracy of the Mad Counties in the Southeast, and the Riots, anarchic remnants of the inner cities, whose debauched citizens are kept supplied with food and joyjuice through the slave labor of the captive Burbs. The hero, James Quincy, was raised in Hattan Riot (most of the poem's place names can be solved as easily as this, but a few are posers), the son of a disgraced Free Countian martial arts expert living in exile. He has a mythical boyhood ("Now that's a dandy story," one character comments on hearing James's account of it, "But I hope you don't mind me saying—it's shot full of holes."), inherits his father's sword Adamant, and escorts his mother back to the family farm in Mohican County. On the way he joins an Ahian military force and earns his first battle stripes. He becomes one of three suitors for the love of the poem's heroine, Ruth McCloud. The first of these suitors is her half-brother Simon (the fruit of an adulterous liaison between Ruth's mother and James's father, whence his exile) and so not a legitimate contender. Simon attempts to rape Ruth, gets caught, is outlawed, and departs for the Mad Counties to perfect his villainy. The second suitor is Antony Manse, a young black whom Ruth loves but who can only marry her if he passes three tests set for him. He fails the third test, and James then passes all three to become her husband.

Up to this point Turner's plot has been as traditional as a nativity pageant or a Harlequin romance. Now it takes a turn that bears the signature of the past decade. Ruth, though friendly toward James and the mother of his son, cannot bear his conjugal attentions and experiences all his ardors as a renewal of Simon's rape. She remains drawn to her earlier lover Antony, but when she is tempted to adultery, she instead pretends a passion for her husband. Then Simon, who has become the false Messiah of the Mad Counties, makes a raid on his old hometown, killing Ruth's father. A war ensues. Simon, as a Parthian shot in the moment of defeat, tells James a lie that makes him suppose his union with Ruth incestuous, and this sends him back to Hattan Riot to consult an oracle called Kingfish, who advises him in this wise:

> "Love de game, boy: de flesh be de life
> ob de spirit, an' de spirit be all a game. But de game
> be all dat dere be, boy, an' dat be better
> dan nothing."

James, returning home, has various adventures very quickly. In just seven pages he's captured by pirates, has good sex with the pirate chief's daughter, is wrecked in the crash of a dirigible, is tempted to become the consort of the queen of the lotus-eating natives of Jorgia's Blue Ridge County, and for a capper takes a job on a starship and works his passage out to the 'Gellan worlds. He returns to Ruth just in time to prevent her from consummating her love for Antony. James, disguised as Antony, at last awakens a reciprocal passion in his wife, and there follows a salute to the seasons and the principle of growth and increase that is a particularly good set-piece. Simon reappears, this time leading a horde of Rioters, and the Free Counties are overwhelmed by the sheer numbers of the enemy. Worse, James's and Ruth's eldest son Daniel is kidnapped by Simon through the connivance of a traitorous servant. Simon demands the father as his price for the son. In the final showdown James sneaks in his sword Adamant for some final hugger-mugger but is killed by the traitorous servant acting under the influence of Simon's last lie. It is left to Ruth and two other women to polish off Simon, and the problem posed by the invading hordes is solved by the suicide of the traitorous servant, Judd, which is misinterpreted by Simon's followers as a sign that all must, after the fashion of Jonesville in Guyana, follow their fallen leader to the grave. Antony becomes Ruth's husband at last.

Laid bare in this way, some of the difficulties of the plot become quite evident. The concluding showdown is a succession of missed bull's-eyes. The Judas figure of Judd is barely sketched by the author, yet the entire denouement hinges on his actions. This misplaced emphasis is symptomatic of a deeper flaw: Simon, who must do double duty as a villain, being the heavy both in the domestic drama and in the larger political conflicts, is a stock figure from melodrama. On one occasion he's given an Iagolike speech asserting the joys of a pure nihilism, but he is without human dimension or features, a Darth Vader. When the forces opposing the protagonist are led by such a bogey, epic is impossible. Epic heroes derive their dignity from having enemies as noble as themselves, for Achilles a Hector, for Aeneas a Turnus.

It is not just in the figure of Simon that Turner fails to do justice to the forces of darkness. He is very scanty in his treatment of both the Mad Counties and the Riots. Three times James appears in the caverns beneath the Hattan Riot to consult the oracle Kingfish, but these visitations more resemble Dorothy's visit to the Wizard than a descent to Avernus. The Riots, though conceptually interesting, remain an offstage threat, their exemplary wickedness a matter of report. The same is true of the Mad Counties. Indeed, both these dystopias come straight from SF's central casting department: the fundamentalist Mad Counties deriving from classic novels by Heinlein, Brackett, and Vidal, the Riots from the sets of movies like *Escape from New York.* These are the lands we love to hate, and Simon is rightfully their lord.

These objections are chiefly to what is absent from Turner's poem, and to a lesser degree to what is present by way of meeting the formal requirements of the epic (the oracular Kingfish, the grab bag of "adventures" before the hero returns to his Penelope), and while they vitiate the poem's claims to epic status, they do not bulk very large against its actual accomplishment. *The New World* may not earn full marks as an epic, but it constitutes a first-rate utopian romance, one that by adopting the costume of Epic outflanks the bane of so many utopian narratives, which is that their plots are dictated by the author's didactic requirements: a Visitor as a stand-in for the reader arrives in Utopia and gets a guided tour by the Polonius in charge of the place. The Visitor raises objections and his guide shoots them down. Turner avoids all this by an astute recognition that poetry is the stuff that utopias should be made of, and that the arguments supporting his utopian theses need not be conducted as formal debates with the dice always loaded in favor of the author's spokesman, but that he can speak in his own poetic voice, as in this passage in which, in the context of Ruth's possible marriage to Antony, the author urges the benefits of miscegenation and of an extension of the marriage contract to the larger kinship group of the extended family:

> We are the holy and dangerous beast that dared
> to domesticate not only our plant and animal servants
> but also ourselves: and not for usefulness only
> but chiefly for beauty, the blazon of expressed shapeliness.
> And so the heroic hang of the Great Dane,
> the pretty baroque of the King Charles Spaniel,
> the deathlike elegance of the Siamese cat, the fire
> of the fighting-fish, bulbous flash of the poi, pout
> and delicate feather of pigeon and dove that Darwin
> admired, crimson petals of rose and peony,
> are only attendants on the sovereign differences given

to this clan of mutated monkeys, to itself by itself.
Once a marriage between a white and a negro
was looked on with horror, for men believed that the races
differed by nature, not, as we now know,
by the choice of persons following, altering what
the cultural rules of beauty dictated. But we
especially prize the unique, and therefore are pleased
when lovers break the habit of choosing a beauty
that resembles that of themselves and their family....
It is our custom also that parents and relatives
should share in the work of consent, and thus help
to make the projected marriage a real one: for marriage
is real so far as it penetrates into the world
of interpersonal verification and gains
the consent of its living environment. Lovers, of course,
as lovers, live in a world of their own, a dream
that need not encounter the touch of reality;
and therefore we reverence them, treating them lovingly
just as we honor the harmless insane. Marriage,
though, is the work of a lifetime, the greatest of arts.
And therefore the kin of the bride and the groom must
set
them tests of their own and be satisfied....

In earlier discursive passages concerning the Free Countian laws of property and inheritance Turner had laid the groundwork for these marriage tests. The tests, when they come to be recounted, would smack too much of the fairy tale if they were not buttressed by these discursive passages, and the discourse is leavened by the traditional ornamentation of the narrative. The wedding of the distinct genres of fable and utopia is an altogether inspired and fruitful union, and does much to mitigate the shallowness of the depiction of the darker forces in the story. For if the task of the poem is to create a utopia rather than an epic, the shorthand environments of the Riots and the Mad Counties suffice for the task. They point to those present-day realities we all recognize—the growth of a permanent criminal underclass in the nation's inner cities and the seemingly dialectical resurgence of a fascistic "Moral Majority"—realities which the utopian arrangements of the ideal city of Mount Verdant are designed to correct.

By casting his utopia in a poetic form Turner avoids having to contend against those literalists who could argue, in a naturalistic utopia, that his commonwealth is demographically or otherwise impracticable, that a Jeffersonian democracy of philosopher farmers doesn't answer to the real needs of the present. Turner's utopia is not literally intended. He is not, for instance, advocating that the problems of the inner city may be solved by mass suicides; rather, as in Dante's *Inferno,* where the punishments of the damned represent their sins viewed under the aspect of eternity, the suicide of the Rioters is a poetic image for the horror of ghetto life as it exists now, and the beauties of Mount Verdant are those of an ideal Middle America stripped of obscuring, inessential blemishes like the arms race, pollution, and sexual inequality. For many readers Turner's *New World* will seem altogether too good to be true, both as overt narrative and as an allegory of an unachievable but ever-to-be-hoped-for polity, but such a judgment reflects a political basis more than an esthetic preference. As a long narrative poem *The New World* has few equals in the English poetry of recent times, and as a work of science fiction there can be no dispute that it possesses an epochal significance. It should be read at once by anyone with a serious regard for science fiction and incorparated into the syllabus of all courses surveying the field, especially at college level. This is a work of singular nobility and excellence; we must all be grateful to Turner for the love and labor that have gone into its creation.

SUNLIGHT, COFFEE, AND THE PAPERS: A POEM FOR OUR TIMES

The Golden Gate: A Novel in Verse
by Vikram Seth
RANDOM HOUSE $17.95 307 PP.

LIKE THE BRIDGE for which it is named, Vikram Seth's *The Golden Gate* is a thing of anomalous beauty: a long narrative poem set in present-day San Francisco, and that is odd enough, but what is odder, a rhyming poem in strict meter that is a "good read" after the manner of the better sort of fiction in the women's magazines. If Mary Gordon had written a contemporary romance that revolved around the "issues" of nuclear disarmament and gay liberation (viewed from an enlightened Catholic perspective) and had then boiled down her prose into eight and a quarter thousand lines of verse, the result would be very like *The Golden Gate.*

The real surprise of this "novel-in-verse" is not that it has been done at all (for there has been a boomlet of narrative poetry lately) but that it has been done so well. Vikram Seth has recently published one slim volume of shorter poems (*The Humble Administrator's Garden,* Carcanet), but for all but the most *au courant* readers of poetry *The Golden Gate* will represent the author's debut, and what a debut it is! Seth writes poetry as it has not been written for nearly a century—that's to say, with the intention that his work should give pleasure to that ideal Common Reader for whom good novelists have always aspired to write. For most poetry professionals earning their living by the teaching of creative writing, Seth's ambitions, and his accomplishment, will be abhorrent if not simply incomprehensible. Does one write Poetry to entertain? Are the affairs and courtships of five Bay Area yuppies—described as such on the very jacket of the book—a suitable subject for Poetry? Are wit and grace and mere cleverness to be counted among the desiderata of Poetry? Dullness forfend!

Yet if you have no vested interest in keeping poetry within the generic boundaries established by academic criticism and by the customary, sanctioned sloth of most poets (slim volumes take less work, after all, than thick), you will almost certainly find *The Golden Gate* an agreeable and judiciously balanced (not too heavy, not too light) tale that has been enhanced by the power of poetry to the narrative equivalent of haute cuisine. This is not to say that there aren't stretches of the story that sag (but isn't that so of most novels, even very good ones?) or that the verse is unexceptionably fine. Some stanzas gush, some lines scan only under duress, and a couple of the larger scenes misfire. Seth's form accommodates most narrative needs naturally, but its artifice does become obtrusive when applied to long speeches and soliloquys. At one point a Berrigan-like priest delivers a nineteen-stanza-long peroration against the arms race, the effect of which was like hearing Schell's *The Fate of the Earth* transformed into rhyming bon mots. Even the converted may become restive with such preaching.

Those few exceptions taken, I thoroughly enjoyed the book, following its quadrangular romance with the same degree of amused involvement or involved bemusement I would give to one of Woody Allen's sedater comedies of sexual intrigue. The plot is simple. Let the sign $\hat{+}$ represent loves-and-is-loved-by and the sign $><$ represent the sundering of love. Then in Act 1, $A \hat{+} B$ and $C \hat{+} D$; in Act 2, $A >< B$ and $C >< D$; and in Act 3, $B \hat{+} C$, while A and D are left with their regrets. The one feature of the plot that may strike some readers as a novelty is that the fourth of the principals, Ed, is gay. But please note, Ed is a good Catholic who initiates his breakup with C from a deeply ingrained sense of sexual guilt. Ed's character is psychologically feasible, as Seth presents it, but his self-sealed fate does beg the question of how the author, as an avowedly Catholic writer, would deal with a gay character who was not supplied with such convenient compunctions.

The chief attraction of *The Golden Gate* is not its story as such, but its ever-recognizable and ever-fresh representation of upper-middle-class life in the 1980s, a life that Seth celebrates with none of the dyspeptic acerbity of such prose chroniclers of the current scene as Ann Beattie or Frederick Barthelme. His characters are not invented to afford his readers the pleasure of knowing themselves to be more knowing. They are all of them quite nice people—good-looking, well bred, prosperous, principled, affectionate—"yuppies" as the jacket copy has it, which is an easily broken code for "people like you and me." The effect of such characters, en masse, together with Seth's chroniclings of representative California pleasures, is like seeing a great many Renoirs all at once. Here, from a hundred possible samplings of Seth's craft, is a single stanza to illustrate this zest for the good ($50,000 per annum) life:

> John looks about him with enjoyment.
> What a man needs, he thinks, is health;
> Well-paid, congenial employment;
> A house; a modicum of wealth;
> Some sunlight; coffee and the papers;
> Artichoke hearts adorned with capers;
> A Burberry trench coat; a Peugeot;
> And in the evening, some Rameau
> Or Couperin; a home-cooked dinner;
> A Stilton, and a little port;
> And so to a duvet. In short,
> In life's brief game to be a winner
> A man must have . . . oh yes, above
> All else, of course, someone to love.

The model for this not-quite-a-sonnet stanza (The rhyme scheme of the fourteen lines is sonnetary, but the meter is four beats per line, not five. A four-beat line—the natural meter of ballads and doggerel—is much easier to sustain over the long stretch for both poet and reader.) is Sir Charles Johnston's superb translation of Pushkin's *Eugene Onegin* (1977), and it is not alone the meter of that marvelous long poem that inspired Seth's emulation. The spirit of Pushkin's verse romance informs Seth's own tale at every turn, and Pushkin's intrusion of his own voice as commentator and master of ceremonies gives Seth a model for the proper balance between narrative momentum and poetic fun and games in his own poem. Rarely has a poetic role model been so sedulously imitated, and even more rarely has such imitation yielded so healthy an offspring. The best that can be said of both Pushkin's and Seth's novels-in-verse is that unlike so many would-be epics theirs are never monotonous. Both portray ordinary life without falling into banality, and one finishes both books with a sense that poetry too rarely yields, a sense that life, however messy it may get from time to time, is really, pretty much, a bowl of cherries.

HISTORY:
THE HOME MOVIE

History: The Home Movie
by Craig Raine
DOUBLEDAY $22.00 326 PP.

LET IT FIRST of all be said that, like Craig Raine's three earlier volumes of poetry, *History* is top-notch, state-of-the-art, and sui generis. Raine, famed as the Tom Swift of England's "Martian School" of poetry, has retooled his copyrighted technique of translating the garage-sale junk of daily life into riddling metaphors and adapted it successfully for epic use. The result is a novel in verse that is both an unputdownable page-turner and a poem distinctively and deliciously Rainean.

Three caveats: that, while item by item the contents of the garage sale are as vivid as the fruit in a Caravaggio still life, their sum-total—the thrust, gist, pith of the book—remains, in large part, an unsolved riddle; that I'm not sure the author of *The Onion, Memory* would have intended any totalizing meaning to be forged from the shards of his tale; and that the contents of the garage sale include reels and reels of X-rated home videos with particular (and obsessive) attention to the practice of masturbation. Readers who prefer poems that keep their flies buttoned will find much to reprehend.

Told in eighty-eight chronologically ordered vignettes set main-ly in the period from the end of the First World War to the end of the Second, *History* offers glimpses of the lives of two star-crossed families, the Raines of England and the Pasternaks of Russia, to whom the poet is related by marriage. Readers of *Rich,* Raine's last collection of poems (1983), have already made the acquaintance of Raine's extraordinary father, Norman, a proletarian prince: champion boxer, wounded war veteran, spiritualist healer, and loving and much-loved father. Craig Raine rivals the playwright Neil Simon in the ardor of his family feeling, and his portraits of parents, grandparents, and uncles are all the more effective for their apparent fascination with warts, both literal and figurative.

Some of these warts, however, like Marianne Moore's emblematic toad, grow on imaginary faces. Raine not only lards his double family chronicle with those usual inferences and probabilities fictionalizers use to bulk out "autobiographical" novels, but has also introduced (as I surmise) some imaginary kindred by which the two stories can be linked so that a branch of the Pasternak family can be rescued from Nazi Germany by their connection to those salt-of-the-earth Brits, the Raines; a redemption myth with enormous box office potential (witness the success of *Schindler's List*).

Comparisons to the Hollywood product should not be considered odious in this connection, for, as its subtitle advertises, *History* is steeped in the mythos and technique of moviemaking. Indeed, if the book has a subtextual thesis to advance, it may go something like this: in our time the effect of the motion picture on the Collective Unconscious has been so pervasive and so penetrating that movies determine not only our imagination of the past (which has become a pastiche of all its cinematic recreations, many of which are tellingly echoed in the poem's vignettes) but also our history-making conduct in the present.

The Pasternak half of the novel is drenched in cinematic and poetic cross-references, thanks to the presence of an earlier self-mythologizer, Boris Pasternak, author not only of the novel *Dr. Zhivago* (source of the epic movie) but of the poems of that same doctor (whom we understand to be Pasternak in disguise). Here in *History* we have the undisguised Pasternak, with his kin, his poetic colleagues and mistresses, being absorbed into a new movie/novel/sheaf of poems by a poet whose four children have taken some significant portion of their own genes from the Pasternak pool; by a poet, furthermore, who artfully and with little apparent fuss revels in these opportunities for an out-Heroding, postmodern self-referentiality.

If this sounds superfluously cerebral, let me insist again on the poem's power to keep you glued to your seat. Raine's art as cinematographer, derived from his alien's-eye-view "Martian" poems, is equal to Bergman's or von Stroheim's, as in this close-up of a German military hat, circa 1915:

> He turns the shako in his big hands,
> solid as a leather motorcar.
> Mudguards back and front,
>
> a radiator badge, spare wheels
> holding the chinstrap double
> like a bumper on the peak.

As a scriptwriter he is also quite accomplished, able to convey paragraphs of exposition in a telling glance.

History is, however, an art movie, and suitable only for mature audiences. Younger readers who lack an internalized time-chart of twentieth-century history may have a hard time assembling the "plot" in their heads, since Raine doesn't do much backgrounding. Finally, of course, as the author, Raine has the edge on all his readers, and I'll confess to having no more well-informed response to a few of his vignettes than, "Where are we? Who? What do you mean by *that*?" Why, in particular, the repeated emphasis on genitalia and "the wanking spanner"?

Raine is not the sort of poet to answer that last question himself, but neither is he the sort to insist on his inviolable mystery as Susan Sontag has advised in *Against Interpretation*. Raine is surely above the Mapplethorpean urge to shock us by violating some heretofore neglected taboo. In any case, in the age of Beavis and Butt-Head masturbation hasn't much to offer in the way of shock value. My theory is that it serves to link the three elements of the title—history, the home, and movies. Raine shows how "history," at the dawn of the movie era, became an opportunity for the average European to ape the movies, specifically in their erotic and fetishistic aspects. Nazis, fascists, Bolsheviks, and ordinary blokes all erected states that were sound stages for the rampant id. In Raine's schema Hollywood was not holding up the mirror of art to the age, but rather, just as crusaders against pornography and violence in movies maintain, the age took its cues from Hollywood.

Other readers will develop other theories, suited to their own puzzlements, for *History: The Home Movie* is, like T. S. Eliot's *The Waste Land,* rich in lacunae and telling erasures, all begging to be filled in. So, while there is still time to read it fresh from the author's pen, unencumbered by the criticism it will surely inspire, have your own private screening.

CHRISTOPHER FRY:
AN APPRECIATION

LOOK UP *FRY, Christopher* in *The Oxford Companion to Twentieth-Century Poetry,* and an arrow will redirect you to *Verse drama,* where both Fry and the art form are given short shrift. Fry's faintly praised as, after Eliot, "the other principal verse dramatist of the time," whose work "has proved similarly to consist of one clear winner against the odds and a number of also-rans." Verse drama is dismissed as being "incompatible" with the regnant dramatic conventions of the twentieth century, "the charged naturalism of Chekhov and Ibsen . . . and a language that purports to be that of 'real life,' in which characters are unlikely to speak poetry."

In practice verse drama has generally been even worse than the *Oxford Companion* hints at. Throughout the nineteenth century it came to be emblematic of everything bogus, antiquarian, and boring in the art of poetry, a tradition that encouraged fogeys of all ages to wrap themselves in bedsheets and imitate the Greeks who'd traumatized them in their public school days. This tradition of plaster of paris sublimity reached its nadir in 1903 in Thomas Hardy's *The Dynasts: An Epic-Drama of the War with Napoleon, in Three Parts, Nineteen Acts, & One Hundred & Thirty Scenes,* a work of over five hundred pages of small print that stands like a pyramid erected over the mummified corpse of verse drama, never (by the author's own pronouncement) to be performed onstage, and perhaps never to be read. (My 1915 edition was virginal when I got it in 1978, not a page cut.) One imagines Hardy muttering all the while he wrote it: "Novels? They don't *deserve* my novels! They'll have *this* instead."

The Dynasts opens, after the manner of *Faust*, in "The Overworld," with the entrance of "the Ancient Spirit and Chorus of the Years, the Spirit and Chorus of the Pities, the Shade of the Earth, the Spirits Sinister and Ironic with their Choruses, Rumors, Spirit-Messengers, and Recording Angels."

The Shade of the Earth asks, "What of the Immanent Will and its designs?" To which, the Spirit of the Years replies:

It works unconsciously, as heretofore,
Eternal artistries in Circumstance,
Whose patterns, wrought by rapt aesthetic rote,
Seem in themselves Its single listless aim,
And not their consequence.

This inspires the Chorus of the Pities to an "aerial music":

Still thus? Still thus?
Ever unconscious!
An automatic sense
Unweeting why or whence?

Was ever entrance to a tomb so securely sealed as this? Was ever any author so well aware of the awesome futility of his endeavor? Already on page fifteen Hardy has delivered his own self-referential verdict on *The Dynasts,* speaking as the Shade of the Earth:

What boots it, Sire,
To down this dynasty, set that one up,
Goad panting people to the throes thereof,
Make wither here my fruit, maintain it there,
And hold me travailing through fineless years

In vain and objectless monotony,
When all such tedious conjuring could be shunned
By uncreation?

The extraordinary thing about *The Dynasts* is that it is the work of a writer who is both a storyteller of proven gifts and a poet ditto. Such is the basilisk influence of verse drama that Hardy's talents were unavailing. Yet Hardy's wasted efforts were not a dead loss, for his example did seem to deter others from riding into the same Valley of Death. With the shining exception of Yeats, poets steered clear of verse drama for a good long time, and those who did eventually rise to the challenge made an effort to avoid historicism and fustian. No more crowns and togas, no more "unweeting why or whence." Hardy's Spirits Sinister and Ironic were upstaged by Mack the Knife and Jenny.

The notable exception to this rule was *Murder in the Cathedral* of 1935, the play the *Oxford Companion* declares to be Eliot's "one clear winner against the odds," a work designed to be performed in cathedrals in the manner of a Solemn High Mass; a Greek tragedy for Anglican worshipers. The form and venue were not Eliot's invention, but a regular feature of Anglican, High Genteel culture in his time, indigenous as cricket. There are notable examples by Anne Ridler, Charles Williams, and Ronald Duncan. *Murder in the Cathedral* has outlasted other such church-sponsored verse plays by virtue of Eliot's greater fame and flair.

Fry's first shy theater pieces were in that same vein—plays designed for churches rather than theaters (*The Boy with a Cart: Cuthman, Saint of Sussex,* 1938), civic pageants, operas for children. He came to such tasks by another route than Eliot, however, having escaped a career as schoolteacher by becoming an actor and director in provincial theaters, for whose stages he also wrote adaptations of well-approved classics. These apprentice years gave Fry an edge over rival writers of verse drama: he had dealt with audiences and knew what worked.

Poets rarely think of themselves as entertainers, except those few, like Dylan Thomas, who have cultivated a dramatic style of public delivery, as against the commoner practice of reading one's poems in a muted, affectless monotone, as though any kind of rhetorical emphasis would be a solecism. Indeed, among the lumpenliterati any acknowledgment of the audience's existence, any effort to cater, inveigle, amuse, or even provoke curiosity is accounted pandering. A proud opacity and the resolute pursuit of an often hidden agenda (as in *The Cantos,* or the longer poems of Wallace Stevens or John Ashbery) are considered the distinguishing marks of truly ambitious poetry, while epic narrative and verse drama tend to be dismissed as compromised and middlebrow, as, indeed, they often are. (Just dip into Maxwell Anderson.)

Fry's first full-length play, *The Firstborn* (1946), is the very model of what a proper modernist has been schooled to suspect of verse drama: a tragedy in three acts, set in ancient Egypt, retelling the story of Moses and Pharaoh up to the time of the Passover. Can such an endeavor come across as anything but an upscale version of Cecil B. DeMille's *The Ten Commandments?* Fry's set pieces do sometimes have the clank of stage armor, as when Moses first demands that Pharaoh let his people go. Pharaoh has declared: "I have put men to a purpose who otherwise / Would have had not the least meaning," to which Moses replies:

> Not the least meaning, except the meaning
> Of the breath in your lungs, the mystery of existing
> At all. What have we approached or conceived
> When we have conquered and built a world? Even
> Though civilization became perfect? What then?
> We have only put a crown on the skeleton.
> It is the individual man
> In his individual freedom who can mature
> With his warm spirit the unripe world.
> They are your likeness, these men, even to nightmares.
> I have business with Egypt, one more victory for her,
> A better one than Ethiopia:
> That she should come to see her own shame
> And discover justice for my people.

This rises to the occasion but not without a noticeable strain; the prosody is rough-hewn, the rhetoric a little too stately, as though Moses were addressing Parliament. Much the same can be said for many of the longer declamations in Fry's later, more familiar plays. If the art of verse drama were to stand or fall by the success of its soliloquies, Fry's would fall.

But the strengths of *The Firstborn* are the strengths of classic theater. It addresses the largest issue of British history in Fry's time— the end of the Empire. His Egypt is the Raj, his Moses Gandhi, and the plagues that God visits on Pharaoh are simply the judgments of History, understood as a Hegelian juggernaut that cannot help but crush the play's title character, Rameses. Rameses is the English public schoolboy in his perfected form: bright, blithe, well spoken and well meaning, who hero-worships Moses and is dismayed that Moses thinks of him as his enemy. Moses, who is tragically blind to what God and History intends, tries to reassure Rameses:

> We're not enemies so much
> As creatures of division. You and I,
> Rameses, like money in a purse,
> Ring together only to be spent
> For different reasons.
> There will be summers to come
> Which need the throne and lotus: a world
> Richer for an Egypt prosperous in wisdom
> Which you will govern.

A tragic theme is not enough to make a tragedy. The theme must be embodied in a story simple enough to be told in two or three acts and readily apprehensible to the audiences available to the playwright. The critic William Arrowsmith, writing about Fry in *The Hudson Review* in 1950, pointed out how the audience may be "too insecure in the form [of verse drama] to judge [the playwright] properly; it is too easy for him to play the poet with his play, to substitute choral trappings and lyric monologues for a working dramatic diction, and the audience is too apt to think these substitutions justified by the mysterious form employed." That says it pretty well not only for *The Dynasts,* but for the efforts of Robinson Jeffers and Archibald MacLeish to write Greek tragedies in modern dress. Fry and Eliot had an edge in writing for the English audience of their time, in that they were the heirs (as Arrowsmith noted) "to the accumulated advantages of the repertory and little-theater movement: a generation of intense activity among both amateur and professional groups, standards of performance incredibly high, serious lay interest and enthusiasm, and now, government patronage and a new (and perhaps dangerous) security from the entertainment industry."

The first audience that a dramatist must please is the troupe of actors who must be persuaded to perform his work, and in that respect Fry was incredibly successful. The first West End production of *The Lady's Not for Burning* in 1949 starred John Gielgud and Pamela Brown, with Richard Burton and Claire Bloom in supporting roles. Olivier directed and took the leading role in *Venus Observed* in 1950. *The Dark Is Light Enough* (1954) was written as a showcase for Dame Edith Evans. The American premier of *The Firstborn* had a cast that included Katharine Cornell, Kathleen Widdoes, Anthony Quayle, and Mildred Natwick. Later productions of *Lady* have starred Derek Jacobi and Kenneth Branagh in the leading role. Stars of this caliber don't choose to appear in the work of a fledgling dramatist without a compelling reason—the script.

Actors know what will work for them, and Fry supplies it. Even the smallest roles in his plays are clearly motivated. That might seem a trivial or self-evident consideration, but it is the sine qua non of drama. Ideally every character one sees onstage should be actively pursuing his own agenda. Even when he is there in the capacity of an attendant lord, his reaction shot should signify something—or else he should not be there. The larger the dramatis personae, the easier it is for a playwright to overlook this necessity. A good director will do his best to get round the problem with blocking and spotlights, but to create the illusion of life, which is theater's first ambition, it is needful to fill the stage with the multiplied energy of (in the words of Fry's Moses) "the individual man / in his individual freedom." *Not* a Greek chorus standing in for the essentially reactive audience, declaiming received wisdom at stately intervals, but distinct characters, each with his own agenda.

This is, of course, a counsel of perfection. But it has been, since Shakespeare, the touchstone of dramatic excellence, and by that measure Fry is a playwright on a par with Congreve, Sheridan, Wilde, and Shaw. Like them, he is—with the notable exception of *The First-born*—a writer of comedies. He is unlike them chiefly in having reverted to verse drama, but from them he has learned one essential lesson: self-defining speech and surreal candor.

In real life, speech more often conceals our motives and ambitions than it defines them, and this is equally true of characters in conventional "realistic" dramas, who are impelled by motives that are buried, problematical, unconscious, or simply fudged. What *is* troubling Hedda Gabler? What makes Lulu run? Every actress has her own answer. In comedy, however, such ambiguities only hinder the action. We need to know what people are about, and we receive that information (ideally) at the entrance of each character. They say who they are and what they want with the clarity and directness that only art allows. Thus, Congreve's Mrs. Marwood declares, with little provocation, that she would carry her aversion (to men) further "by marrying; if I could but find one that loved me very well, and would be thoroughly sensible of ill-usage, I think I should do myself the violence of undergoing the ceremony." She knows herself, and we know her at the same moment.

Shaw went on to perfect the artifice of the preternaturally self-aware character, so that philistines and burglars should possess the same powers of instant self-definitions. Fry was the final heir of that tradition, so antithetical to the kitchen-sink naturalism that would take hold in England even as Fry was being acclaimed the country's leading dramatist.

Fry orchestrates the entrance of each character as though he or she might be, as in his or her estimation he or she is, the whole show. Read just the first page of *The Lady's Not for Burning,* as Thomas intrudes on Richard, the mayor's clerk, who demands of him, "Can I have your name?" "It's yours," says Thomas. "Now, look—" "It's no earthly / Use to me. I travel light," Thomas cuts in, and off we go, having as quickly as that established, in Arrowsmith's phrase, "a working dramatic diction," a way of moving back and forth between the prosaic and the metaphoric that is colloquial, terse, and readily assimilable.

Thanks to this artifice, even Fry's most rustic characters speak in poetry—that is to say, with a transparent honesty and directness—without a bump of incongruence. For example (again in *Lady*), the feather-headed Chaplain who's been asleep by the fire awakes to propose a stratagem that will be the plot-hinge of the second act. The problem is how to persuade the protagonist, Thomas (who longs to be given to the hangman), *not* to confess to a murder for which the authorities would rather burn the Lady of the title. Torture has not succeeded with Thomas. The Chaplain's solution:

> If he cannot be stayed with flagons, or comforted
> With apples—I quote, of course—or the light, the ocean,
> The ever-changing . . . I mean and stars, extraordinary
> How many, or some instrument or other—I am afraid
> I appear rhapsodical—but perhaps the addition
> Of your thumbscrew will not succeed either. The point
> I'm attempting to make is this one: he might be wooed
> From his aptitude for death by being happier;
> And what I was going to suggest, quite irresponsibly,
> Is that he might be invited to partake
> Of our festivities this evening. No,
> I see it astonishes you.

It is only a cameo role, but so finely carved and warmly lighted, that any character actor of a certain age is bound to appear to advantage.

Fry at his farthest stretch, when his plot makes its greatest demands of the leading characters, succeeds by the same device of perspicuous self-definition and lucidity. The highpoint of *Lady* comes when Jennet Jourdemayne, the Lady of the title, faced with being burned at the stake, is offered another choice by the lecherous Humphrey Devize:

    You mean you give me a choice:
To sleep with you, or to-morrow to sleep with my fathers.
And if I value the gift of life,
Which, dear heaven, I do, I can scarcely refuse.

"Isn't that sense?" Humphrey urges. She answers:

    Admirable sense.
Oh, why, why am I not sensible?
Oddly enough, I hesitate. Can I
So dislike being cornered by a young lecher
That I should rather die? That would be
The maniac pitch of pride. Indeed, it might
Even be sin. Can I believe my ears?
I seem to be considering heaven. And heaven,
From this angle, seems considerable.

Jennet Jourdemayne is a recension of Shakespeare's Isabella in *Measure for Measure,* a wise virgin for modern times; not a nun and with no theoretic commitment to chastity; indeed, a woman with a more skeptical and reasoned view of the world than any of the medieval figures about her. The period aspect of the play becomes, thereby, an essential part of the ironic machinery of the plot, as in Shaw's historical dramas, where the past is prized not for its grand opera pomps and pageantries but for absurdities more easily seen as such than those of our own time. Jests at the pieties and patriotic guff of Egyptians and Druids can provoke a smile; jests at our own provoke controversy.

For centuries poetry was the prerogative of tragedy kings and queens, but then World War I put an end to noble sentiment and modernism held sway with its intolerance of high rhetoric. Verse drama, even when it abjured the archaic hokum of *The Dynasts,* became next to impossible, and nobility was relegated to the slums of the silent movies, to those who knew no better. But it remained, even so, a possibility, slumbering like Arthur in his burial mound. And so it was that Fry, a provincial thespian who knew no better, who only knew that audiences had never stopped enjoying Shakespeare's plays, accomplished the resurrection of verse drama.

Temporarily, it would seem. Only *The Lady's Not for Burning* still gets revived on a regular basis. The later plays are neglected: *Venus Observed, The Dark Is Light Enough, A Yard of Sun, Curtmantle.* Each has a claim on intelligent consideration equal or superior to the best work of Osborne and Pinter—or of, for that matter, Fry's American contemporaries, Miller and Williams. That they are comedies (all but *The Firstborn* and *Curtmantle,* a play that chronicles the life of King Henry II) has told against them. In theory tragedy and comedy are supposed to be esthetic equals; in practice comedy is dismissed as fluff.

Fry's penchant for costume drama has also alienated critics, particularly since he became, in his later years, a rather undistinguished Hollywood hack, writing scripts for *Ben Hur* (1959), *Barabbas* (1962), and John Huston's lamentably wooden *The Bible* (1966). Other good playwrights (and novelists) have had equally lusterless track records as filmwriters. There does seem to be a natural limit of about fifteen years during which a playwright does his signature work. Fry's fifteen good years commenced in 1946 with his one-act comedy based on an anecdote from Petronius, *A Phoenix Too Frequent,* which represents Fry at his most Shavian, and it comes to an end in 1961 with *Curtmantle,* a good play that had the misfortune to appear at exactly the time of a better play on the same historic theme, Jean Anouilh's *Becket.* During the same period, in addition to his own plays, Fry translated and adapted five by Giraudoux and Anouilh that show him to be as capable, witty, and stage-smart in prose as in poetry. Altogether it is a track record quite as commendable as that of his major contemporary rivals for theatrical laurels—Miller, Williams, Pinter, and Osborne (all of whose oeuvres respect the same fifteen-good-years rule of thumb).

Fry's dramas merit revival and full-scale critical evaluation beyond the scope of this essay. Lacking that, let me urge that you read the plays. No play can be complete until you've seen it staged, but books are still a wonderful second best. I read Fry's plays when I was in high school in the fifties and was knocked out. I like them better now, though many of my enthusiasms of that time make me blush. That's how the classics are supposed to work: they get better as their readers get older.

IV

SNAPPED PROSE IN SLIM VOLUMES: A REVIEW OF RECENT POETRY

FIRST, A PUZZLE. The four blocks of words below are excerpts from books recently brought out by major publishers. For reasons of space (and to support my later contention) the four excerpts have been reconstituted into ordinary, justified prose. In order of their probable sales, the poets and their books are: Rod McKuen, *Suspension Bridge* (Harper & Row, $9.95); Alice Walker, *Horses Make a Landscape Look More Beautiful* (Harcourt Brace Jovanovich, $10.95); Philip Schultz, *Deep Within the Ravine* (Viking, $14.95); Gerald Stern, *Paradise Poems* (Random House, $12.95). Some helpful hints: McKuen, whom the poetry establishment treats as a nonperson, is, since Ogden Nash's death, the most popular (i.e., best-selling) poet in America. Walker has had a best-seller of her own, the Pulitzer Prize–winning novel *The Color Purple*. Schultz received good critical notices for his first collection, *Like Wings,* and this second book bears a blurb from Norman Mailer declaring Schultz to be "a hell of a poet, one of the very best of his generation, full of slashing language. . . . " Stern, whose fifth book this is, teaches at the University of Iowa's Writer's Workshop, the nation's primary training facility for creative writing. The puzzle is simple: match the writer with the bit of poem he or she has written. (Answers are on page 127.)

(1) Joe, I read your advert on the shithouse wall at Morro Bay. I didn't write the number down for I had nothing I could give to one so desperate and needing. But I thought you ought to know that all of us who deal in words are only writing advertisements for ourselves.

(2) To be warm, to be dry, to be writing poems again (after months of distraction and emptiness), to love and be loved in absentia is joy enough for me. On these blustery mornings in a city that could be wet from my kisses I need nothing else. And then again, I need it all.

(3) Returning may be a step forward, but now the question is how much we can bear to question. Change, I think, happens almost always too late. Yes, I still miss the way you washed your hands before undressing & how your green eyes darkened with desire. I remember what was promised. That once I believed I could die of love. That, like fate & youth & weather, it continued forever.

(4) I look up through the branches dreaming of fate. My old enemy the blue sky is above me. My old enemy the hawk is moving slowly through the string of white clouds. One day I will wake up at dawn and philosophize about my state as I get ready. I will put on my heavy shirt and think of the long and bitter day ahead.

Readers with allergic sensitivity to bathos, banality, and gush will not be surprised to find such qualities in the work of Rod McKuen, whose commercial success has earned him an obloquy denied to most other poets, who, if notably bad, are politely ignored. But the point of the puzzle is how little there is to distinguish between McKuen's glop and that of his compeers. Of course, it would be possible to find in each poet unmistakably characteristic poses, as when Walker inveighs against her enemy the Wasichu, or white man, killer of buffalo, "murderous and lazy." Or Schultz when he gets to kvetching about the terms of Existence ("yes, he thinks, pain is existence & he is bounded in light, stuck deep within pain's ravine, his mind is infected.") Stern, when he is fussing in the garden ("Today I'm sticking a shovel in the ground and digging up the little green patch between the hosta and the fringe bleeding heart. I am going to plant bee balm there and a few little pansies till the roots take and the leaves spread out in both directions.")

[Answer: the excerpts are presented in the same order in which the poets are named.]

Yet beneath these ostensible differences the four are in essential agreement both as to the craft of poetry and the service a poet may render his or her audience. Their craft is easily summed up, and its simplicity has made of poetry what Whitman dreamed of, the most democratic of the arts:

Take any piece of prose you like
and snap it into lines of verse
like this, using the end of the line

as a kind of comma. You can create
a further sense of shapeliness
by grouping the snapped prose in stanzas, so.

As to the purpose such snapped prose may serve its readers, the poets agree that it is to provide them an idealized persona (the poet's) for use as a psychological role model, a *style* of thinking suited precisely to one's gender, class, and temperament. To achieve this the poet must take care to be sincere, likable, and (so that the reader feels that the poet *needs* his readerly attention) a little lonely.

What such a conception of poetry omits from its view is: (1) that poetry should differ from prose by virtue of meter, rhyme, and other formal requirements; (2) that the language be somehow heightened, different in kind from that of daily speech and newspaper prose; and (3) that it should be self-transcending rather than self-revealing, universal in its tendency rather than personal and parochial. Many good poets, even today, would concur with the latter two traditional prescriptions, and a few with the first, but the common ruck of writing school apparatchiks still live in fear of the curse that modernism pronounced against our poetic ancestors. A convenient fear, since most of them, if they ventured on deeper waters, would surely come a-cropper, as McKuen does, when he aspires to what he thinks of as the grand manner. Consider the conclusion of the eighth of nine "sonnets" (rhymed, but in irregular, mostly four-foot meters) that are given a place of honor at the end of his collection:

> I always thought a river should
> Be like a lifeline in a way.
> Not always altogether good
> But not so much the other way.
> The Platte, she's not like Robin Hood,
> What she brings in she takes away.

In lines like that McKuen almost becomes memorably bad, and that is better, in a way, than being mediocre.

There is also, throughout his poetry, a pastel mistiness of image. Fogs are dear to him as emblems of the state of reverie that is the source of his poetry, a state in which (and this may be the secret of his success) he and his reader are most closely akin. In a steamy mirror all men are twins. Had Rod McKuen been sent to one of the creative writing schools, his second lesson (after the sonnets had been beaten out of him) would have been to abjure his love of imprecision and ineffability for a sparrow's-eye view that concentrates on clear outlines and telling details—and the writing school would have been wrong. Even when his verses are lame, McKuen's instincts are right—or, at least, he shares them with some irreproachably Serious poets (to one of whom, John Ashbery, McKuen, in a collegial spirit, dedicates a poem).

Indeed, the unequivocally best of the batch of poetry collections sent me—John Koethe's *The Late Wisconsin Spring* (Princeton University Press)—fits this bill precisely. "What I want in poetry," Koethe writes, "is a kind of abstract photography / Of the nerves, but what I like in photography / Is the poetry of literal pictures of the neighborhood." Koethe (pronounced *Katy*) gets what he wants in poem after poem, and if your first reaction was, like mine, an impatient surmise that the emperor was once again exposing himself in public, look again, for in fact he's dressed quite *comme il faut* after the manner of Wallace Stevens (but without the loud neckties of that gentleman's jackdaw vocabulary), with even a hint of Wordsworth in the fabric and the cut. This is good stuff, and its goodness depends not at all on solidarity with the poet's politics or lifestyle, neither of which could be inferred from his poems. Except that he had an unhappy childhood and still tends to glory (like McKuen) in wandering lonely as a cloud, the reader won't learn much about John Koethe. It's no way to win a popularity contest, but even so he has my vote as Most Likely to Succeed.

Finally, from England, a world away, a book-length poem by the redoubtable Geoffrey Hill. *The Mystery of the Charity of Charles Péguy* (Oxford University Press, $19.95 hardcover, $7.95 paperback) consists of an even hundred quatrains of off-rhymed pentameter verse that asks, but can't quite answer, the question put in the fourth quatrain, "Did Péguy kill Jaurès? Did he incite the assassin?" Readers whose memory of the news, and of French poetry, doesn't stretch back to 1914 and earlier will need more than the footnotes and two-page biographical sketch provided by Hill in order to fathom what the poem is talking about. Reading it cold the first time through, I came away with a sense that it was gorgeous poetry but that the title was all too apt. Then I did some homework so that Péguy came into focus and returned to the poem enough better informed that I could make sense of most of it, but to convey that sense and then to ponder the justice of Hill's account, as distinct from its panache, lies beyond the scope of this review, and perhaps of this reviewer.

Here in a nutshell (which I won't pretend to try and crack) is the situation that provokes Hill's concern. Péguy belonged to the first generation of the French peasantry that got a crack at higher education. He became a Dreyfusard and a Socialist of utopian tendencies, supported himself by running a bookstore near the Sorbonne, edited a much-respected and little-read magazine, and wrote poetry of an increasingly mystical bent, including a long verse drama, *Le Mystère de la Charité de Jeanne d'Arc,* whence Hill's title. The mystery in Péguy's case is that the mystical poet should have been, as well, a literary warmonger, whose single most famous line is a paraphrase of one from Horace and translates as: "Happy are those who die for their fatherland." Péguy's fulminations against the Socialist leader Jaurès, who did not share this sentiment, inspired one young idealist of the day to assassinate Jaurès, and so Péguy has the unusual distinction for a poet of being one of the proximate causes of World War I. Hill's question is, therefore, an interesting one: Are the opinions of poets exempt from the rules governing other kinds of discourse? It is no idle question. One need only read such a book as Alice Walker's to see that her publisher certainly thinks so, for if one repaired her poems into prose, much of what she has to say would certainly have to be judged racist—or at least as (I prefer the old-fashioned word) prejudiced. But as it is published as "poetry," we are not supposed to take exception. Hill never does render a verdict clear as history's: Péguy was one of the first victims of the war he may have caused. Talk about poetic justice!

POETS AS FRIENDS AND NEIGHBORS

In Other Words
by May Swenson KNOPF $16.95 128 PP.

A Schedule of Benefits
by John N. Morris ATHENEUM $16.95 55 PP.

New and Collected Poems
by Richard Wilbur HARCOURT BRACE JOVANOVICH $27.95 397 PP.

The Rain in the Trees
by W. S. Merwin KNOPF $16.95 78 PP.

The Muse of Distance
by Alan Williamson KNOPF $8.95 (PAPERBACK) 69 PP.

WE PICK THE poets whom we read (supposing we read poetry at all) as we pick our friends, for a disposition, sensibility, and sense of humor that complements our own. This simple fact of readerly life is often a source of distress to particular poets and their partisans, who feel that esthetic merit should be commendation enough. They live in that fantasy world created at the universities, the Republic of Letters, where every two or three decades constitutes an Age with its own roster of canonical Authors. Almost all the teapot tempests of the world of poetry revolve about questions of admission into the shortlist of candidates for canonical status in our own, as-yet-unnamed Age, to be one of the poets destined to be discussed for an hour on PBS, poets we are supposed to read, as we take medicines, whether we like the taste or not.

The five poets here under review are all of a competence and (relative to their ages) recognized stature sufficient to qualify them as canonical contenders, yet I cannot imagine a single reader of so catholic a taste as to relish all five. Here it is not only safe, but true, to say that admirers of X will be delighted with X's new book. If X = May Swenson, they will be delighted with *In Other Words,* which James Merrill praises on the back jacket with undisguised equivocation: "Wonderful May Swenson . . . Without her to write them, who could have imagined these poems?" Well, Marianne Moore for one, and Moore's protégée Elizabeth Bishop for another, nor can I imagine Swenson taking umbrage at having answered Merrill's question so, for her poems are as clearly in that line of descent as any Akita to its pedigreed ancestors. Readers who love to see the curious and lovely objects of the world, its flora and fauna and choicer collectibles, catalogued and anatomized will admire Swenson's skills at such tasks much as they would Moore's or Bishop's. She is a magpie of rare proper nouns: "palo verde, teddybear cholla, ocotillo, bristlebush, and organpipe" are strung together in one catalogue. Words are her Tinkertoys: "The roldengod and the soneyhuckle / the sack eyed blusan and the wistle theed" is the beginning of the relentlessly playful "A Nosty Fright." She commemorates all of life's smallest occasions just as she collects string, as witness the first stanzas from "A Thank-You Letter":

> Dear Clifford: It took me half an hour
> to undo the cradle of string in which
> your package from Denmark came.
>
> The several knots tied under, over, and
> athwart each other—tightly tied and looped
> and tied again—proved so perplexing. When,
>
> finally, the last knot loosened, letting
> the string—really a soft cord—fall free,
> the sense of triumph was delicious.
>
> I now have this wonderful cord 174" long
> although your package is only 13 × 10 × 2. . . .

Swenson can be spinsterish in larger-spirited, less cozy ways than this, but "spinisterish" is the operative adjective throughout, and readers who do not wish to adopt a maiden aunt into their imagination's extended family won't get on with her. It's their loss.

John N. Morris, by a happy polarity, is archetypally avuncular. Crustier and grumpier than Swenson (but no less Fundamentally Decent), Morris is all business. The very title of his book, *A Schedule of Benefits,* alludes to an accident insurance policy, while other poems crystallize about such metaphoric donnés as a museum shop catalogue, a will, the alteration of a suit, the poet's entry in *Who's Who,* and "good" tourists who follow their guidebooks. Morris takes his stand some few steps back from his own feelings, making wry comments tinged with knowing self-reflectivity, as in these lines from a poem about photo albums:

> . . . everywhere we are smiling. Always
> The idea seems to be to turn our backs on
> Something tremendous—the South Rim, say,
> Or Niagara ruining [*sic*] behind us.
>
> Now we all stare with my stare.
> For I am here chiefly as the point of view—
> Invisible but the without-which-nothing.
> My business is composition, keeping
> Us close together inside the hard edges
> Where we pause for these moments of reflection.

It is always hard to know of someone who is notably modest if he is being modest to a fault. If Morris repressed his diffident, hobbyist's smile and faced the grand canyon or waterfall that he imagines himself ignoring, he might well be a larger poet, but a better poet? There's no telling.

Yet if he wanted a role model for such an effort, Richard Wilbur would do handsomely. If he had not been the second to hold the office of America's poet laureate, Wilbur could lay claim to the unenviable title of being the country's most neglected poet of the first rank.

The cause for that lies partly in the decorum and finesse of his work: the jacket of his book diminishes him with the piffling epithet: "He is the master craftsman of our times . . ." Decoded, that means Wilbur is a formalist and, without making any fuss about it, an antimodernist; perhaps, in his happy appropriation of a range of poetic models from the entire intelligible span of English (and French) literature, a postmodernist. But there is nothing in his *New and Collected Poems* a publicist might latch on to and ballyhoo: no hints of scandal or suicide notes, no howling jeremiads, nothing *newsworthy.* Even worse, in terms of academic renown, Wilbur's poetry is lucid, rarely requiring explication or footnotes. There is no system, no *Summa* accreting, no Pounding at the door to sell us a set of encyclopedias. What there *is* he tells us in a translation of Baudelaire: "There, there is nothing else but grace and measure, / Richness, quietness, and pleasure."

Wilbur writes poems one would not be surprised to find shuffled into Palgrave's *Golden Treasury,* completely flensed of the blubber of the inessential self, beautiful as bones. Often enough, one of his poems will begin, like one of Swenson's, in the kitchen or the garden, but Wilbur's property abuts the Elysian Fields and within a few stanzas he's hopped over the fence into the neighboring sublimity. Here he is, for instance, peering into a hole that a carpenter has cut in the floor of his parlor, marveling at the joists and pipes that have been revealed, then asking himself what he's looking for in that hole, and offering this answer:

> . . . the buried strangeness
> Which nourishes the known:
> That spring from which the floor-lamp
> Drinks now a wilder bloom,
> Inflaming the damask love-seat
> And the whole dangerous room.

Simply to catalogue all Wilbur's salient, but so diverse, merits would require enough column inches to build a small temple, and in any case such a demonstration would be superfluous as describing every painting in a retrospective of another luminously tranquil artist,

Henri Matisse (who also translated, into paint, Baudelaire's *luxe, calme, et volupté*). The Elysian Fields don't need a Baedeker. Enough to say that the new poems, comprising a fifth of this volume, are solidly Wilburtian, the grandest of the lot being the libretto for a long, lilting patriotic cantata, "On Freedom's Ground," which would alone entitle him to the peppercorns and all other emoluments of laureatedom. As for the poems of Wilbur's yesteryears, they are *all* here, sturdy as the day they were built. The only omissions are the lyrics he contributed to Bernstein's *Candide* and his superb and thoroughly playable translations of Molière and Racine, which I hope his publisher will soon bring out in a complementary volume.

Admirers of "deep image" poetry will undoubtedly want to plunge into *The Rain in the Trees* by W. S. Merwin, one of the doyens of that school. "Deep image" poetry is the poetic equivalent of minimalism in fiction. Its plain style is presumed to conceal, like still waters, hidden depths. In the schools of creative writing, whose students and alumni probably constitute the single largest audience for contemporary poetry, it is the dominant mode, being easy both to teach and to fake. However, that does not mean that its practitioners are charlatans, and Merwin sometimes does generate poetic magic with a modicum of shamanistic ingredients, a feather, a puff of smoke. More often, to my mind and ear, his poems come off as formulaic rather than incantatory. The poetry becomes a bully pulpit for the more-holistic-than-thou Merwin to inveigh against the traditional bugbears of the counterculture, airports and automobiles and the horrid spectacle of wage slaves heading to their—Ugh!—offices, as in "Glasses":

> There is no eye to catch
>
> They come in uniforms
> they cross bridges built on cement arches
>
> . . .
>
> they pay the electric bills
> they owe money
> all the stars turn in vast courses around them

unnoticed
they vote

they buy their tickets
they applaud
they go into the elevator
thinking of money
with the quiet gleam of money. . . .

Etc., etc., one cheap shot after another, the assumption underlying each mini-diatribe being that Merwin and his readers *notice* the stars in their vast courses and connect with them in a silent communion of which his poems are the almost-mute witness. If you buy that, you might also be the kind of person to benefit from acupuncture. Millions do.

If there were such a school as Maximalism in poetry, Alan Williamson would be on the board of directors. His poems in *The Muse of Distance* aim at a high, Rilkean sublimity, and his aim is usually good. But though his ambitions are Orphic, his building materials are contemporary, the curriculum vitae of an American childhood that finds ineffable significances in the industrial and suburban landscapes that elicit from Merwin only sniffiness. Williamson explains what he's after better than I can in the opening lines of his book's splendid, fifteen-page-long title poem, a memoir of the long summer auto trips on which his father took the Williamsons when Alan was a boy:

What composes a life? Mine comes, too much, from
books;
but also the sense that, if you climbed high places,

you would see the streets go on with nothing to end them
and be driven to, perhaps even desire,

whatever they withheld: a flight of smokestacks past water;
a girl in a mean, dawn-blue room; a glimpse of the terrible

engines, or giants, it took to make such a world . . .

Williamson's main *modus operandi,* even in shorter poems, is spiritual autobiography, in the vein of Wordsworth or Robert Lowell, with whom Williamson once studied and who is the subject of his critical work, *Pity the Monsters: The Political Vision of Robert Lowell.* Lowell's influence has rarely taken such a happy form. Too often his epigones have imitated the crabbed diction, the Laocoönish posturing of One Who Suffers Greatly, the urge to get back to the confessional in every poem. Williamson eschews all this. What he has derived from Lowell, and from his own intensely cultivated talent, is a way of gleaning spiritual meanings from the residues of daily life. Not the preshrunk instant numinousness of *The Rain in the Trees,* but well-weighted words about those things most difficult to speak of. A public poem, for instance, on our era's most awful and most thought-numbing theme, the prospect of atomic annihilation, "Recitation for the Dismantling of a Hydrogen Bomb," in which he describes everyday life in Nuclear America with an exactitude of dread and dismay that should make the poem a touchstone for the age of anxiety. The better the poem, the more frustrating it is to offer only an excerpt, but I hope these opening lines may motivate you to seek out Williamson's book:

From under the flat surface of the planet,
where we know, by statistics, you are waiting,
the White Trains sliding you through our emptiest spaces,
the small grassy doors to you trimly
sunk in the earth by desert or cornfield . . .

We have seen you, as in the mirror of a shield,
suddenly standing tall on so many sides of us
like beautiful ghosts—able to hold completely
still on your columns of smoke, then making
a slight lateral tilt to take direction.
And then we realized—everything standing, the rattled
watch on the table a-tick—we were the ghosts,
and you, your power, our inheritors.

And turning from the shield, we saw the world
glare back, withholding; as if a nothingness
already lived in bird and twig, and they
turned their backs on us, to know it.

POETS OF EXILE

A Part of Speech
by Joseph Brodsky FARRAR STRAUS & GIROUX $12.95 152 PP.

The Sinking of the Titanic
by Hans Magnus Enzensberger HOUGHTON MIFFLIN $11.95 98 PP.

IN THE EARLY years of modernism James Joyce commended silence, exile, and cunning as the foundations of a career in literature. Now modernism is the orthodoxy of every English department, its battles won, its founders canonized, even its epigoni mostly dead or moribund, and of Joyce's triad of virtues only exile continues to be central to the modernist creed. (Writers are never to be believed when they recommend silence, and cunning too uncomfortably resembles careerism for it to be openly celebrated in academia.) Having appointed himself conscience of his race, a poet's most certain path to glory is public outrage, ridicule, and interdiction. In a word, exile.

But literal exile has become almost impossible to achieve—for American poets, at least. The public has learned to look elsewhere for the pleasure of being scandalized. Modernist writing, whether prose or poetry, only befuddles and bores them. To be unread is disheartening but doesn't amount to exile.

Russians, however, are exiled, quite regularly, though usually for writings more actionable than a modernist poet might be guilty of. Exposé, denunciation, and broad satire are more likely to earn publication in, and a ticket to, the West. To write opaque, hermetic poetry in a country that honors plain speaking both in its tame poets (Yevtushenko) and in its proscribed novelists (Solzhenitsyn) is to court martyrdom *and* obscurity. Such, however, has been the chosen course of Joseph Brodsky, who now, in his eighth year of exile from Russia, bids fair to inherit the position lately vacated by Robert Lowell as Sovereign Pontiff of "serious" (i.e., avant-garde, modernist) poetry. From the point of view of the small College of Cardinals empowered to elect a pope, Brodsky is heaven-sent: he is just such a poet as each of them would choose to be—dense, allusive, unremittingly morose—and, as well, a bona fide exile from the fabled hemisphere hidden behind the Iron Curtain, a veritable Lazarus. What an endorsement for modernism that Brodsky should adopt it as his esthetic creed and that Russia should authenticate that choice by banishment! Just when it seemed the pope was dead, we can shout *Viva il Papa!*

Brodsky's celebrity as a refugee from the Gulag Archipelago was one precondition for his present réclame, but talent was necessarily another. His poetry, modernist or not, is the real thing. Brodsky writes long lyric lines, often gnomic in meaning and gnarly in syntax, but smooth on the tongue as sour cream. Some of the credit for this must belong to his translators (among whom are numbered such worthies as Wilbur, Moss, and Hecht), just as some of the blame for certain screeching half-rhymes (halter/footballer, take them/suffocation) may be laid at their door. But Brodsky, defying and transcending that pain of exile keenest to a poet, the pain of divorce from his native tongue, has collaborated in many of these translations and in a few instances, most notably the long title poem of *A Part of Speech,* has undertaken the work of translation himself. A single voice seems to sound from all the poems, and the resulting collection has an authority and finality uncommon among translations.

His subject matter is—what else could it be?—exile. Even before leaving Russia, he begins a long poem, "When you recall me in that land ... and when you duly sigh ..., pondering the blinding number / of seas and fields flung out between us. ... " When he strays from the subject of exile it is to meditate on death and the decline of civilizations, dark themes as darkly rendered.

Sometimes, in a narrative poem or travel chronicle, he will so far descend from the highest seriousness as to allow himself flashes of mordant wit, as when, moving through Mexico, we descry his native, Russian nightmares looming behind a scrim of Aztec civilization:

> Little gods of clay who let themselves be copied
> with extraordinary ease, permitting heterodoxy....
> What would they say if they could speak once more?
>
> Nothing at all. At best, talk of triumphs snatched
> over some adjoining tribe of men, smashed
> skulls. Or how pouring blood into bowls
> sacred to the Sun God strengthens the latter's bowels;
> how sacrifice of eight young and strong men before dark
> guarantees a sunrise more surely than the lark.
>
> Better syphilis after all, better the orifice
> of Cortés' unicorns, than sacrifice like this.
> If fate assigns your carcass to the vultures' rage
> let the murderer be a murderer, not a sage.
> Anyway, how would they ever, had it
> not been for the Spaniards, have learned of what really
>   happened.

Better (the paraphrase is irresistible) America, for all its vulgarity and brutality, than the systematic human sacrifice of the gulags. (The one puzzler in those lines—What are Cortés' unicorns?—is glossed in a footnote at the back of the book: They're a kind of cannon.)

Not all Brodsky's poems yield up their sense so readily. At his most abstruse and metaphysical, as in "A Song to No Music," he can tease a metaphor beyond all reckoning and give even John Donne lessons in plane geometry. He can brood over the vasty abyss for, it would seem, weeks at a stretch, and never in all that while speak of anything more concrete than Space and Time:

Time is far greater than space. Space is a thing.
Whereas time is, in essence, the thought, the conscious
                                 dream
of a thing. And life itself is a variety
of time. . . .

Sometimes, in a mood of exemplary modernist futility, Brodsky produces a poem the effect of which is of a Samuel Beckett monologue chopped into quatrains:

What then shall I talk about?
Shall I talk about nothingness?
Shall I talk about days, or nights?
Or people? No, only things,

since people will surely die.
All of them. As I shall.
All talk is a barren trade.
A writing on the wind's wall.

Happily, such moods don't often get the better of him, and the proportion of portentous nonsense to live poetry is respectably low. Even Rilke nods, after all. My own preference is for a poetry more secured to quotidian experience, more willing to indulge a mood of mere ebullience, less given to complainings of suffocation, but for those readers who read poetry as a kind of secular Sabbath, Brodsky provides a month of Sundays in the best tradition of Puritan New England.

    Hans Magnus Enzensberger would also like to be a poet of exile, but being native to West Germany he has had to settle for spells of expatriation. *The Sinking of the Titanic,* a book-length poem in thirty-three cantos with sundry interpolations, was begun in 1969, when the author was self-exiled to Castro's Cuba, having previously sojourned in the United States and Norway. The translation is the author's own and flavorful enough at its best moments to have persuaded me that its *longueurs* derive from the original. The English title does fail to capture the Spenglerian resonance of *Der Untergang der Titanic,* but the text leaves us in no doubt that nothing less than the entirety of Western Civilization is being figured forth in the *Titanic*'s demise.

Given such a dire theme, and no plot to speak of, one might expect this to be tough sledding indeed, but Enzensberger addresses his readers as an audience to be entertained, rather than (as Brodsky) the ineffable twin of his own stricken intelligence, and his book is as accessible and ingratiating as a good thriller. The ship's inexorable doom is played off against this or that unsuspecting vanity, rather in the manner of these German woodcuts illustrating the Dance of Death. Finally Enzensberger has little more to say about the fatal demise of absolutely all of us than that we are still waiting for it to happen and meanwhile nothing much can be done, icebergs being so little responsive to reason. The twenty-seventh canto opens:

> "In actual fact nothing has happened."
> There was no such a thing as the sinking of the *Titanic.*
> It was just a movie, an omen, a hallucination.

Scenes of carnage and rescue are imagined, erased, reimagined, like vaudeville turns in a macabre nightclub. Sometimes the poet's self-importance disguises itself as irony, as in this swatch from a long bolt of Dantesque equations:

> This is a man who believes he is Dante.
>
> This is a man everybody, except Dante, believes to be
> Dante.
> This is a man everybody believes to be Dante, only he
> himself does not fall for it.
> This is a man nobody believes to be Dante, except Dante.
> This is Dante.

In fact, that was not Dante, but Hans Magnus Enzensberger searching in vain for an editor. Usually his ironies are less clanging, his wit brisker, his language better corseted.

Comparisons are both odious and irrelevant. The music is better at Brodsky's church services than in Enzensberger's cabaret, but the jokes are undeniably funnier, the atmosphere more relaxed, and everyone has more fun *chez* Enzensberger. As for which of them would win a Dante look-alike contest, the photos on the back covers leave no doubt at all—Brodsky gets the laurel crown.

OUT OF THE MURK PLECTRUM

Flow Chart
by John Ashbery KNOPF $20 216 PP.

STAND AROUND IN the Cubist corner of any well-touristed museum and inside of half an hour you will surely hear a discussion of where in his pictures Picasso has hidden the guitars or wine bottles or the ears and noses of his models. Paintings even less representational than his get the same treatment. Is this particular pink smoosh by de Kooning meant to be thought of in the same way one thinks of the thighs of a Rubens Venus? Is this grid of erased lines by Diebenkorn somehow the blueprint of a domestic interior in a world of alternate geometries? Purists will insist that such unsophisticated speculations have nothing to do with the art of painting, but they will say the same of Venus's thighs. The painters themselves, to judge by the titles they affix to their paintings, have not forsworn the idea of referentiality; they have only allowed a greater degree of slippage between their subject and its representation.

Perhaps no poet of the present day has been more actively involved, both as critic and collaborator, in the "project" of modern American painting in its glory days than John Ashbery; and none, with the significant exception of Gertrude Stein, has made such a determined effort to apply the lessons of painting to his own art and to free poetry from its servitude to referentiality, to make poems that are as abstract as paintings. In many of the poems in his most rebarbative and Steinish collection of 1962, *The Tennis Court Oath,* there is simply no way to wrest a plain discursive meaning from the poet's utterances. "Yellow curtains / Are in fashion," one poem begins, and continues, "Murk plectrum, / Fatigue and smoke of nights / And recording of piano in factory." That "Murk plectrum," though it continues to reverberate through the poem, resists interpretation as sturdily as any of Stein's "Tender Buttons." For instance, her "An Umbrella," which read, in its entirety: "Coloring high means that the strange reason is in front not more in front behind. Not more in front in peace of the dot."

Stein's effort to adapt Cubism's techniques of fracture and reassembly to literary purposes did not generate readerly poetry, and even Ashbery abandoned a Murk-plectrum degree of nonreferentiality in later work. However, he'd discovered another and more utile form of abstraction, one that can be found, in an embryonic form, in the prose of Henry James and Hemingway: the perpetually suspended referent. Ashbery's absolutely favorite word is "It," as in "Get it?" or "What's it mean?" or as it appears in the following self-contained and self-referential segment of his new book-length poem, *Flow Chart:*

> Without further ado bring on the subject of these
> negotiations. They all would like to collect it always, but
>   since
> that's impossible, the Logos alone will have to suffice.
> A pity, since no one has seen it recently. Others crowded
>   the opening, hoping
> to catch a glimpse, but the majority saw the occluded
>   expatriate ragtag representation and
> decided to not even try. To this day no one knows the
>   shape or heft of the thing,
> and that's the honest truth thrown out of court, exhibiting
>   abrasions,
> muffled. And the story of how we ran out of it.

Ashbery certainly has *something* in mind here, but the "subject of these negotiations" is constantly in flux. Is it, for instance, the "it" of the next line that we all would like to collect always? And is the "it" no one's seen recently, the same "it," or, as grammatically likely, the Logos? The poem doesn't go on talking about the same thing long enough for the poet ever to be pinned down, though that's not always so since Ashbery can also be lucid to the point of banality for lines at a time:

> So what's
> to feel nervous about? We all know that we have to live
>   for a certain time and then
> unfortunately we must die, and after that no one is sure
>   what happens. Accounts vary. But we
> most of us feel we'll be made comfortable for much of
>   the time after that, and get credit
> for the (admittedly) few nice things we did, and no one
>   is going to make too much
> of a fuss over those we'd rather draw the curtain over,
>   and besides, we can't see
> much that was wrong in them, there are two sides to every
>   question. . . .

Most of *Flow Chart* inhabits a rhetorical region more well-lit and apprehensible than the first excerpt quoted, and more lyrical and "sincere" than the second (though in its handling of a tone of Mortimer Snerd-ish common sense that passage is a fair sample of the poem's drollery). The most remarkable thing about the book, for me, was simply how enjoyable it was to read. Ashbery is generally regarded, and even dreaded, as one of those poets who can't be read without making a major intellectual effort, on the principle, No pain, no gain. One can dip into *Flow Chart* anywhere with a good likelihood of being either amused or beguiled or simply astonished at the way he zips down the page, like a skier negotiating moguls, with a major swerve from the oracular to the demotic to some other antithetical tone in almost every line.

That ability to change the subject quickly, at high speed, without ever really stating it, has become, for many contemporary poets, the litmus test of true lyricism, thanks almost entirely to Ashbery's inspiring but, alas, almost inimitable manner. It is the illusion that knack induces, especially in this latest book, of almost limitless profusions of poetic statement that puts Ashbery into contention with the immortals. In the words of Harold Bloom, quoted on the book flap: "No one now writing poems in the English language is likelier than Ashbery to survive the severe judgments of time . . . He is joining that American sequence that includes Whitman, Dickinson, Stevens, and Hart Crane."

That's as may be. My own highest praise for Ashbery would be that alone among contemporary poets he has succeeded in creating a body of work that defeats the effort of Criticism to preside over the reading of poetry. Ashbery's poetry is vaporous and steamy and eludes the hermeneutical grasp. To understand Ashbery one can only read more Ashbery, and if the insights that accrue to that reading seem somehow insubstantial once one has departed the text, that is not to be wondered at, for Ashbery is the poet laureate of Spaciness, that touchstone of the sixties Zeitgeist that here has found its mandarin apotheosis.

THE LAST WORD ON DEATH

The Transparent Man
by Anthony Hecht
KNOPF $18.95 75 PP.

Collected Earlier Poems
by Anthony Hecht
KNOPF $22.95 272 PP.

POETS ARE OUR best authorities on death. Religion would like to have the job, but by its very doctrinal confidence it avoids the nagging question pondered by Hamlet, that archetype of the poetic character: What if, after we're dead, there isn't anything else, just our actuarial allotment and then the Big Sleep? Is that a consummation to be wished? One of poetry's tersest answers is to be found in a chorus from Sophocles' *Oedipus at Colonus:*

> Not to be born is, past all yearning, best.
> And second best is, having seen the light,
> To return at once to deep oblivion....

Among contemporary poets writing in English none has fixed a more unwavering gaze on this cheerless theme, nor sounded that Sophoclean note so truly as Anthony Hecht (from whose latest collection, *The Transparent Man,* the above translation is drawn).

Hecht does have other notes to sound: he paints admirable land- and seascapes; he has a Mozartean vivacity in depicting affairs of the heart; he can be consummately civilized and witheringly cruel. But in all these other modes there is a darkness to Hecht's poetry that derives from his lifelong intimacy with death, as though paintings by Boucher or Monet were to be filtered through the palette of Marsden Hartley.

We Americans are supposed, as a rule, to be squeamish about death, but that rule surely doesn't apply to American poets. Hecht is one of a long honor guard that was led off by William Cullen Bryant, Edgar Allan Poe, Emily Dickinson, and Walt Whitman. That lineage noticeably thins out with the advent of modernism (except for the separate category of the suicides: Crane, Plath, Berryman, et al.). Perhaps a pronounced interest in death is essentially at odds with the modernist injunction to make it new. Hecht, at any rate, is the most adamantly old-fashioned of all contemporary poets of the first rank. This has been evident since his first collection of 1954, *A Summoning of Stones,* which manifests his traditionalism not only in the topiaried elegance of its formal verse but also by its donnish allusiveness to the whole gamut of West Civ. Hecht jests with Plato, tells a ballad tale of eighteenth-century London, discourses on a painting by Memling, and writes a rhymed epistle in the manner of Byron's Childe Harold, which begins:

> I write from Rome. Last year, the Holy Year,
> The flock was belled, and pilgrims came to see
> How milkweed mocked the buried engineer,
> Wedging between his marble works, where free
> And famished went the lions forth to tear
> A living meal from the offending knee,
> And where, on pagan ground turned to our good,
> *Santa Maria sopra Minerva* stood.

To appreciate such poetry one must first of all have read enough history to know what is being discussed, and enough poetry to appreciate the Augustan balance of "A living meal from the offending knee" and to relish the double-take set up by that archly precise "offending." Readers not schooled for such tasks (most, probably) or those who prefer poetry to serve as an introduction to new friends (the commonest mission of poetry in our time) will resent Hecht for being such a smartypants or feel miffed by his reticence. Even when he writes about himself, as he does, unsparingly, in "See Naples and Die," the long centerpiece poem in his new collection, Hecht is not at pains to have us like him. Indeed, he comes across as a difficult person. But what a poet!

Poem by poem, Hecht must be reckoned the peer of Richard Wilbur and James Merrill. At that level of dependably near-perfect accomplishment further comparisons are as nugatory as between Byron, Keats, and Shelley. Hecht has been less prolific than Wilbur or Merrill, but that can be an asset from a readerly point of view, as it allows one the pleasure of surveying Hecht's oeuvre without assuming the rigors of a graduate seminar, a civility not to be enjoyed in the company of busier writers.

It is a commonplace in reviewing poetry to salute each subsequent book as better than the last, but Hecht's last, *The Venetian Vespers* of 1979, was so good that virtually every poem in it (except the translations of poems by Joseph Brodsky) seems destined for decades of anthologization. Not *every* poem in *The Transparent Man* is of the same unequivocal excellence, only a majority. But on his peculiar theme of death Hecht has produced a quire of elegies, the fifth section of the book, that are quietly, sublimely beyond all praise. Perhaps not to be born is best, but second best is to have lived long enough for Anthony Hecht to have written one's epitaph.

BARROOM BUDDY AND PROM KING

Where Water Comes Together with Other Water
by Raymond Carver RANDOM HOUSE $13.95 130 PP.

Cats of the Temple
by Brad Leithauser KNOPF $7.95 PAPER 70 PP.

WHEN, IN PRAISING a poet, it is said that he has "found his own voice" what is usually meant is that he has developed a manner of self-dramatization sufficiently consistent that a single persona seems to be the source of all his poems. "Voice" in this sense equates with a manner of delivery, a stance, a style that the audience may not share but that it can at least recognize from a distance, like a traffic sign. Raymond Carver is a poet who sings the song of himself with a consistency and confidence that leaves us in no doubt at all as to what it's like to be Raymond Carver, a task made easier by virtue of the short stories he's written, many of which reflect the same experiences that the poems assure us have been his. He has been a drunk, but, redeemed by a good woman's love, now lives each day as it comes. He likes to hunt and fish (indeed, nothing else seems to get him out of doors). He worries that his children will come to no good like him and his old man, and, lest we forget, he worries a lot about death, as in the conclusion to a short poem cataloguing his favorite fears:

> Fear of waking up to find you gone.
> Fear of not loving and fear of not loving enough.
> Fear that what I love will prove lethal to those I love.

Fear of death.
Fear of living too long.
Fear of death.
  I've said that.

Carver's poems are usually short, telling anecdotes from his life told in a no-bullshit tone of barroom confidentiality, as if by a country-western Marmeládov. His heart is always on his sleeve, whether he is apostrophizing his married daughter:

You're a beautiful drunk, daughter.
But you're a drunk. I can't say you're breaking
my heart. I don't have a heart when it comes
to this booze thing. Sad, yes. Christ alone knows . . .

or recounting a late-night phone call from an old drinking companion:

I love you, Bro, you said.
And then a sob passed between us. I took hold
of the receiver as if
it were my buddy's arm.
And I wished for us both
I could put my arms
around you, old friend.
I love you too, Bro.
I said that, and then we hung up.

Readers who don't suffer toxic reactions to Carver's mixture of machismo and vulnerability may enjoy his poems for their anecdotal value. He tells good stories, has an easy-going sense of humor, and usually a little more verbal crackle than those excerpts indicate. There will be some readers for whom Carver may serve as a role model (the commonest purpose of poetry in our time), but his audience is more likely to be those like myself who only imagine the honky-tonk half of the world. Charles Bukowski's poetry has similar appeal, and indeed its voyeuristic attraction is even greater, since Bukowski is an unreformed reprobate with claims to being America's premier dirty old man. Bukowski reveals himself as one might by opening a trench-coat; Carver's self-revelations have more the character of testimony at an AA meeting. Potentially Carver's poems could be as popular as those of Robert Service—and for not dissimilar reasons.

When Brad Leithauser's first collection of poems, *Hundreds of Fireflies,* appeared in 1982, he was generally acclaimed as the Prom King of American poetry. As the first poet to advertise himself as a Preppie, Leithauser became the spokesman for the Ivy League gentry who had once *owned* poetry, along with the other arts, and then seen it taken over by successive immigrant hordes. Leithauser is too much a gentleman to inveigh against any minority's aspirations, but in the autobiographical centerpiece poem of that first collection, "Two Summers," he celebrates his talent, his job in a Wall Street law firm, and his $200 suits as candidly as Bukowski would a six-pack. Many readers found his candor beguiling, and even those too spiritual or too genteel to approve overt paeans to class advantage could admire the young urbane professional qua poet. Here were formal poems produced on a variety of templates, witty when wit was called for, and uniformly well crafted, some exquisitely so.

In his second collection, *Cats of the Temple,* Leithauser has decided to concentrate exclusively on being exquisite. Though the circumstances of his life are richer than ever (he has spent several years in Japan at the Kyoto Comparative Law Center), we only learn of this in a postscriptive author's note, not in his poems, or not directly. He does some Japanese "scenes," but they are as generic in their *japonaiserie* as any painted fan. Nature has taken over, and Nature, for Leithauser, comprises zoos, formal gardens, and vacation spots— even the very benches in those environs where earlier poets have been known to sit and write their poems. He has no anecdotes to tell, and his jokes fall as flat as the following bit of sub–Ogden Nash:

Poet's Lament

Why must gainful
Employment be so painful?

When he's in his exquisite vein, he can still gild refined gold, but too often his diction gets knotty in proportion as the thought is thin.

For all that this particular (very slim) volume is a disappointment, and for all that Carver's was consistently more readable, Leithauser's awareness of the formal demands and possibilities of language—and even his willingness to do without the charms of blarney—bode well for his future. Having left off being "Brad Leithauser," he is in a good position to become a poet.

PRODUCTS OF THE
WORKSHOP

White Paper: On Contemporary American Poetry
by J. D. McClatchy COLUMBIA UNIVERSITY PRESS $39.50 351 PP.

Poets for Life: 76 Poets Respond to AIDS
Edited by Michael Klein CROWN $18.95 244 PP.

God Hunger
by Michael Ryan VIKING $17.95 79 PP.

"EIGHTY YEARS AGO, or even half that number," queries critic J. D. McClatchy, "what did the fledgling poet face? A few lions, the long shelf, the solitary charge. And today? A babble and an industry." A babble because "there is no national standard, no single voice with which our poets aspire to speak." McClatchy allows as how diversity may be a good thing, but in practice he doesn't have much truck with it. The individual writers he celebrates in the main body of this collection of essays, *White Paper: On Contemporary American Poetry*, represent McClatchy's own sense of a national standard and a single voice, or if not quite that, then two well-harmonized choruses, one celestial (Lowell, Bishop, Berryman, Plath), the other our most Augustan elders (Merrill, Howard, Hollander, Clampitt, Hecht). In unraveling the varied relevances of a favorite poem, McClatchy is an accomplished analyst, but as a polemicist presenting his "white paper" on the condition of poetry he comes across as simply another defender of the canonical against the hordes outside the gate.

In lamenting the influence of the poetry workshops, which are now a feature of virtually every college and university, with a faculty, accordingly, of several thousand nationwide—each a published poet with at least one slim volume behind him or her—McClatchy is scarcely alone. Joseph Epstein published an essay in the August 1988 *Commentary* titled "Who Killed Poetry?" which also blames the creative writing industry for an unwanted plethora of poetry such that it has become impossible to observe the decorums of rank and precedence. This essay was reprinted in the industry's own trade paper, the Associated Writing Programs' *Chronicle,* where the creative writers were allowed to respond, which they did with various degrees of outrage and wounded dignity. "Living poetry," declared Toi Derricotte, "is made up of those taking the risk, not those making judgments about whether or not poetry is alive." Not all the symposiasts took Derricotte's closed-shop approach, but almost all of them shared, with Epstein and McClatchy, the mistaken assumption that the purpose of creative writing courses is to train armies of accomplished poets and novelists.

Creative writing courses have many legitimate raisons d'être, but they can't teach anyone to be a first-class poet. Indeed, by inculcating a proficiency in the current fashionable style, they may well encourage those talents with too ready a knack for emulation. And talent of the larger sort doesn't need workshops, as the history of literature bears ample witness. Teaching creative writing has another purpose: in school systems that offer no formal training in rhetoric or elocution, a poetry "workshop" is often the only school for eloquence.

Learning to write with eloquence—i.e., with wit, feeling, and a bit of flair—is an empowering experience, and one that should be part of everyone's education. Kenneth Koch has shown in his books about teaching young children and nursing-home residents to write poetry that everyone *can* do it. Creative writing courses serve many of the same educational purposes as athletic programs. They channel excess energies to harmless, healthful purposes, promote a sense of well-being, and develop real skills. They also encourage a portion of the students to suppose they can be contenders; inevitably, those who don't make it into the major leagues often stay on at the universities to conduct the athletic departments and the writing workshops.

The difference is that in poetry the process of elimination and ranking is less decisive than in sports. It has become the kind of noncompetitive contest in which every child goes home with a prize. Criticism is often an exchange of favors and courtesies, written in the bloated language of blurbs, as when Stanley Kunitz, the master of the meaningless encomium, praises the (innocuous at best) poems of Michael Ryan as "boldly conceived, with an unsparing honesty and a clarity of focus that invest them with a shattering reality." this form of positive thinking extends even to critics as capable as Helen Vendler, who never discusses what she can't applaud. McClatchy is even more remiss in this regard, since his position paper lambastes only nameless mediocrities and sneers, by allusion, at poets he ought to name—at "mad housewives, Detroit factory workers and Vietnam veterans" and their "unrelieved tedium of speechliness."

It can be a tedious business to criticize the work of tedious poets, but if one disdains to do so, one should not be surprised to find them in time decked with the praises of a Stanley Kunitz and weighted with the prizes that poets give one another. The sensible thing to do in this situation, and what most readers of a literary bent have already done, is to deal with poetry as with other no-longer-living arts: Reserve it for those holidays of the spirit when one takes a favorite classic volume down from the shelf, blows off the dust, and is delectated.

In some respects all poets are equal, and the anthology *Poets for Life* illustrates the most unarguable of those respects. It contains poems on the theme of AIDS by seventy-six poets of the most varied backgrounds and capabilities. Many are elegies for specific victims of the plague. A few of the poems might pass the McClatchy litmus test for formal beauty, but many—including McClatchy's "The Landing"—strain to rise to a solemn occasion and fall flat. Many more are stiff or shrill: a good elegy is at least as hard to write as a note of condolence. A few are bathetic and whiny. But I can't imagine any critic considering *Poets for Life* as suitable grist for the critical mill. The book possesses a documentary force that transcends aesthetics. Like the great AIDS quilt, the book becomes a kind of metaphor for the mass grave the plague is busy filling.

Grief is by no means the only equalizer in the republic of letters, only the one least likely to be controverted. Any sincere emotion, expressed with candor and a modicum of skill, commands a humane if not always an aesthetic respect. And this is precisely the kind of poetry encouraged by the workshops, a poetry of naive, earnest self-expression and self-discovery, endeavors that have an undoubted role in the educational process, regardless of the merits of the poems that may be their by-products. Indeed, a heart worn candidly on one's sleeve is one of the best devices known to avert the evil eye of critics.

Which brings us to Michael Ryan, whose third collection, *God Hunger,* was so lavishly praised by Stanley Kunitz. Ryan strikes me as the very model of the workshop poet, in the pejorative sense. He comes with many laurels: His first book was nominated for a National Book Award; his second was selected for the National Poetry Series. This book is published by Viking, and its poems have appeared in such venues as *Poetry, The New Yorker, The Nation,* and *American Poetry Review,* where Ryan is a regular contributor. Despite all this, so large has the kingdom of poetry grown that I'd not heard of Ryan before reading *God Hunger,* and I can take an oath that my poor opinion of his poems is based strictly on their internal evidence. Yet, since Ryan writes about almost nothing except himself and his various foul moods, from self-pity to reproachfulness, it is hard to speak of his poems as though they had an existence independent of his personality as he has chosen to dramatize it. In disliking his poems I feel I am disliking a person, and this bespeaks a kind of mimetic achievement: were Ryan a worse poet, one might have less cause to dislike the self he depicts.

Ryan is often concerned to show himself in his uniform as a poet, as when, in his account of "Meeting Cheever" (Iowa City, 1973), he sees himself as a "wounded-by-the-world angry young poet / who became me as strangely as years become today." In another poem reproaching a doppelgänger who committed suicide, we see the same face in the mirror: "a pushy kid who loved poetry, / one more young man alone in his distress." Ryan the Wounded Poet truly comes into his own in the book's longest poem, "A Burglary," which begins with a moment of immortal false modesty: "It was only of my studio at Yaddo / a twenty-by-twenty cabin in the woods / whose walls are nearly all windows, and all they got was a typewriter and stereo." Ryan admits this is "a loss / which even to me did not sound great / within the world's constant

howl of misery," but he is wretched anyhow, and can substantiate his
woe with a quotation from Hannah Arendt's *Thinking:*

> with my underscoring and stars in the margin—
> "Solitude is being with oneself. Loneliness
> is being with no one."—I felt again
> a desolation I had almost forgotten.
> At Yaddo I could hear it whisper
> like the voice of another person
> mocking all I said outwardly calm or kind,
> and for months, teaching classes or at dinner with friends,
> my mind might blank as if slammed
> by a wave, and I'd struggle to pretend
> I wasn't somersaulting underwater unable to breathe.

Ryan escapes his desolation by attending a party to which he'd been
invited by two dentists' wives he'd met at a local disco. At the party,

> The guests were all dentists, their wives, and hygienists;
> all had long been curious about Yaddo
> which stands like a Vatican in their midst.
> In twos and threes, all twenty of them talked to me
> ("You're a poet? What do you *do?*"),
> and someone's unemployed kid brother
> who could have passed for Arthur Bremer
> recited his own personal poems to me
> endlessly. I tilted my ear toward him and listened.
> I thought this something I could do.
> Maybe for this reason, if for no other,
> everyone came to seem to feel pleasure
> in my being there. I began enjoying myself, too,
> until we heard, from the den this time,
> the host dentist screaming at his wife:
> "What the hell are you doing inviting to our *home*
> some strange guy you met in a bar?
> To humiliate me? Or are you crazy?"

Ryan considers sticking around but, recalling a knife fight he'd witnessed in a Mexican movie theater, thinks better of it and goes back to the disco, where he guzzles "shot after shot of bourbon" and then drives back drunk to Yaddo, where, switching to six-packs, he drinks till dawn. At the end of the poem he learns that the dentist whose party he'd visited is divorcing his wife. The tone throughout the poem, throughout the book, is self-aggrandizing, lachrymose, and condescending toward all who are dentists and not poets (but who, even so, must see Yaddo as "a Vatican").

And these qualities, I would submit, are precisely the ones that have won Michael Ryan the approval of his peers. For if self-portraiture and self-mythologizing are his only competence, then it must be that the self Ryan exhibits is one that registers as not only viable but worthy of emulation. And it is not an unfamiliar myth: the hard drinking, the hints of having been a brawler, the womanizing and litanies of reproach to the women who won't put out but just lie there: "your luminous eyes wide open, three miles deep in yourself / rooted in poison." This is Hemingway country, denuded though it may be of those narrative virtues that make Hemingway worth reading, but even this territory is considered genuinely admirable by some readers, because they either live there or suppose they'd like to. In pop music there is Bon Jovi and Guns N'Roses; in the movies there's Chuck Norris and Sean Penn; in poetry there is Michael Ryan, and doubtless many more.

In the prospect of eternity, to which poetry properly belongs, it doesn't make a scrap of difference. Cream generally rises, and when it does not, it isn't for lack of room at the top.

Why bother panning the likes of *God Hunger* at all, in that case? Because sometimes, as one watches the emperor's latest fashion show or reads reports of it in the press, it is reassuring to hear someone else echo one's own sense of the event. This can't be done for *every* show, just as one could not work up a passion of indignation over each headline reporting on perpetual scandals such as Watergate or HUD. I also feel that every critic is obligated to give his or her aversions at least a regular airing, if not equal time with the enthusiasms, for to do otherwise is to take part in a conspiracy of silence.

POMPES POSTMODERNE

Poetic License: Essays on Modernist and Postmodernist Lyric
by Marjorie Perloff
NORTHWESTERN UNIVERSITY PRESS $29.95 345PP.

MARJORIE PERLOFF HAS a relationship toward the "postmodern" poetry she champions as a critic much like the relationship of Donna
Elvira to Don Giovanni in Mozart's opera. She has a passionate enthusiasm for its potential that the repeated experience of its unwor-
thiness never dampens. Perloff is a capable critic, who sometimes
marvels unduly at rudimentary prosodic skills, but who has a basically
serviceable sense of what is wheat and what chaff. She is, however,
a professional critic, and these days in academia that often entails a
fealty to French models of discourse and valuation that are antithetical
to literary common sense.

"Postmodern" is an epithet that can encompass almost anything
written since 1950 that might strike admirers of Eliot or Stevens as
odd or, ideally, baffling (and so, needing professional decoding assistance from a critic). Gertrude Stein is, for Perloff, the wellspring of
this esthetic, the *"côté postmoderne,"* as she styles it with a glaze of
authenticating French. One of the best essays in *Poetic License* is an
appreciation of the various verbal textures to be found in Stein's work
from the smooth to the rebarbative. She is an okay unriddler of a
rune like Stein's "portrait" entitled "Jean Cocteau":

Needs be needs be needs be near.
Needs be needs be needs be.
This is where they have their land astray
                    Two say.

Even here she is prone to discover spurious double meanings (she'd
have us believe "needs be" a pun on "kneads bee") and misses obvious
ones (she glosses "Two say" as a pun on "to say," and not the obvious
French verbal tic, "*tu sais*").

This kind of critical filagree-work has two serious limitations:
(1) it can be applied equally well to a text purposing a meaning as to
one generated randomly; (2) it cannot succeed as advocacy (i.e., a sore
is a sore is a sore, and festers the same by any other name). These
are limitations only as they apply to the text under scrutiny, however.
A critic may actually appear to advantage in defending unworthy
texts, much as defense lawyers shine brighter in proportion as the
defendants' sins are black. The basic myth of the avant-garde (a myth
implicit in the "postmodern" label) is that art progresses by historical
stages, and each advance is perceived by the uninitiated rabble as
sacrilege or nonsense. Painting provides the best paradigm: impres-
sionism, postimpressionism, cubism, abstraction, pop, and then the
Babel of the postmodern.

Squeezing poetry's feet into this conceptual slipper is not an
easy task, since the formal options open to poets have not changed in
the last forty years or even longer. There are, rather, operational
modes and rhetorical strategies that have appealed to roughly the
same intellectual strata of readers over the last century or more. One
such strand combines high prophetic utterance with demotic speech
and populist sentiment—the Whitman-Ginsberg axis. Perloff has a
sharp ear for both what is good and what is blague in this vein. Her
essay on Ginsberg is a model of how to write a rave: "To read Ginsberg's *Collected Poems* in 1985 is something of a shock—a *frisson* of
pure pleasure. Was our poetry really this energetic, this powerful and
immediate just a few short decades ago?" She also does a good job
of vivisection on the corpus of Paul Blackburn, a beat of a different

(dumber) character. She is withering toward one of W. C. Williams's heirs, W. S. Merwin, and full of applause for another heir, Lorine Niedecker. The catholicity of her tastes encompasses just (or justifiable) estimates of Sylvia Plath, D. H. Lawrence, John Ashbery, and various epigones of Ezra Pound.

However, every critic wants to carve out some new intellectual territory, which will thereafter bear a plaque, "Discovered in [year] by [critic's name]." It is here, where she chooses to plant the flag of discovery, in the purlieus of "language poetry," that Perloff will fail to convince any but the converted. Here is a snippet from a poem she particularly extolls, Lyn Hejinian's *The Guard:*

> Yesterday the sun went West and sucked
> the sea from books. My witness
> is an exoskelton. Altruism suggestively fits.
> It is true, I like to go to the hardware store
> and browse on detail. So sociable the influence
>
> of Vuillard, so undying in disorder is order....

Of this, and of poems no better, she claims that they have "less to do with the Romantic conception of poetry as 'an intensely subjective and personal expression' (Hegel) . . . than with the original derivation of *lyric* as a composition performed on the lyre." To which my own immediate and unmediated response is: "Lyre, lyre, pants on fire!" Or, in adult parlance, bullshit.

Nothing can excuse dullness, except a critic intent on originality.

Marjorie Perloff has poets more dire than Lyn Hejinian whom she'd extenuate: she has Steve McCaffery, the author of *Panopticon,* from which she quotes:

> Again and again. And so on. And so forth. And back
>   again.
> And once more. And one more time. Again and again
>   and
> through and through. Over and over again and again.

Moments anticipatory of. Then cancelled. And then again.
And again and again. And over and over . . .

"And," Perloff notes, "this prose unit ends with two pages of 'and on
and on and on,' the two words forming a kind of concrete poem
made of successive columns."

Perloff is not entirely comfortable with McCaffery's Goofy (in
the Disney sense) koans. His writing provokes her to address "the
question of style": "Like many of the poets loosely associated with
the 'language' movement . . . McCaffery writes a critical prose that
seems, on a first reading, irritatingly jargon ridden—indeed, downright ugly:

> The cipheral text involves the replacement of a tradi-
> tionally 'readerly' function . . . by a first order
> experience of graphemes, their material tension and
> relationships and their *sign potentiality* as substance,
> hypo-verbal units simultaneously pushing towards, yet
> resisting contextual significations."

In other words, McCaffery is leery of texts possessing an ascertainable
significance, and, since his own lack any worth decoding, this is a
shrewd tactic for him to pursue.

To her credit it may be said that Marjorie Perloff herself eschews such pseudo-scientific silliness, and even knows enough to be
embarrassed by it. Why then does she praise those who traffic in it?
Because, like Everest, it's there. The English departments of the better
universities these days are controlled by tailors who design clothes for
the same naked emperor. One either salutes their fashion sense
or perishes. Increasingly, the emperor's wardrobe is acclaimed.
Thousands of English majors who know, as Perloff does, that such
piffle is not poetry also know on which side their bread is buttered.

And why is the piffle written at all? Because the myth of the
avant-garde still has enough currency to make obscurantism a profitable enterprise. If one can create a jargon sufficiently impenetrable
and portentous and then refuse to speak any other language, one will

be secure against most criticism. Deconstructive critics and related charlatans have been profiting from this insight for many years. Now poets have realized there is a similar ecological niche for them in academia. As Perloff points out, in a moment of inspired matchmaking: "the poems of a Charles Bernstein or a Lyn Hejinian, not to speak of Leiris or Cage, are more consonant with the theories of Derrida and de Man, Lacan and Lyotard, Barthes and Benjamin, than are the canonical texts that are currently being ground through the poststructuralist mill." She would have such critics forget about Wordsworth and Wallace Stevens and write about poets like themselves.

This is a suggestion I heartily endorse. If deconstructive critics would only leave real literature alone and devote their entire attention to the likes of the language poets, solipsism will have achieved its masterpiece, an academic ghetto that can do double duty as a quarantine ward.

THE HIGH PRIEST OF HIGH TIMES

Charles Olson: The Allegory of a Poet's Life
by Tom Clark
W. W. NORTON $27.95 403 PP.

SPECTACULARLY DISMAL OR dishonest lives often make for great reading, as witness this biography of the minor league poet and beatnik guru Charles Olson (1910–70). Olson's poetry was either ignored or reviled by the poetic tastemakers of his own generation, including writers of such diverse tendencies as James Dickey, Robert Bly (who termed *Maximus,* Olson's magnum opus, the work of "a *Babbitt* in verse," and "the worst book of the year"), Thom Gunn, Louis Simpson, Louise Bogan, and Marianne Moore, who labeled Olson's patented postmodern "projective verse" as "weedy and colorless like suckers from an un-sunned tuber."

That Olson managed to carve out his own special place in the history of postwar American literature, despite a virtual critical consensus against his poetry, is a tribute to his knack for creating disciples. If his peers would have none of him, he knew how to appeal, in a Pied Piperish way, to the nascent counterculture of the fifties and sixties. At Black Mountain, an experimental college in rural North Carolina, Olson was a pioneer in the dismantling of the college core curriculum and its replacement by a kind of autodidacticism that differed little from autointoxication. He was, in short, the high priest of High Times, and Tom Clark's biography is a balefully fascinating account of both the man and the milieu he did so much to form.

Olson grew up in Worcester, Massachusetts, the son of a Swedish immigrant postal worker—to a height, by age eighteen, of six foot eight. His accomplishments as an undergraduate at Wesleyan earned him a fellowship to that university's graduate school, where he selected as the subject of his M.A. thesis Herman Melville, an author only then beginning to receive his critical due. Olson's most lasting achievement over his entire lifetime may well be having tracked down 124 books, some heavily annotated, that had constituted the core of Melville's library.

Once he had his M.A., Olson began to lose steam. He taught awhile, then entered Harvard, where long stretches of sloth and procrastination were followed by manic bursts of overexcited, underdeveloped brainstorming, a pattern he would maintain throughout his life, with sloth the ascendant force. With the exception of three weeks on a fishing boat at age twenty-six (which he mythologized to Melvillean dimensions in his poetry), and an office job during the war, Olson scarcely did a lick of work, except to write poetry and prose only marginally publishable and to "teach" in the filibustering manner of a barroom philosopher. His domestic requirements were met by his two common-law wives. In their absence, he mooched meals where he could. He was an egregious sponger and a tenacious uninvited guest. His professional life was one long applications grant. To his credit, he could be generous with the alms he took in: a substantial part of his first Guggenheim was spent on a horse that the poet gave to a girl who loved riding. She kept the horse but dumped the poet. Later women were not so wise.

After dropping out of Harvard, Olson took up a bohemian life in New York, trying to write an ever-more-inchoate tome on Melville (who came to look more like Olson with each draft) and living on the savings of his doormat of a girlfriend Connie Wilcock, who would continue for over a decade to be the very model of the adoring, acquiescent, and ill-used wife that feminist legends are made from. When the war began, Olson, terrified of military service (needlessly, for he was to rejoice in 4-F status, thanks to his height), took a job in the Office of War Information, at the invitation of New Dealer Alan Cranston. This led in turn to a role in FDR's 1944 election campaign. When FDR won and Olson wasn't given the job of post-master general, Olson initiated his career as freeloader and professional guest. When these resources failed, he had Connie, who took a series of menial jobs. "Connie's jobs would not only provide their economic wherewithal," Clark notes, "but reinforce the compartmentalization of their domestic patterns. . . . Charles now routinely remained at his desk over his books and papers until dawn, seldom stirring from bed until midafternoon . . . as Connie wearily trooped in from her long day of breadwinning. . . . 'Charles himself did absolutely nothing but write, talk, and read,' says a friend [Frank Moore]. 'I do not recall his once washing a dish or sweeping the floor. Connie did everything.'"

He was, of course, unfaithful—at first only in an epistolary way, but eventually on a one-night-stand-per-annum basis with a woman, Frances Boldereff, who had won Olson's heart by reading and admiring his poems. Only now, pushing forty and having given years to his 119-page book on Melville, did Olson turn to poetry in a serious way. Many of these early poems served a double purpose, addressing his Muse with a calculated ambiguity such that both Connie and Frances could suppose themselves the Muse in question.

Olson made his real mark—i.e., acquired most of his disciples—at Black Mountain, an experimental college, meagerly funded, but with a remarkable track record for attracting both faculty and students who were to set the style for the avant-garde arts in the next decades. Within the faculty Olson made few friends and was openly at odds with such competing geniuses as Buckminster Fuller, John Cage, and Franz Kline. Clark's biography reaches its anecdotal zenith in the Black Mountain chapters, as Olson sinks to his moral nadir. He gets rid of Connie when his daughter by her becomes too great a nuisance, then takes up with a student by whom he produces a son, whom in time he'll dispose of similarly. As Olson deteriorated so did Black Mountain, losing more students each year from 1950 through 1956, until at last he presided over its bankruptcy as its official rector.

Clark's account of Olson's last years as a tenured professor in the academic equivalent of Skid Row gives Olson something he always lusted after but could never achieve on his own—mythical stature. The poet's life becomes, as the book's subtitle proclaims, a cautionary parable concerning the price to be paid for megalomania, a hunger for sycophants, and too much booze and drugs.

This lesson seems to have been lost upon some of those who contributed blurb copy for the back jacket, for they interpret what Clark pretty clearly represents as an unmitigated disaster as, rather, cause for rejoicing, a celebration of "a classic American genius" (Robert Creeley) or "a grand American genius" (Andrei Codrescu). Edward Dorn, one of Olson's students at Black Mountain and the loyalest of his acolytes, writes: "Let us rejoice that some long standing assumptions about this great literary figure have been swept away by Clark's long-anticipated portrait!" Does this mean there was still worse news that Clark omits? I would find that hard to imagine, for there is scarcely a page in the book, excepting those where Clark glosses the poetry and offers it qualified praise, in which Olson doesn't one way or another disgrace himself. Yet there persists a hunger for Olson's kind of self-anointed "genius," for the poet as a self-destructing mad fool, a Jim Morrison without music. Love, as another poet has noted, is blind.

THE OCCASION OF
THE POEM

Heaven and Earth: A Cosmology
by Albert Goldbarth
UNIVERSITY OF GEORGIA PRESS $20.00 CLOTH $9.95 PAPER

What Work Is and *New Selected Poems*
by Philip Levine
KNOPF $19.00 AND $24.00

Between the Chains
by Turner Cassity
UNIVERSITY OF CHICAGO PRESS (NO PRICE GIVEN)

Someone Going Home Late
by Daryl Jones
TEXAS TECH UNIVERSITY PRESS $16.95 CLOTH $9.95 PAPER

Madoc: A Mystery
by Paul Muldoon
FARRAR STRAUS & GIROUX $14.95

ONCE A POET has mastered his instrument, once he *is* a poet, he is judged—cherished, respected, or ignored—chiefly for his sense of poetic opportunity, for the ways he welcomes or courts his Muse; for his availability, as a poet, to the plenum of experience. Poets distinguish themselves one from the other less by the formal characteristics of their voices than by the occasions they elect to share with us, and while some poets are admired for their judicious cultivation of the same Parnassian half acre, in general the poets we prize most, and read most faithfully, are those whose lives, as reported, seem largest; who are able, in the most diverse moods and circumstances, to map a wide range of experience while maintaining the special alertness and afflatus poetry requires.

By this criterion, Albert Goldbarth must be accounted one of our most considerable poets. Though only forty-four years old, he has already amassed a body of work that would dwarf that of most poets now approaching retirement age, and while his gifts have undoubtedly been ripening since his first collection, *Under Cover,* of 1972, Goldbarth has been no late bloomer. He lisped in numbers and, poetlike, proclaimed his sometime fame in even his first flawed, verbose, but already inspired poems. "I am the timepiece of my generation," he wrote in "Coprolites" (1972). "You could write a poem about my body. / You could dedicate it to my contemporaries / aging as I age."

From the first, as well, Goldbarth's poetry has been as notable for its humor as for its afflatus. Indeed, it can be argued that the two are nowadays inseparable. The informing conceit of "Coprolites" equates the title artifact ("a scientist cracks open human feces / fossilized ages ago, a clock / stopped once and saying its message / forever") and what it is the poet leaves behind, and Goldbarth gets away with it, because, like Whitman who looms over him, he *respects* feces and takes an intelligent interest in them, as in virtually everything else his magpie mind lights on. Witness the opening lines of "Some Things" in *Heaven and Earth,* where he declares:

> I'm tired of writing about the gods,
> those causal winds we snap in.
> Tired of reading their signs in the entrails
> when the guts themselves, the fat swags
> of an animal, are eloquent enough.

The language has more power now, surely, but its vector hasn't swerved. He's still snapping in the breezy dichotomy between Essence and Somethingness, still quarreling with gods and guts and undecided which will have his final allegiance, what he thinks or what he sees. He does both very well.

For all the flamboyance of his language, Goldbarth's primary gift (as with Ammons or Keats) is visual. He's as attentive to textures and patternings as Holbein or Holman Hunt. In the same poem he notes, of a goat that has just given birth, that her vulva is "one engorged carnation / with paprika-spots of blood." He observes, in "12th Century Chinese Painting with a Few Dozen Seal Imprints Across It," that

> The sky
> has opened. Out of it, as large as temple gongs
> yet floating as easily as snowflakes, pour
> transistor circuits, maps of topiaries, cattle brands,
> IUDs, the floorplans of stockades, cartouches,
> hibachi grills, lace doilywork, horsecollars,
> laboratory mouse-mazes, brain-impressions. . . .

And these patterns imprint themselves on human nature, human flesh, as when you

> press your forehead to the russian olive there, its trunk
> unyielding, a thing not you but able to texture you,
> a hardness to hold to, a firm true specific event.
>   "Reality Organization"

In his superb phantasmagoria, "The Niggling Mystery," he imagines Newton dissecting the cadaver of a giant emblematic of the whole creation, and each slice of the dissection is a new cinematic coup:

he'll slice beyond the surface slick of fresh fawn organs
rainbowsheen heart-casing, pudding brains, past even

the cilia-oared confetti microtenants
of the blood, and find, and formularize for all time,

spectrum-regular and gravity-clasped, whatever niggling
mystery it is in such a beast that makes the poets slobber

As the giant's fileting continues, Goldbarth leads Newton into his
own favorite realm of "smaller and deeper": "Uterine / vesicles, retinal
nubs and sub-nubs, lung grains, mucilloids . . ."

An uncommonly large number of the poems in *Heaven and
Earth* are of a quality meriting their inclusion in any *Selected Poems*
the poet might publish. Readers of *Poetry* can determine for themselves if my praises seem reasonable, since five of his best have recently
appeared in those pages: "A Monument," "In the Midst of Intrusive
Richness," "Steerage," "Sentimental," and "A Letter." As to my initial
contention, that a poet most defines himself by the range of occasions
that trigger his poems, Goldbarth would seem to be on twenty-four-
hour alert. Among the Goldbarthian occasions in *Heaven and Earth*
are the poet's bemusement by a televised Intertribal Pow-Wow that
he relishes because it's incomprehensible ("The Dynamics of Huh");
a statistic from *Harper's Index* that notes that Henry David Thoreau
received ninety direct-mail solicitations at Walden Pond in 1988,
which prompts the poet to write his "Letter" to Thoreau; a phone
call from his ex ("Little Burger Blues Song"); the faces of missing
children printed on milk cartons ("The Children of Elmer"); and a
book on "The History of Buttons." In his longest and richest poems,
the initial occasion is not always identifiable among the Mandelbrot
Set foliation going on. In "The Nile," for instance, Goldbarth covers
a lot of anecdotal territory—Rabbi Lehrfield's Hebrew School; Edgar
Rice Burroughs's Barsoom; his niece's infant babblings, jazz, glosso-
lalia; his cousins' escape from Nazi Germany; and scenes from a noisy,
drunken party at the poet's home, all the disparate elements braided
together with the casual narrative felicity of such a professional mono-
loguist as Spalding Gray.

Range of occasion is not limited to external cues; it is also a matter of affective generosity, of revealing the self in the diversity of its weathers and habiliments. The commonest form of poetic self-censorship is the privileging of certain moods and modes as "po-etic"—usually, among those who favor "Serious" as preeminently valorizing, moods of solemnity and moroseness. Such poets we know only such times as they are angry or in pain or in love. Goldbarth is too rambunctious, too full of his own endorphins, to confine himself to those occasions generally considered proper to poetry. To some this may make him seem unserious and lightweight, but only to such as are inclined to question the propriety of laughter, brio, and a large appetite.

And to such I commend the latest collection by Philip Levine, *What Work Is.* Levine and Goldbarth are as unlike as two good poets well might be. Goldbarth is expansive, Levine inspissated. Goldbarth writes long, loopy lines full of deliberate dazzle; Levine writes a terse poetry that aspires to the self-effacing plainness of the furniture one finds in the waiting room of an emergency ward. Goldbarth is more often than not in a celebratory mood; Levine usually writes from a sense of grievance, and there's no wound too old or small but that he doesn't still nurse it. Nothing happens but it is an occasion for remorse or guilt or intimations of death. A teenage drinking bout ends like this:

> first the bottle had to be
> emptied, and then the three boys
> had to empty themselves of all
> they had so painfully taken in
> and by means even more painful
> as they bowed by turns over
> the eye of the toilet bowl
> to discharge their shame. Ahead
> lay cigarettes, the futility
> of guaranteed programs of
> exercise, the elaborate lies
> of conquest no one believed,

forms of sexual torture and
rejection undreamed of.

                                                    "Gin"

Everyone he knows seems to share his temperament—especially his
family. His poem "Soloing" opens so:

My mother tells me she dreamed
of John Coltrane, a young Trane
playing his music with such joy
and contained energy and rage
she could not hold back her tears.

In 1947 he crashes a New Year's Eve party with his brother,
who threw his drink on the wall of the hotel room, and forty years
later Levine is writing a poem about it. Indeed, the book could as
aptly be titled *40 Years Ago,* since it is about that era that Levine
writes by preference, the present having little to interest him except
with respect to the ways it is even smaller and meaner than the
garbage pits of yesteryear. Thus, he observes, of the hotel where the
drink was thrown: "The Book Cadillac is still going, though it smells
/ like a steam bath, and the rooms are tiny and gray."

Gray is Levine's favorite color. His mother cooks gray roast
beefs and sits, blind and crying, beside a TV set that is "gray, expres-
sionless." He drives past "closed warehouses / of gray cotton cloth,"
and past the gray oaks of US 24. He wakes to a dawn "gray and
weak," spades gray soil, and imagines his brother, in a moment of
transcendence, from a boat in "On the River":

so he can see with a painter's eye
the hulking shapes of warehouses define
themselves, the sad rusts and grays
take hold and shimmer a moment
in the blur of air until the stones
darken like wounds and become nothing.

. . .
He does this for me, who long ago
stopped seeing beneath the shadows
of concrete and burned brick towers
the flickering hints of life, the colors
we made of fresh earth and flowers
coming through the wet smells of houses
fallen in upon themselves. . . .

This could mean that the poet has become, literally, color-blind, but I take it rather to be a declaration of temperament, one that *won't* be cajoled into smiling or making any accommodation with a persecuting universe. The very earliest years of childhood had moments of deceptive ebullience, which tempted the young poet to jump off a roof, thinking he could fly ("Roofs," in *New Selected Poems*); he learned he couldn't. Now, contemplating a class of bored fourth graders in Flint, Michigan, he writes, in "Among Children,"

You can see
already how their backs have thickened,
how their small hands, soiled by pig iron,
leap and stutter even in dreams. I would like
to sit down among them and read slowly
from *The Book of Job.* . . .

And at recess, for a special treat, some wormwood flavor Kool-Aid?
Temperament is not a matter of taste, and those who share Levine's morose outlook will receive such poems with hosannahs, as do the reviewers quoted on the back jackets of both books, Edward Hirsch ("In a reactionary and forgetful time these radiantly human and memorializing poems can help us understand our lives.") and John Martone ("Of all contemporary poets, he has probably remained most faithful to the world of the American underclass and working class, who know as he does what it is to endure 'a succession of stupid jobs.' ") I confess that I react to a book-length quantity of Levine's poems as I might to the nonstop bitching and moaning of an ordinary

person. If you don't like blue-collar labor (I keep wanting to tell him), find some other kind of work. In fact, he did, decades ago, move to Fresno where, as poets do nowadays, he teaches the writing of poetry, and presumably leads a happier life, albeit one that offers fewer opportunities for his sorrowful Muse.

In only one of the poems in *What Work Is* does Levine represent himself as having a good time. In "The Right Cross" the occasion of the poem is a workout with the heavy bag hanging from the rafters of his California garage:

> I pull on the salty
> bag gloves, bow my head, dip one shoulder
>
> into the great sullen weight, and begin
> with a series of quick jabs. I'm up
> on my toes, moving clockwise, grunting
> as the blows crumple, the air going out
> and coming back in little hot benedictions.

This for Levine is demi-Eden, and it leads him to recall his boxing coach of "forty years ago," Nate Coleman.

> I could feel his words
> —"like this"—falling sweetly on my cheek
> and smell the milky sweetness of his breath
> —"you just let it go"—, the dark lashes
> of his mysterious green eyes unmoving.

After his workout and these reminiscences Levine even notices there are "grave vines and swelling tomatoes" behind his garage. Could it be that Levine needs physical exercise and even a certain amount of aggression to overcome his general sense of the grayness of things? (At the end of the poem, just before bed, "the earth goes gray.") This is received wisdom from Group Therapy 101, where those who complain about their depression are encouraged to release their pent-up anger by battering pillows ("Just let it go"), but it does seem to work.

"Burned," the longest and quite the best poem in *What Work Is,* succeeds because, like the biblical lamentations that are its model, its despair rises above mere complaint to horror and invective.

As to the merits of *What Work Is* relative to the twelve earlier volumes from which the contents of *New Selected Poems* have been gathered, Levine must be credited with being one of our most consistent poets. The jobs he couldn't stomach forty years ago and complains of today are the same jobs he's been complaining of, in the same barebones language, throughout his poetic career. As reviewers are wont to say, in praise as faint as it is true, the author's devoted fans will love his latest work.

A thought (concept, notion, bright idea) can be the occasion for a poem, but poetry these days more often springs from the feelings of poets or their remembrances (Levine) or from the stream of the poet's consciousness in a state of afflatus (Ashbery preeminently, but Goldbarth, too). For a poem to have issued from discursive impulses tends to be accounted unambitious, and poets who work in this way are generally written off as minor, especially if their poetry is also formal in its character. They are said to write poems rather than poetry. This is a defensible esthetic preference, but it tends to diminish the accomplishments of those, like Turner Cassity, who write poems, each of them peculiar to itself and not ostensibly part of a larger oeuvre.

But there is another way to think of it, Shelley's, who thought that poets were our unacknowledged legislators. Lacking that, at least we might let them write eternity's Op-Ed page, and that is what Turner Cassity consistently does. He reports from around the world, with pithy commentary from such varied locales as Istanbul, Indochina, South Africa, Polynesia, Kansas City ("A lot of Sodom in a little rain, / Sin's most accomplished City of the Plain"), the Caribbean, and the moon, and always in that tone of insider authority that makes us defer to his considered judgment and concinnate wit. "Immurings" begins by telling us:

> The land walls of Byzantium, the Maginot
> Line of their time, and that time was a thousand years,

Expressways parallel today and on-ramps breach.
The highways, frankly, have the more impressive scale,
And certainly are more an obstacle, as in
Berlin the structures for the viewing of the Wall
Exceed the Wall.

"When in Doubt, Remain in Doubt" begins with a moral derived from history:

Not even on the eve of Salamis
Did Delphi give a competent response.
No oracle does, ever. That is why
Great Men consult them. Oracles are doubt
Objectified, but left ambiguous,
So as to force a choice.

Fully half the poems in *Between the Chains* declare their themes with the same straightforward, virtually journalistic clarity, and he reaches closure with the same authority. Here is a sampling:

If lava grips who uses it, it is no eagle's claw.
It is an Oversoul in pleasure taking back its own.
                              "Prometheus in Polynesia"

Or this from a poem called "Against Activism," which seems simply to describe the mechanical action of a concert grand:

The right-hand pedal, all things which sustain,
Do so at least in part by doing nothing.

A poet so consistently epigrammatic can be dismissed, by those incapable themselves of wit, as unserious, as though to be serious one must always be in fog. Cassity never writes a poem without knowing exactly what he means to say—crisply, pithily, and, very often, cruelly. No contemporary poet of the first rank is less politically correct. Witness the title poem, "Between the Chains," which I quote in its entirety (including its epigraph, from John R. Shorten's *The Johannesburg Saga):*

> *Brokers and their clients and hangers-on would congregate in the short section of Simmonds Street between Market and Commissioner streets. The Mining Commissioner had posts erected and chains hung between them in order to close the area. Hence the 'open air Stock Exchange' and the phrase 'Between the chains.'*

It neither shames us nor is gain,
The broker's cry from chain to chain.

It is the human urge to trade,
Our standoff with the urge to aid.

If by it bleeding hearts are wrecked
I am not; you aren't. Nor was Brecht.

Up, Mahagonnay in the claims,
And dig. Life has a digging's aims.

Here is the only city built
On neither trade nor sand nor silt

But on the rock itself of gold.
It is not, it will not be, old.

It holds much guilt, some hope, all pains,
Between the chains, between the chains.

Blake, while he might have disagreed with that, could not have taken exception with the delivery, and might well feel flattered for having been so deftly echoed.

A simple test of any collection's merit is this: supposing you were editing an anthology of the year's best poems, how many of these would you be tempted by? For me, three-quarters of those in *Between the Chains* would have a claim to be included. Or here's

another test. Joseph Epstein has recently lamented the dearth of poems with single, memorable lines as once there were in the days of
Yeats and Eliot. Let him read Turner Cassity, and begin to memorize
again.

Daryl Jones is the chair of the English Department and dean of the
College of Arts and Sciences at Boise State University in Idaho. He
is, as well, the recipient of an NEA Creative Writing Fellowship
Grant, and an earlier version of *Someone Going Home Late* was a
finalist in the 1987 National Poetry Series Open Competition, while
this version comes with a foreword by Philip Levine, whose praises
are unstinting, if somewhat nebulous: "Jones's work is deeply rooted
in the richest strains of poetry in the American language, and it con-
tinually pays homage to those who have come before and given us a
timeless literature. . . . For me the great thrust behind these poems is
related to the author's need to face the worst, the furies if you
will. . . . He writes about the daily world that troubles us all, and
what's more he can capture the nights in all their fury." And here's
the passage Levine quotes to demonstrate Jones's fury-capturing art:

> Undressed, the sleeping bag
> pulled up against our chins, we hear the sudden
> darkness closing in. Amid the soft
> moaning of wind through nylon,
> the flip flop of the tent
> inhaling, exhaling,
> we listen to the first faint
> click of a snowflake falling,
> hold each other closely, sleep.
>   "Riding It Out on Elk Mountain"

These lines also illustrate, according to Levine, how "His characters
have the determination to face the worst and survive." He's got to be
kidding. This is a camping trip, one cautious step away from fireside
coziness and triumphant domesticity, which are, much more than the

furies of the night, Jones's typical themes. His last poem in the book, "Thanksgiving," begins

> If it is true
> that what we wish most
> will happen
>
> that we will
> after all
> wake
> in that other place
> and walk
> arm in arm
> a man and a woman
> in orchards of light . . .

and it ends with

> the sun going down
> in cranberry
> in plum
>
> and you
> seated across from me
> pulling one half
> of the wishbone

Jones is not to be disparaged for leading a comfortable, homey life, nor for his many expressions of conjugal and parental love, nor even for being a sentimentalist—if only he managed to bring some art to bear. All I can see in these lines is a false exigence, and I hear the Voice of the Poet, hushed with self-reverence, delivering each minuscule line as though it encoded some immense secret significance.

When Jones is not celebrating the warmth of hearth and home or the rigors of the great outdoors, he offers, like Levine, vignettes of an impoverished childhood and of at least one early blue-collar job, the earthly life he has departed for the asphodel of Academe. These

memory poems show more exertion and are less full of veiled compliments to the poet's self, but they are but a few in a book that gives
rather scant measure in any case—fifty-six pages, with a lot of white
open spaces.

Paul Muldoon's *Madoc* is a book-length, narrative poem in the frac-
tured, montage manner that has become, since modernism, the conventional way in which poets tell a story. Rather than going to the
bother of setting a scene and peopling it with characters, who then
reveal themselves by their speech and actions (how humdrum that
would be!), Muldoon offers a series of vivid images and gnomic observations, many no more than two lines, few longer than a page,
from which the diligent reader will be able to infer a larger action,
which, in brief, goes like this:

In an alternate Anglo-American past, the poets Coleridge and
Southey set off with family and servants to establish a Pantisocratic
utopia in the New World (an intention they happily never carried
out in this universe). Coleridge and the woman fall into the hands of
Indians, who turn Coleridge on to peyote and other Native American
medicaments, while Southey degenerates from youthful idealism to
being a sadistic petty tyrant, who entertains himself by having Cayuga
women flogged for witchcraft. There is a science-fiction framing narrative that rarely impinges on the frontier adventures and isn't very
interesting in itself. Less escapable is a system of chaptering each small
mosaic of the tale with the bracketed name of a great philosopher, so
that *Madoc* recapitulates the history of Western thought from Thales,
Anaximander, and Anaximenes at the beginning to the very latest
celebrity intellectuals at the end: Foucault, Chomsky, Derrida, Noz-
ick, Kristeva, and Hawking.

The great thinkers look down from their brackets over the
events of *Madoc* like deities under order not to interfere in human
affairs. They are present (I suspect) to assure those who demand difficulty of poetry, especially poetry offering the readerly luxury of
linear narrative, that Muldoon bears pondering, that there are her-
meneutic depths and coulisses of allusiveness where only adepts and
initiates may dare to tread. Muldoon's attitude toward the figures in

his pantheon is much like that toward the figures in his poem, an informed contempt. Thus, the penultimate tessera of the poem, titled [Kristeva], reads, in its entirety, "Signifump. Signifump. Signifump." While [James] (William, presumably) presides over these two lines:

> The pile of horse-dung at the heart of Southeyopolis
> looks for all the world like a dish of baked apples.

As a gloss on James that may be inadequate, but as a descriptive cameo it's okay, and if one is willing to read the book as a series of stills and short clips from a movie by Ken Russell, it offers equivalent decadent pleasures. Muldoon's camera, like Russell's, never misses the opportunity to zoom in close on grisly details or to gaze spellbound on scenes of torture. Such morbid fascinations are the stock in trade of many other historical novelists, and it is part of human nature to be unable to resist looking at atrocity photographs. The question remains, does *Madoc*'s helter-skelter narrative pattern, with its excursions into such parallel lives as those of Thomas Moore, Lord Byron, Lewis and Clark, Aaron Burr, Thomas Jefferson, and George Catlin, add up either to a memorable drama or to a coherent vision of history? I don't think so.

Yet I did enjoy many of the epic's noncohering set pieces, and admired Muldoon's often densely impacted and riddling free verse and his connoisseurship in the discovery and deployment of rare old words. Here is a sampling: brank, smoot, sawyer (in the navigational sense), piggin, milty, sudatory, bleb. They're all to be found in the dictionary, each a neat (or nasty) surprise, and in that they are emblematic of Muldoon's antiquarian sifting of the dust of early U.S. history. The scattered tesserae of *Madoc* may not add up to much more of a statement about history than, "Weren't they awful?" but each one has its special oddity or charm, so that unlike most modern long poems, *Madoc* continues to be readable for its entire length.

A NASHIONAL
INSTITUTION

I Wouldn't Have Missed It: Selected Poems of Ogden Nash
Selected by Linell Smith and Isabel Eberstadt
Introduction by Anthony Burgess
Deutsch £9.95 407 pp.

FOR THE FORTY years of Ogden Nash's career as America's foremost white-collar humorist, the popular success of his books of light verse expressed the consensus view of the reading public anent poetry: they, too, disliked it. Disliked, that is, the oracular assumptions that most poets make, their claims to a higher wisdom, a more finely tuned awareness, and larger emotions than are found to obtain elsewhere in the middle class. Nash had no such pretensions. He wrote his verses about just those subjects that a well-behaved dinner guest might use for conversational fodder in mixed company. He was the very beau ideal that Emily Post commended to her genteel readers in her per-durable *Etiquette:* "What he says is of no moment. It is the twist he gives to it, the intonation, the personality he puts into his quip.... Our greatly beloved Will Rogers could tell a group of people that it had rained today and would probably rain tomorrow, and make everyone burst into laughter...."

But while Mrs. Post approved humor, she feared, justly, the subversive power of wit: "The one in greatest danger of making enemies is the man or woman of brilliant wit. If sharp, wit tends to produce a feeling of mistrust even when it stimulates.... Perfectly well-intentioned people, who mean to say nothing unkind, in the flash of a second 'see a point,' and in the next second score it with no more power to resist than a drug addict has to refuse a dose put into his hand!" It was by his shrewd abstention from saying anything that might give offense, by his spirit's entire accord with the principles set forth in the Post decalogue (the first edition of *Etiquette* appeared in 1922, when Nash was twenty), that Nash secured for his verses an audience (and for himself an income) larger than that enjoyed by any American poet of his time.

In the first poem Nash placed with *The New Yorker* (where he would soon after be employed), he already defined himself as the spokesman and representative of the white-collar audience that felt a kindred complacent malaise about the terms of their employment and the dimensions of their lives:

> I sit in an office at 244 Madison Avenue
> And say to myself You have a responsible job, havenue?
> Why then do you fritter away your time on this doggerel?
> If you have a sore throat you can cure it by using a good
> goggeral,
> If you have a sore foot you can get it fixed by a chirop-
> odist,
> And you can get your original sin removed by St. John
> the Bopodist,
> Why then should this flocculent lassitude be incurable?
> Kansas City, Kansas, proves that even Kansas City needn't
> always be Missourible.
> Up up my soul! This inaction is abominable.
> Perhaps it is the result of disturbances abdominable.
> The pilgrims settled Massachusetts in 1620 when they
> landed on a stone hummock.
> Maybe if they were here now they would settle my stom-
> ach.
> Oh, if I only had the wings of a bird

> Instead of being confined on Madison Avenue I could soar
> in a jiffy to Second or Third.
> "Spring Comes to Murray Hill"

Already in these first magazine verses Nash displayed all the tricks and tropes that were to become his trademarks: orthographic deformations for the sake of a rhyme-forced hyper-pun; the use of the archaic vocabulary and syntax of inspirational schoolroom poetry, a venerable gambit, which Nash deploys to mock his own pretensions and aspirations; and (a device that Nash virtually copyrighted, though he did not invent it) the elastic couplet, or Nash Rambler, which can grow to any length provided it's stopped by a rhyme. Anthony Burgess gives the Rambler its due in his very brief pastiche "Introduction," in which he declares: "I am trying to imitate him here, but he is probably quite inimitable. / My own talent for this sort of thing being limited and his virtually illimitable." For Burgess, as toastmaster, Nash transcends all forms of criticism but polite applause: ". . . In the face of the unanalysable I must not be analytical. / And when a writer is beyond criticism it is stupid to go all critical." Or, as Thumper's mother advised: "If you can't say something nice about someone, you shouldn't say anything at all."

Nash had another mode, not so patently his, but one no less essential to his position as laureate to Middle America—the mini-maxim. "In the Vanities / No one wears panities" and, apropos of Baby, "A bit of talcum / Is always walcum" are fair samples. The object of these Ad Age adages is not so much to be witty and epigrammatic as to be remembered and produced at the appropriate cue, to become a suply of verbal small change for those whose sense of humor is limited to rote performance. In my childhood, in the forties in Minnesota, Nash's most famous mini-maxim, "Reflection on Ice-Breaking" ("Candy / Is dandy / But liquor / Is quicker.") was trotted out on all occasions of ceremonial imbibing, always with the same preliminary chuckle of obeisance to the god of mirth and catchphrases.

Time has not been kind to these jingles, since it is difficult to

be at once pithy and innocuous, but even Nash's most skillful droll-
eries suffer for being heaped together into a "Selected Poems." Candy
may be tasty one piece at a time, but this is a gross of Snickers. Very
soon the sameness of the product will cloy even the avidest consumer.
If there must be a big book, why not go whole hog and give us
Nash's Complete Poems? There is no rationale given for the poems
excluded (of the 101 poems from *Versus* of 1949, 41 are reprinted) and
no attempt to produce a semblance of variety by including the lyrics
Nash wrote for the musical *One Touch of Venus* or any sample of his
books for children. Anything to take the curse of sameness off the
enterprise would have been welcome.

Measured against the general level of accomplishment of hu-
morous verse in any standard anthology, Nash's limitations are glar-
ingly evident. Narrative is not in his line, nor comic monologue (one
must observe to be able to mimic), nor (least of all) satire, nor yet
parody. His frame of intellectual reference remained, until his death
in 1971, that of a well-brought-up eleven-year-old, and his allusive
power is limited accordingly. His attention to public events is nil. He
has no bêtes noires, only pet peeves: uncomfortable beds, incompetent
caddies, anything smelly or noisy or odd-tasting. He has but a single
persona—Dagwood.

What is left, and what Nash was best at, is wordplay, as in
"The Lama," where, after doubting whether a "three-lllllama" anywhere exists, he caps his verses with a prose footnote: "The author's
attention has been called to a type of conflagration known as the
three-alarmer. Pooh." Yet for every poem that's genuinely risible, *I
Wouldn't Have Missed It* offers a dozen that range from perfunctory
to bromidic.

Finally it was not Thalia, that sharp-tongued shrew, who was
Nash's muse, but Emily Post, who advised, concerning "The Code of
a Gentleman": "Exhibitions of anger, fear, hatred, embarrassment,
ardor, or hilarity are all bad form in public." No one can say of Ogden
Nash that he was not a gentleman.

LIGHT VERSE

The Norton Book of Light Verse
Edited by *Russell Baker* NORTON $17.95 447 PP.

Light Year '87
Edited by *Robert Wallace* BITS PRESS (CLEVELAND) $13.95 267 PP.

A CHILD'S FIRST experience of poetry, after graduating from diapers
and lullabies, is likely to be light verse. I still remember the look of
pleasure that would come over my father's face each time a new bottle
of ketchup was opened and he could recite Anonymous's rhyme,
"Shake and shake the ketchup bottle / None'll come out and then a
lot'll." This is included in Russell Baker's splendid new anthology of
light verse, but—*Caveat emptor!*—in a sanitized version approved by
ketchup manufacturers that begins, "*If* you do not shake the ketchup
bottle..." In either version, there is something as pleasing to the
tongue as ketchup itself in that rhyme of *bottle* and *lot'll,* and should
the time come when ketchup is only available in single-serving pack-
ets, Anonymous's lines will survive, like Miss Muffet's tuffet, for the
beauty of the rhyme alone.

Among the separate subanthologies into which *The Norton Anthology of Light Verse* has been organized is one titled "PG," which
offers a sampling of all those poems a child first learns to giggle at—
poems that may cause those of maturer years to cringe. Even at the
age of six I thought Eugene Field's "Wynken, Blynken, and Nod" as
mooshy as Cream of Wheat, and Russell Baker, for having purveyed
such treacle, should hear nothing but its droning repetition for a week

of insomniac nights. To be fair, most of the other warhorses of the nursery that Baker gathers are remarkable for having a double valence, a resonance beyond the firecracker popping of the "joke" that is the hallmark of great light verse.

"PG" is the most tradition-bound of the book's nineteen subsections, but even here Baker makes room for such living or only lately deceased voices as those of Stevie Smith, Theodore Roethke, Shel Silverstein, and Allen Ginsberg. In itself, "PG" constitutes an ideal anthology of poems for children, striking just the right balance between inevitability ("Jabberwocky" and two of Eliot's cat poems) and freshness, which is the balance that the book strikes in general. Indeed, for its range of taste, for the proportion of hot buttered popcorn to old chestnuts, and for sheer prevailing good fun, Baker's anthology may be the best all-purpose anthology of light verse going, and it is certainly light-years ahead of the original such anthology from 1938, Auden's ill-conceived and famously unreadable *Oxford Book of Light Verse.*

The problem with Auden's collection, and to a lesser degree with later shuffles of the deck by Kingsley Amis (*The New Oxford Book of English Light Verse,* 1978) and by Gavin Ewart (*The Penguin Book of Light Verse,* 1980), was diagnosed some time ago by A. A. Milne: "The trouble with most of the anthologists [of light verse] is that, even if they have an understanding of their subject, secretly they are still a little ashamed of it. They try to give it the blessings of legitimacy by tracing its ancestry back to some dull fourteenth century poem beginning '*Lhude sing cuccu*' or '*Merry swithe it is in halle.*' " Auden was the worst offender in this regard, and his anthology so abounds in ballads, nursery rhymes, and folk songs that half the contents are the work of Anonymous, an author especially beloved of anthologists in that he doesn't fuss about proper acknowledgment or demand royalties, virtues he shares with other deceased authors from the Venerable Bede to Thomas Hardy. On this subject, Russell Baker in his introduction gently tweaks the noses of Auden and Ewart by recounting his agonies in deciding whether to include, as they did, a large chunk of Chaucer: "Wouldn't professors be shocked by a book of light verse that didn't include Chaucer?" In the end he opts for a book that will be "like an amusement park, . . . A book for people who were looking for fun." He foregoes arranging all the poems in chronological order, and invites us to consider William Shakespeare side by side with Phyllis McGinley, Leigh Hunt next to Ogden Nash. Not every old song is resuscitated by this means, but it's certainly an improvement on an obstacle course commencing with fifty pages of Anglo-Saxon riddles and ribaldry in Middle High English, and sometimes the great dead speak to uncannily topical effect, as in "Köln," by Samuel Taylor Coleridge:

> In Köln, a town of monks and bones,
> And pavements fanged with murderous stones,
> And rags, and hags, and hideous wenches,
> I counted two-and-seventy stenches,
> All well-defined, and separate stinks!
> Ye nymphs that reign o'er sewers and sinks,
> The river Rhine, it is well known,
> Doth wash your city of Cologne,
> But tell me, nymphs, What power divine
> Shall henceforth wash the river Rhine?

In making odious comparisons between rival anthologies, weight is the first consideration, even for light verse, and with 400 or so poems by some 230 authors, Baker gives much better measure than Amis. Ewart's book, with 350 poems by 150 authors, actually contains more lines of poetry, since Ewart credits his readers with a longer attention span and includes hefty extracts from Byron, Pope, and Chaucer, and bushels of ballads. All good stuff, with lots of fiber for a healthy diet, but I think most readers will prefer Baker's snacktray philosophy.

In the matter of hilarity, Baker's English rivals are more risqué, and Ewart has some limericks and one "rugger song" by that dirty old bugger Anon that would surely bring a blush to any maiden's cheek. Baker has undoubtedly had prudential reasons for excluding X-rated language from his selection, but though he may be some snickers the poorer for omitting the choicest graffiti of our era, no one can otherwise fault America's Official Humorist in his sense of what's funny. There were a score of poems that had me laughing aloud, both alone at home and in public places, and a dozen more beside which I wrote "QUOTE!" including a comic epic by Anne Tibble done in the language of phrase books, which begins:

It is three o'clock in the morning.
I am in a hurry.
I will have some fried fish.
It does not smell nice.
Bring some coffee now—and some wine.
Where is the toilet? There is a mistake in the bill.
You have charged me too much.
I have left my glasses, my watch and my ring in the toilet.
Bring them.

The comic catastrophes mount up to a height that is Alpine. That poem alone is worth the price of admission, and there are four hundred more. Not all of them as apt as Ms. Tibble's to make one head for a Xerox machine, but the general level is high, and there are not many of the genteel suburban, Ogden-Nash-on-an-off-day sort that used to appear in the back pages of the *Saturday Evening Post* and have given light verse a bad name.

Indeed, Baker's greatest service as an editor is having ferreted out so much good light verse from the last two or three decades, when it has been living far from its old haunts in the editorial pages of major newspapers and in such magazines as *The New Yorker* and *Vanity Fair*. Light verse still lives, and some of the best "literary" poets in America are dab hands at it: X. J. Kennedy, George Starbuck, Anthony Hecht and John Hollander (coinventors of the double dactyl, a form that can rival the glories of the limerick), Marge Piercy—all writers better known to the readers of literary quarterlies than to the general public, but all right at home in Baker's pages.

It may be that the times are a-changin', and that the editor who will assemble *The New Norton Book of Light Verse* some time in the twenty-first century will not have quite so hard a time of it as Baker, for much of the work will have been done for him by Robert Wallace, who has, for the last five years, been editing an annual of light verse, the latest of which, *Light Year '87,* contains a roster of nearly two hundred poets, many of whom also appear in the Norton anthology. Wallace's editorial standards are high, and he casts his net wider with each succeeding volume, bringing light verse to light from such obscure nooks and crannies as *Wisconsin Restaurateur* and *Hollow Spring Review.* Indeed, so many of the poems in the Light Year series appear in those pages for the first time that it has probably become the principal venue for original light verse in this country. So, when you've exhausted Baker's snacktray and the cupboard is otherwise bare, the Light Year series is the likeliest source of what we all can never get enough of—more.

HAVING AN OEUVRE

Selected Poetry
by John Hollander KNOPF $27.50

Tesserae and Other Poems
by John Hollander KNOPF $20.00

Collected Poems: 1953–1993
by John Updike KNOPF $27.50

What We Don't Know About Each Other
by Lawrence Raab PENGUIN $12.00 PAPER

Sweet Ruin
by Tony Hoagland
UNIVERSITY OF WISCONSIN PRESS $12.00 PAPER

The Palms
by Charlie Smith W. W. NORTON $18.95

IN A POETRY culture in which the McPoem so much preponderates that many middle-aged poetry bureaucrats have never tasted anything else, the poetry of John Hollander is dinner at Lutèce. It may not necessarily be more nourishing; sometimes, indeed, the sauces can be so rich as to seem sinful, especially to those who regard tofu and brown rice as the poetically correct alternative to hamburgers. But to those readers who seek in contemporary poetry the pleasures they have learned to value in the canonical poetry of the great dead white males, from Pindar through Swinburne, Hollander, of all the language's living poets, is probably the most masterful in terms of the refinement of his execution and, in an instrumental sense, purity of tone. He can be exquisite at the drop of a pin—and he can keep on being exquisite till even the best-tutored appetite must cry, "Hold! Enough!"

For Hollander is quite aware that one of the requisites of greatness in poetry is stamina, and he has produced, at regular intervals, long lyrical sequences that range in scale from daunting (the 75 unrhymed tercets of the dream travelogue, "The Head of the Bed") to the googolplex lapidary wonders of his 1984 Pelion-on-Ossa special, *Powers of Thirteen,* a work of 169 thirteen-line stanzas, each line being thirteen syllables long, so that by the poem's own calculation it contains (excluding the subtitles appearing at the bottom of most of the numbered stanzas) 28,561 syllables. Hollander, the most self-reflexive of all poets, spells this out at the end of stanza 27 ("*At the End of the Line*"):

> Twenty-eight thousand, five hundred sixty syllables
> Here breathe hotly down the neck of some ultimate one
> That may not demean their manyness. Means to some end,
> They have been awaiting death. Endings mean meaning's
> > end.
> So the final monosyllable, with a volume
> Thunderous and inaudible brings us to a close.
> In the end as in the beginning will be the word.

Perspiration alone is no guarantee of good poetry, much less of genius. Sheer doggedness has been responsible for lots of long dull tomes. There must be, as well, a constant welling-up of inspiration, if the poet is to overcome our natural tendency to say, "Okay, okay, I get the idea." In Ashbery's long poems, this leavening takes the form of the flux of different kinds of demotic speech and the interference patterns that result as they are whirled about in the Jacuzzi of his art. In Hollander it is the music. He exults in all those formal artifices that those who are maladroit in their use deplore—meter, rhyme, and such overdetermined verbal embroidery as that in the third and fourth lines above. Eager to proselytize for his art, he has written the definitive taxonomy of traditional poetic forms, *Rhyme's Reason,* in which each verse form and rhetorical device is called on to describe itself. Like this:

> Translating Omar Khayyam's *Rubaiyat,*
> Edward Fitzgerald, it would seem, forgot
> To rhyme the third line with the other ones.
> (The last line underscored its lonely lot.)

Wit is not, in itself, music (though melody cannot be without it; witness the title of Hollander's last volume of criticism, *Melodious Guile*). Music is of and for the senses, a tongue that licks the inside of one's ear, that reminds us of what we like to eat, of sunsets and evening breezes, as in these Khayyám-flavored quatrains from the long verse sequence, "The Tesserae," that forms the core of his latest new collection:

> The flaming *mullah* in his house of lead
> Raves fruitlessly among the faithful dead.
>   The Persian melon cooling in the shade
> Keeps summer's wisdom in its sleeping head.
>
>   . . .
>
> Tinged with false promise, edged with polychrome,
> The sunset's red drips up along its dome;
>   Tuning the corded jibsheet to the strum
> Of evening air we make a run for home.

There are 144 such quatrains in *Tesserae,* all in the same vein of luxurious, Fitzgeraldine equanimity. There is probably no other poet today who could so well capture and sustain that tone; there is surely no other who would aspire to.

For not only does Hollander possess extraordinary gifts, his po-etry also reveals him to be a poet of a peculiar temperament: unruf-fled; imperturbable; Olympian. A sensualist, yes, sprawling dreamily across the sheets, but they are (he keeps reminding us) sheets of *paper*. Hollander, of course, has examined his own poetic conscience in this matter of the view to be had from an ivory tower and of verse that "smells of the lamp" (no critic can hope to outflank the poet on his ever-ongoing tour of his own premises), and stanzas 134–35 of *Powers of Thirteen* offer a typically mellow assessment of "the ways of lamps":

> As hot as it is bright; sun, moon and constellations
> That guide our works and nights, your lamp smells of
> M's poems, yes,
> And all the other nifty redolences of the world.

Dinner at Lutèce is notable not only for being tasty; it is also expensive. Is there an equivalence in Hollander's poetry? In terms of pages or epiphanies per dollar, the *Selected Poetry* surely represents a better bargain than most McPoetry take-out orders, and in his Khay-yám persona Hollander can be as accessible as a wheelchair ramp. But one must have done a lot of graduate study to savor all the dishes as the chef intends. Yet his allusiveness is not the highest hurdle. The music itself demands a trained ear. Unless one has tried to perform on the same instrument (or studied, at the very least, its repertory), virtuosity can become irksome. The patrons of four-star restaurants are not, usually, aspiring chefs, but most readers of poetry these days are poets themselves of a sort—rarely of Hollander's sort. They tend rather to be whiners than winers and diners, and for them the prices on the menu will seem exorbitant.

The selection from Hollander's six earliest volumes of poetry is largely the same in this new volume as in *Spectral Emanations: New and Selected Poems* of 1978. A handful of poems have been added, a double-handful deleted, and there is no longer a sampling from Hollander's typo-graphic collection, *Types of Shape* (1969). I regret their absence, as I do that of his 1976 book-length seminarrative tour de force, *Reflections on Espionage,* though I can see why Hollander would prefer to include the even more juggernautical *Powers of Thirteen* to represent his full stretch in the long poem. For that matter I wish there were a sampling of his double-dactyls, the light verse form he coinvented with Anthony Hecht. Indeed, except for the fact that, on the evidence of *Tesserae,* Hollander is still working at full throttle, I think the poet would be better served by a *Complete Poems* than by a second *Selected,* generous as it is. But half a loaf of Hollander is still a surfeit of riches.

It is difficult to approach John Updike's *Collected Poems* as the work of a poet—indeed, of one of the best poets writing today. Updike enjoys such preeminence as a novelist that his poetry could be mistaken as a hobby or a foible, and the poet himself has encouraged such a misperception by packaging his poetic self as a writer of verse; even of "light verse," which Updike has carefully segregated from his poetry, consigning it to the last one hundred pages of this collection. He explains, in his preface, that ". . . I wanted to distinguish my poems from my light verse. My principle of segregation has been that a poem derives from the real (the given, the substantial) world and light verse from the man-made world of information—books, newspapers, words, signs. If a set of lines brought back to me something I actually saw or felt, it was not light verse."

By this odd criterion, Updike includes among his nonlight, realworld poems "The Beautiful Bowel Movement," a droll tribute to

> . . . a masterpiece: a flawless coil,
> unbroken, in the bowl, as if a potter
> who worked in this most frail, least grateful clay
> had set himself to shape a topaz vase.
> O spiral perfection, not seashell nor
> stardust, how can I keep you? With this poem.

By any other rule of thumb, this would certainly be considered light verse. Meanwhile, in his back-of-the-book light-verse ghetto, there is this quatrain, titled "Upon Shaving Off One's Beard":

> The scissors cut the long-grown hair;
>   The razor scrapes the remnant fuzz.
> Small-jawed, weak-chinned, big-eyed, I stare
>   At the forgotten boy I was.

Surely this was something Updike actually saw and felt (one sees and feels it with him). If he accounts it light verse, it can only be for formal or psychological reasons. Four tetrameter lines in rhyme capturing a moment of commonplace chagrin: what else could it be?

Updike's dilemma is that there is no rule of thumb by which to distinguish light verse from poetry, for there is no matter so trivial it cannot serve as the occasion for a weighty poem, nor any form so strict or so free that it can't be employed for flippancy. Further, there is a continuous poetic spectrum from Allegro to Penseroso, and only the most resolutely twee (Ogden Nash) or solemn (Wordsworth) can escape all imputation of consorting with the enemy. Updike does, characteristically, write poems that, even when not ostensibly light, are buoyant, richly conceited, musical, and entertaining. Novelists are still permitted to entertain (though they get extra points from serious critics to the degree that they eschew such a low ambition), but the entertainment quotient of poetry is almost never referred to. And it is this aspect of Updike's poetry, finally, that offends the poetry establishment and provokes its resolute inattention to his work.

His poetry, in turn, has almost no relation to his contemporaries, nor is it much interested, as Hollander's is, in itself. It is a poetry of civility—in its epigrammatical lucidity; in the matters it treats of, which neither overstep the bounds of polite confidence nor provoke an impatient listener to ask "What's your *point?*"; and in its tone of vulgar bonhomie and good appetite. Updike has written a brief manifesto on this subject, "Taste," which concludes:

It makes one blush to be credited with taste.
Chipmunk fur, wave-patterns on sand, white asters—
but for these, and some few other exceptions,
Nature has no taste, just productivity.
I want to be, like Nature, tasteless,
abundant, reckless, cheerful. Go screw, taste—
itself a tasteless suggestion.

This in its way is disingenuous, for one might dismiss taste in much more tasteless terms than "go screw." Updike wears the emblems of his class with the same grinning confidence that a burgher in a Frans Hals painting wears his starched, bleached, and pleated collar. He vacations in Greece, Italy, and the Caribbean and responds with a voluptuary alertness. He cares for his property, visits museums, and, everywhere he goes, pays close attention to the patterns and textures of his surroundings and tries to capture these in quick, accurate sketches. "Penumbrae" begins like this:

The shadows have their seasons, too.
The feathery web the budding maples
cast down upon the sullen lawn

bears but a faint relation to
high summer's umbrageous weight
and tunnellike continuum—

black leached from green, deep pools
wherein a globe of gnats revolves
as airy as an astrolabe.

The thinning shade of autumn is
an inherited Oriental.
red worn to pink, nap worn to thread.

It ends:

And loveliest, because least looked-for,
gray on gray, the stripes
the pearl-white winter sun

hung low beneath the leafless wood
draws out from trunk to trunk across the road
like a stairway that does not rise.

Updike's attitude toward this world of *luxe, calme,* and *volupté* is like
that of the skier imagined in the middle of the same poem: he is
"exultant at the summit." This translates, in poetic terms, into high
energy.

Beneath the brio and lustrous surfaces, there is something else,
or, more accurately, there isn't. With the exception of a 1960 poem,
"Seven Stanzas at Easter," which takes an unequivocally neo-
orthodox stance on Christianity's major wager ("Make no mistake:"
it begins, "if He rose at all / it was as His body . . ."), Updike's view
of ultimate reality is stoically positivistic. His universe, like the ocean
in his poem "On the Island," is:

sleepless, inanimate, bottomless, prayer-denying,
the soughing of matter cast off by the sun, blind sun

among suns, massed liquid of atoms that conceives
and consumes, that communes with itself only,

soulless and mighty; our planes, our islands sink:
a still moon plates the sealed spot where they were.

There may be even in Updike's atheism a kind of WASP-ish gentility.
I have the sense that the author of "Seven Stanzas at Easter" would
not so openly declare entropy the victor at Armageddon if Bonhoeffer
and our more advanced Protestant divines had not created a theology
that accommodates the death of God. Because Updike, finally, aspires
to be the voice of his generation and of his social class. Already, in
his Phi Beta Kappa Poem of 1973, "Apologies to Harvard," he had

donned the robes of a commencement speaker and proclaimed, with rueful resonance,

> We thought one war as moral as the next,
> Believed that life was tragic and absurd,
> And were absurdly cheerful, just like Sartre.
> We loved John Donne and Hopkins, Yeats and Pound,
> Plus all things convolute and dry and pure.
> Medieval history was rather swank;
> Psychology was in the mind; abstract
> Things grabbed us where we lived; the only life
> Worth living was the private life; and—last,
> Worst scandal in this characterization—
> *We did not know we were a generation.*

If the class that Updike addresses so cogently were in the habit of reading poetry, he would be America's Philip Larkin. But they do not, and so the merits of his poetry have been by and large unacknowledged. And even that lends the poetry an additional Ozymandian grandeur, as though one were to come upon a tastefully appointed dinner for eight in the middle of a toxic waste dump. Everything is as it should be: china, crystal, flatware, napery; the food exquisitely prepared, the wine well chosen. But there are no guests and the air is unbreathable.

The three remaining collections differ so greatly from the work considered above that they require an entirely different critical apparatus. Here, especially in the poems of Raab and Hoagland, there are no formal challenges, no musicality, no effort to find the *mot juste* or the telling epithet. There is simply candor, an effort to enlist the reader's sympathy in the circumstances of the poets' lives. All three poets have been awarded prizes for their confidences, and all three offer thanks to Yaddo on their acknowledgment pages, so however little regard this reviewer can muster for their work, their esthetic respectability is an established fact.

What We Don't Know About Each Other, winner of the 1992

National Poetry Series, is Lawrence Raab's fourth collection. He was born in 1946 and has taught at Williams College since 1976. His physical circumstances seem to be roughly similar to those enjoyed by Updike and Hollander, but he doesn't manage to take much pleasure in them. He is given over to worries (often imagining traffic accidents that might happen), to self-pity ("Can you understand how sorry / I felt for myself, / how much I wanted to go inside?" one poem trails off morosely), and to unresolved emotional confusion ("How does it make you feel? / he asked, although he did not know anymore / what he wanted them to say"). He is afflicted with low self-esteem and has a "bad muse" who suggests that his

> is the same old life a thousand people
> have had the good sense to keep to themselves.
> Who wants to hear what it was like
> to turn forty, or the strange thing
> your dog did last week? So relax.

He takes his bad muse's advice in most of his poems, which are pointedly diffident and full of "artless" repetitions. He has in one poem, within eight lines of each other, a river "where they've planted flowers, / so many beautiful flowers" and people strolling "with their children, many children." "This or that" and its variants are among his preferred locutions. His language is flat as Kansas in August, and his spirits low as a barometer before a hurricane. Indeed, the hidden agenda or secret narrative of Raab's poems is one of veiled threats, as in the self-portrait in the bathroom mirror, entitled "The Sudden Appearance of a Monster at a Window."

> At any moment he could put his fist
> right through that window. And on your side:
> you could grab hold of this
> letter opener, or even now try
> very slowly to slide the revolver

out of the drawer of the desk in front of you.
But none of this will happen. . . .

Sweet Ruin, Tony Hoagland's first collection of poems, won the
Brittingham Prize in Poetry. His publisher provides a shorter CV
than Raab's, but the acknowledgments page shows the poet to have
been industrious at the craft of poetry, for in addition to Yaddo he
has thanks to pay to five friends who helped with his manuscript, to
the Provincetown Fine Arts Work Center, the Arizona Commission
on the Arts, and the National Endowment, *plus* sundry friends and
publishers.

Each of the book's four parts has its own epigraph, so we know
the poet has read Franz Kafka, Umberto Eco, Rumi, Van Morrison,
and Wallace Stevens. His manner is artfully tousled, like Raab's, with
lots of "sort of's" and "kind of's" (know what I mean?), and his
matter the lure of self-destruction. The title poem describes, with
gossipy relish, how his father "hail[ed] disaster like a cab," and sees
a similar cloud looming over his future:

> Like a smudge on the horizon. Like a black spot
> on the heart. How one day soon
> I might take this nervous paradise,
>
> bone and muscle of this extraordinary life,
> and with one deliberate gesture,
> like a man stepping on a stick,
> break it into halves. But less gracefully
>
> than that. I think there must be something wrong
> with me, or wrong with strength, that I would
> break my happiness apart
> simply for the pleasure of the sound.
> The sound the pieces make. What is wrong
>
> with peace? I couldn't say.
> But, sweet ruin, I can hear you.

There is always the desire.
Always the cloud, suddenly present
and willing to oblige.

That's a fair sample of both Hoagland's vices and his virtues. It's lazy poetry. The lines and the stanzas break only so that the page may look like a poem. Sentences are kept as simple as possible by frequent recourse to repetition. Such metaphor as the poet allows himself is Tin Pan Alley boilerplate. The interest of the poems is entirely anecdotal. Reading them is like listening in on someone who's mastered the art of group therapy. He has some good stories to tell and he's *vulnerable* to just that degree that can win the approbation of his peers. Better yet, he's got a sense of humor and, when that fails, a winning smile. One can look forward to his next book of poetry in much the same way one follows the life history of a distant relative, whom one visits at intervals of five or ten years, time enough to make out the exact size and shape that the smudge on the horizon has become.

The Palms, Charlie Smith's third collection of poems, did not win any prizes, but his 1987 collection, *Red Roads,* was selected for the National Poetry Series and won the Great Lakes College Association for New Poets award. He has also written four novels. A year younger than Raab, Smith seems older by two or three lifetimes. His poems, more ambitious and accomplished, are also more predictable by virtue of their successful emulation of approved models.

Like Hoagland, Smith likes to exhibit the family skeletons. In the first poem in the book, "My Parents' Wedding," he pictures his parents in Hawaii, making love, "wild for each other's bodies, packed / with energy like the bombs the Japanese planes / twirled through gaps in the windward mountains." The poem, a single page in length, concludes:

Her hair is long and black and ripples like a river
and he is dressed in a white uniform; she is stretching

her body up to take his lips with hers, and it is one week
before he will find her in bed with his best friend.

As a poet, Smith, like Raymond Carver, is at his best when he
is writing short stories that happen to lend themselves to the com-
pressions of poetry. Lacking the armature of plot and character
revelation, he's often at a loss for words. An apostrophe "To Lautreamont" begins, ominously, "I don't know what to say to you" and
maunders a little while in a vaguely lyrical way, like this:

> I forgot you at times, chased wounded birds
> into the thickets, small, yellow-eyed hawks
> and less important creatures, and it was
> not only from despair that I stayed away
> from your palaces: I came to love the woods
> and the small declivities in which cool
> water stood calmly as if sleeping

As if sleeping: that much I believe. But the wounded hawks, the
despair, and the palaces come across as poetry, in the pejorative sense
of that word.

There are enough scandal-peppered, Carverish poems in *The
Palms* to recommend it to those readers who like that vein of workshop poetry, but I cite the lines from "To Lautreamont" by way of
reemphasizing the artistry of Hollander and Updike, who know how
to write the kind of poem that Smith here hazily, lazily aspires to—
the poem of lyric afflatus. It's a skill that can be learned—but not by
those who are always away from the palace.

POETRY ROUNDUP

Imperfect Thirst
by Galway Kinnell Houghton Mifflin $19.95

Worshipful Company of Fletchers
by James Tate ECCO $20.00

Sunday Skaters
by Mary Jo Salter KNOPF $20.00

Winter Numbers and *Selected Poems, 1965–1990*
by Marilyn Hacker NORTON $17.95 AND $22.00

Late Empire
by David Wojahn UNIVERSITY OF PITTSBURGH $22.95 CLOTH,
$19.95 PAPER

The Glass Hammer: A Southern Childhood
by Andrew Hudgins HOUGHTON MIFFLIN $18.95

And For Example
by Ann Lauterbach PENGUIN $14.95 PAPER

The Darker Face of the Earth: A Verse Play
by Rita Dove STORY LINE $10.95

Firekeeper: New and Selected Poems
by Pattiann Rogers MILKWEED $12.95 PAPER

Selected Poems
by C. K. Williams FARRAR, STRAUS & GIROUX $22.00

READERS WITH ONLY a casual, or dutiful, interest in poetry seek out poets they can be comfortable with. Shades of the schoolhouse begin to close round such readers when poems require too much deciphering. So, according to their temperaments, they will gravitate to poets of amiability or moral earnestness, whose work they will reward with a knowing chuckle or an approving nod.

Among contemporary poets few can rival Galway Kinnell for sheer amiability. The press kit accompanying his twelfth collection, *Imperfect Thirst,* declares, "One of the foremost performers on the poetry circuit, Kinnell inevitably draws enormous crowds with his readings." He is a Pulitzer winner, a MacArthur fellow, and the poet laureate of Vermont, where Hugh Schultz, who owns the Wheelock Village Store, has saluted the poet as "a hometown body" and "a heckuva nice guy, real easy going, low-key." If ever a poet had to be found to endorse a new brand of bran flakes, here is the man.

In the world according to Kinnell death is, unproblematically, an aspect of life in Vermont.

> In the other animals the desire to die comes when existing
>   wears out existence.
> In us this desire can come too early, and we kill ourselves,
>   or it may never come, and we have to be dragged away.
> Not many are able to die well, not even Jesus going back
>   to his father.
> And yet dying gets done—and Eddie Jewell coming up
>   the road with his tractor in the back of a truck and
>   seeing an owl lifting its wings as it alights on the ridge-
>   pole of that red house, Galway, will know that now it
>   is you being accepted back into the family of mortals.
>   "The Biting Insects"

One might ask of such a death where its sting is, but surely a poet is entitled to imagine his own death in whatever terms he likes. There is nothing wrong with being comfy. Comfy feels good, and it is Kinnell's mission as a poet to share his good feelings with his readers, as

when at the close of another poem, "The Music of Poetry," Kinnell
finds himself.

> ... here in St. Paul, Minnesota, where I lean
> at a podium trying to draw my talk to a close,
> or a time zone away on Bleecker Street in New York,
> where only minutes ago my beloved may have
> put down her book and drawn up her eiderdown
> around herself and turned out the light—
> now, causing me to garble a few words
> and tangle my syntax, I imagine I can hear
> her say my name into the slow waves
> of the night and, faintly, being alone, sing.

If Kinnell's amiability is a late-night snack of milk and cookies,
James Tate's *Worshipful Company of Fletchers,* which won the 1994
National Book Award for Poetry, is a whole box of Little Debbie
Snack Cakes. Kinnell was born in 1927, Tate in 1943—a generation
gap that is reflected in their divergent sense of a becoming diffidence.
Each approaches his audience aiming to reassure them that the poet
is no stuffed shirt or fruitcake but a regular kind of guy. In Kinnell's
case this doesn't rule out a degree of relaxed dignity and old-fashioned
lyricism. For Tate poems must eschew the poetical altogether. His
esthetic is one of false-naive candors and surrealistic whimsies. He is
an underground cartoonist without portfolio, as in these opening lines
of "Jim Left the Pet Cemetery with a Feeling of Disgust."

> We hope to avoid everlasting mistakes.
> We had a custom-made coffin for the boa.
> It was fifty times longer than a pencil box.
> As for the parakeet, she fit inside a snowball.
> Music played, *Jim's Total Health Book* was read.
> "Mind your eggs," was all it said.
> Jim walked around the snowfield and photographed eggs.
> We installed a birdfeeder over the gravestone.
> The deceased seemed pleased.

A woman no one knew tried to buy socks from everybody.
She said, "This is a town made out of nothing,"
and no one disagreed. Dagwood drew faces on the eggs.

This is to the poetry of the academy as *Beavis and Butt-Head* is to
prime-time sitcoms, an artificial burp whose artful subtext is the suggestion that good table manners are arbitrary and undemocratic; that
serious poetry is equally silly; that, just like Dylan said, everybody
must get stoned.

If Kinnell is a cup of mulled cider and Tate a toke on a sixties
bong, Mary Jo Salter is an above-average Beaujolais nouveau. She has
yet to win a Pulitzer, but she surely will. Already she's had fellowships
from the NEA, the Guggenheim, and the Ingram Merrill Foundation.
Her poems regularly grace the pages of *The New Yorker,* and were
they paintings they would be just at home in the interiors we may
glimpse in its ads. When Salter looks about for a metaphor, it often
takes the form of domestic appurtenances. A cloud becomes "a rough-
hewn rug of nubbled shearling, thrown / perilously near the sun, as
if on / the floor before a fire." In Iceland rain and hail fall together
"as if from one combined / salt and pepper shaker." Most telling is
the metamorphosis noted in "Boulevard du Montparnasse":

> Once, in a doorway in Paris, I saw
> the most beautiful couple in the world.
> They were each the single most beautiful thing in the
> world.
> She would have been sixteen, perhaps; he twenty.
> Their skin was the same shade of black: like a shiny Stein-
> way.
> And they stood there like the four-legged instrument
> of a passion so grand one could barely imagine them
> ever working, or eating, or reading a magazine.
> Even they could hardly believe it.

In its rapt estheticizing of *les Nègres* this is more French than all
Gaul, where blacks signify, in the cabarets of Montparnasse, the jun-

gly side of love. Surely, Salter's beast with four legs is a lineal descendant of Josephine Baker. Were Salter to have seen the same couple in a doorway in Harlem, would they have shone like a Steinway, and would her inability to imagine them "ever working, or eating, or reading a magazine" have had the same pastoral quality?

Class distinctions are the great dividing line in American poetry, all the more divisive for being, officially, invisible. Readers attuned to the genteel decorums of Salter's poetry would gravely resent questioning the privileges she enjoys with such a patrician grace. One's class, like one's color, is a fact of life, not to be altered but rather accepted, as Salter does, with demure thanks and occasional moments of dread. Salter says as much herself in her "Letter from America":

> ... A cozy life, and safe—
> we still have Avon ladies, scout troops, still
> let in a man who claims to want to check
> a meter in the cellar. But hop into
> the car, and five miles south it's something else.
> Boarded-up windows. Crack vials and broken glass.
> An old mill town, now poor and Puerto Rican
> mostly, though to us they may as well
> be ghosts....

The same ghosts, and others closer to home, haunt *Winter Numbers,* the latest collection from Marilyn Hacker, which has been released in conjunction with her *Selected Poems, 1965–1990.* Among the poems in the latter, admirable book are many that celebrate those pleasures of hearth and home, including the bedroom, that are Salter's customary environs. Hacker's poems in this vein exhibit both a greater gusto and a higher poetic polish, to that degree that the poet's gifts are more in evidence than her good breeding. Indeed, in her novelistic sonnet sequence, *Love, Death, and the Changing of the Seasons* (which has not been excerpted for the *Selected Poems*), Hacker's erotic (and culinary) adventures are chronicled with a lip-smacking candor that has made it a landmark of lesbian literature. If only the book had been funded by the NEA, it would surely have won for her the most excited condemnations of Jesse Helms and his ilk.

Winter Numbers represents a darker soulscape. She has had breast cancer, surgery, and chemotherapy. Many friends have died— from AIDS, cancer, and suicide. She confronts her trials and losses as best she can—with stoicism; with a muted and sometimes scatter-shot anger (how *ethically* cognate are AIDS, cancer, and the Holocaust as enemies of life?); and with an unfailing mastery of syntax. In the last particular she demonstrates how rhyme and meter may be not only a refuge but a strength, for the habit of thinking enforced by formal poetry, with a respect for contingency, paradox, and nuance, is of value not simply in dealing with a complex rhyme-scheme but in being able to treat of matters that are, in their nature, turbulent and destabilizing. In the Horatian ode, "Against Elegies," that leads off the book, Hacker bears witness "for my own dead and dying," commemorating the deaths of her peers, while noting, ruefully, how "irremediable death is farther away from them," i.e., from "my old friends, my new friends who are old, or older, sixty, seventy . . ."

> . . . they seem to hold
> it at bay better than the young-middle-aged
> whom something, or another something, kills
> before the chapter's finished, the play staged.
> The curtains stay down when the light fades.

"Against Elegies" is one of those rare poems in which a poet's sorrow and a public occasion find perfect congruence. There are many other poems in the book almost as perdurable, one of which, "Elysian Fields," offers an instructive contrast to Salter's averted gaze before similar street scenes. After a closely observed inventory of venders and the wares they've spread on a Broadway sidewalk, Hacker points her moral in quietly underplayed couplets:

> . . . What we meant by "poor,"
> when I was twenty, was a tenement

with clanking pipes and roaches; what we meant
was up six flights of grimed, piss-pungent stairs,
four babies and a baby-faced welfare
worker forbidden to say "birth control."
I was almost her, on the payroll
of New York State Employment Services
—the East 14th Street Branch, whose task it was
to send day workers, mostly Black, to clean
other people's houses. Five-fifteen
and I walked east, walked south, walked up my four
flights. Poor was a neighbor, was next door,
is still a door away. The door is mine.
Outside, the poor work Broadway in the rain.
The cappuccino drinkers watch them pass
under the awning from behind the glass.

David Wojahn's poems in *Late Empire* bear an almost parodic
resemblance to Hacker's, in that they unite a penchant for strict form
with a simmering political correctitude that, in the case of Wojahn's
collection, seems almost encyclopedic in its outrage. In the course of
the ten poems that comprise Part I of the book: "A skinhead waves
a broken bottle at / a scared Bengali kid" ("Late Empire"); Dutch
sailors hunt dodos to extinction, and grade school children are herded
under their desks for a cold war–air raid drill ("Extinctions"); an
abortion clinic worker is stoned by a mob of protesters ("Clamor"); a
guileless Polish immigrant removes asbestos under the aegis of mob
contractors ("Hive Keepers"); the poet as a child discovers his father's
stash of porn ("My Father's Pornography"); more porn, this time
fueling the random gunfire rebel forces in Luanda in 1975 ("Homage to Ryszard Kapuscinski"); a Boston cop cudgels two fighting
swans to death with "blow after blow after blow after blow" ("Vid-
eotape of Fighting Swans, Boston Public Gardens"); a concentration
camp prisoner is beaten to death ("Xerox of a Photograph of Bergen-
Belsen"); and at a city beach a "doctor/lawyer/investment banker"
scores crack from "a black guy" ("Human Form"). Ten poems, ten
different buttons pushed.

The next two parts of the book are sonnet sequences—one set fairly strict, one sonnetary in length only—in which the poet tries to come to terms with his memories of his working-class parents. Unfortunately, compassion is not Wojahn's strong suit, and what comes across is less an adult poet's reconciling vision than a teenager's unrelenting resentments. Wojahn has a knack for poetry of high dudgeon, but in *Late Empire* he lacks the anecdotal and imaginative focus that distinguished the poems in *Mystery Train* (1990), particularly the series of imagined rock 'n' roll vignettes that form the memorable title sequence.

The quality specifically missing from *Late Empire* is the basis of Andrew Hudgins's conspicuous success in *The Glass Hammer,* a verse memoir of the poet's childhood, which Wojahn himself has reviewed in *Poetry* (January 1995), where he notes that Hudgins writes about "a distant father and alcoholic mother straight from central casting"—parents, in that respect, just like his own. But what a difference in their portraiture. While Wojahn portrays his parents at moments of emblematic anomie ("Her gin / Glass sweating on the table, I watch her doze, / The book dropped to the floor." Or, of his father: "Just an arm now, lifting bourbon / To the disembodied mouth. . . . "), Hudgins is an inspired gossip, zooming in on the telling details, the anecdote at once particular and universal, as when his nightmarish Granny Raines plants her kiss of death on his toddler lips. Sometimes he simply offers a catalogue of family catchphrases, or jokes, or, as here, "Threats and Lamentations":

> I'll jerk a knot in your tail, boy.
> Jack's staring at me. He's touching me.
> Mom, George is breathing on my face.
> What *am* I going to do with you?
> Go shake the dew off your lily.
> We won't be stopping every five yards
> for you to pee. Don't try me, boy. . . .

Again and again, Hudgin's instinct for buried psychic treasure would trigger congruent memories of my own childhood, an effect that Wojahn's reminiscences never had, even though we both grew up in Minnesota with similar social backgrounds. Hudgins is southern in that enviable sense that imparts to the work of Eudora Welty or Carson McCullers a cruel humor and linguistic crackle that derives (as do those lines above) from a *community* of, if you'll forgive the pun, wise crackers. One can imagine *his* relatives, even the fearsome Granny Raines, reading his poems avidly, resenting them bitterly, and laughing aloud from start to finish. For Hudgins is very funny, one might even say mercilessly. (Wojahn writes, reprovingly, "Sometimes these gestures make us wince.") One splendid poem, "The Needs of the Joke Teller," recounts, as Wojahn has it, "an interminable string of singularly non-PC (and often singularly unfunny) entries from the Hudgins Joke Book." He just doesn't *get* it, though Hudgins's poem goes out of its way to explain:

> Punch lines are cheerful bullies. They trip
> the taboos, knock them to the dirt,
> sit on them and tickle them
> until the unwilling laughter begs
> in tears, for mercy. That's why, at sixteen,
> this was my favorite joke: . . .

It is for Hudgins to tell you the rest. Readers who can relish ribaldry without experiencing PC guilt or watch a good sitcom without worrying that their neighbors might think them lowbrow will have a ball with *The Glass Hammer*.

Ann Lauterbach lives in another universe, far from rage or pain or unwonted mirth; a place stripped bare of furniture and history and all other vulgar points of reference. A philosophical universe where the big epistemological questions get asked over and over again: What is real? Who am I? What's happening here?

> Then the real is a convincing show? Of course
> the beam looks real, but is more melancholy
> an inhalation of breath moving across

to a charged little image.
It's like looking at a forest
through the eyes of a needle
        "For Example (5): Song of the Already Sung"

A literalist might want to ask what kind of beam moves its melancholy breath across charged little images (of what?), before having to deal with the question of how the real-seeming beam resembles a forest seen through the eye of a needle. To such a literalist the poet of *And For Example* has this to say:

upon the asylum/of course/ into something/for
repressively/of patients/to five or six hundred
of that sort/on the edge/on all sides
from the semantic/against moral treatment/with it

Of course! This is that on-the-edge, with-it poetry that works by erasure and fragmentation, and, in the words of Lauterbach's leading blurb writer and role model, John Ashbery, "goes straight to the elastic, infinite core of time." Does that make it clearer? No? Then, let Bin Ramke, another blurbist, explain: "Ann Lauterbach works at an intersection between the esthetic and the activist. Her poetry makes the material world a part of the grand glamour of dangerous words." A privilege that the material world has been longing to attain ever since the elastic, infinite core of time began.

If that seems flippant or lacking in respect, let me note, as a matter of plain fact, that Lauterbach is an official MacArthur genius and the head of the writing faculty in the MFA program at Bard College.

Rita Dove can trump that: she is the poet laureate of the United States, not to mention the winner of the Pulitzer Prize for *Thomas and Beulah* (1986). Her current offering, *The Darker Face of the Earth: A Verse Play,* is a recension of the Oedipus legend set in South Carolina in the days of slavery. Am ambitious undertaking, all the more so in that it can't help but challenge comparison to one of the most remarkable theatrical successes of the 1980s, Lee Breuer's and Bob

Telson's musical, *The Gospel at Colonus,* not to mention the challenge to such translators and adapters of Sophocles as Yeats, Cocteau (twice), and Fitzgerald.

In the event, Dove's play is so wanting in theatrical imagination and poetic vigor that, competitively speaking, it doesn't even leave the gate. A *Booklist* reviewer quoted on the back cover claims that this is "a classic tragedy, in blank verse," but it evidences no closer acquaintance with Sophocles' original than might be gathered from a paragraph of plot synopsis, nor is it in blank verse, but rather in the laziest sort of free verse—at once short-winded and overblown. Here is how Augustus, Dove's Oedipal hero, raises the banner of revolt:

> That's all right, old man;
> I have no quarrel with you.
> You've fought your battle and now
> you just want to live out your life
> in peace. But there's a new breed
> growing up in this New World—
> and if the white folks don't
> give us our freedom, we'll fight for it!

And here is the climax of the action, the moment when the Jocasta figure is compelled to reveal to her son and paramour the secret of his birth:

> Haven't you figured it out yet?
> Yes, Louis did take to slave girls;
> ask any of them. Diana has his eyes.
> But you—
> AUGUSTUS: Diana my sister?
> AMALIA:—you are not his son!
> Hector knew;
> that's why he went to the swamp.
> And I never touched him again.
> (AUGUSTUS looks slowly, desperately at her.)

Now do you understand?
I—am—your—mother!
   (bursts into wild laughter)
Your mother!
   (begins to reel through the room, laughing incessantly)
Your mother!
AUGUSTUS: NO!

Finally, two volumes—a Selected, and a New and Selected—that will commend themselves not only to thrifty readers but to those who prefer poetry that ventures beyond the perimeters of a poet's private life and daily weathers. Such distillations of an entire career (to date) ought to receive much more than a passing commendation; a Festschrift might be more in keeping, not only for Pattiann Rogers and C. K. Williams but, as well, for Marilyn Hacker's *Selected,* noted above. On the other hand, for readers who have missed a matured author's earlier harvests, by dint of inattention or simply youth, what a smorgasbord such books can be!

Pattiann Rogers writes in that richest indigenous vein of American poetry that combines scientific discourse (particularly natural history) with a sublime, raptured egotism, a tradition stemming from Emerson and Whitman and continued in our time by poets like A. R. Ammons and Albert Goldbarth (Who appears among the poet's blurb writers on the back cover of *Firekeeper*). If one excludes the prose writer, Annie Dillard, Rogers is the most notable contemporary female writer in that tradition.

Her poems are not so hyperkinetic as Goldbarth's, not so apt to carom from one end of the galaxy to the other in a few lines. They lack the rigor of Ammons's analytic discourse, but they make up for that with almonds, currants, and other savory sweetnesses, as in these opening stanzas from "The Power of Toads," which takes its cue from Marianne Moore's prescription for poetry:

The oak toad and the red-spotted toad love their love
In a spring rain, calling and calling, breeding
Through a stormy evening clasped atop their mates.

Who wouldn't sing—anticipating the belly pressed hard
Against a female's spine in the steady rain
Below writhing skies, the safe moist jelly effluence
Of a final exaltation?

There might be some toads who actually believe
That the loin-shaking thunder of the banks, the evening
Filled with damp, the warm softening mud and rising
Riverlets are the facts of their own persistent
Performance. Maybe they think that when they sing
They sing more than songs, creating rain and mist
By their voices, initiating the union of water and dusk,
Females materializing on the banks shaped perfectly
By their calls.

Of all the collections reviewed here, C. K. William's *Selected Poems* was the one I kept returning to most often, as I might phone a friend who's always home, always welcoming, and always has a new angle on What's Happening. Williams's signature long, long (eight-to ten-beat) lines and looping syntax seem to be generated more by a liking for lucidity than by a lyrical impulse, yet one never feels, as one does with Kinnell or Hudgins, that his poems are simply inspired conversation. They have the force, rather, of the best journalism—human interest stories, editorials, news flashes from around the world and across the street, all of it rendered in a level tone that one is surprised to find so surprising.

Here was my relation with the woman who lived all last
                    autumn and winter day and night
on a bench in the Hundred and Third Street subway sta-
                    tion until finally one day she vanished:
                              . . .
we regarded each other, scrutinized one another: me shyly,
                    obliquely, trying not to be furtive;
she boldly, unblinkingly, even pugnaciously; wrathfully
                    even, when her bottle was empty.

So begins "Thirst," a poem that puzzles over "the dance of our glances" for six more stanzas that are notable less for their rhetorical energy (though it suffices) than for the poet's determination to imagine an inner life for a figure we all know and dread to think of. For Salter she would be a "ghost" among the crack vials of drive-thru slums; for Hacker and Wojahn a comrade at the barricades. For Williams she is one among literally hundreds of characters whom he has imagined as intensely as Pattiann Rogers has imagined her red-spotted toads.

The dramatic gift is not a requirement for writing good poetry. Some poets, like Ann Lauterbach, lack it entirely; their mental horizon stops at their own hairlines. Others, like Rita Dove, aspire to drama, but have no gift for speaking in other voices than their own, so that "characters" can speak only in the clockwork accents of received wisdom.

But those poets fortunate enough to possess a dramatic gift, like Williams or Robert Browning or Richard Howard, live in a larger and more blessed universe, a fact reflected in the largeness, psychological complexity, and variety of their oeuvres. "Thirst" is a single poem among some 150 that bulk out 279 pages of a book that is most notable for its social and discursive range. Poetry, Williams would seem to be saying, between his lines, can be *about* something. It can matter.

REVIEWING POETRY:
A RETROSPECT

THERE IS A good reason most reviews of poetry are so dull, and it's not just because the same can be said for most poetry. It's true that review editors tend to assign the books of dull poets to critics of congruent dullness, but even zany poets are likely to inspire dull reviews.

The reason is this: poets are regarded as handicapped writers whose work must be treated with a tender condescension, such as one accords the athletic achievements of basketball players confined to wheelchairs. Poets don't make the best-seller lists; they don't expect to earn a living from their poetry. Their jobs at the fringe of a bloated educational bureaucracy benefit neither the larger economy nor the little commonweal of poetry. Rather, like other forms of "special education," poetry workshops exist to foster a self-esteem that, in its fullest flower, verges on delusions of reference.

The woeful "marginalization" of poets has nowhere been celebrated with more heartfelt self-pity or greater conviction of self-righteousness than by Adrienne Rich in her book-length manifesto, *What Is Found There* (Norton, 1993). "Poets in the United States," she writes, "have either some kind of private means, have held full-time, consuming jobs, or have chosen to work in low-paying, part-time sectors of the economy. . . . " Indeed; and what options does that omit? Only dereliction, crime, and prison. In addition to having to earn a living, poets have also to contend with "the shrinkage of arts funding, the censorship-by-clique, the censorship by the Right, the censorship by distribution." Add all these forms of hardship and censorship together and the grim outlook is this: *some poets may not be published!*

Rich's sense of entitlement is unusual only in her having given it expression at book length. Her attitude of sanctimonious *ressentiment* is typical of the professional poet and, by now, so familiar as to constitute a comic archetype as recognizable as Blond Starlet, Redneck Demagogue, or Computer Nerd. It is in the nature of such comic figures that they are deaf to argument and beyond reformation. Mr. Macawber will always be Mr. Macawber. The only way to deal with such people is not to deal with them at all.

And that is how the larger intellectual culture has learned to deal with poetry. Recently I've had a ringside seat at the process when I served on the board of the National Book Critics Circle. Some of the most articulate and discerning members of the board, when confronting the prospect of selecting the shortlist in poetry, recused themselves, not from any lack of poetic responsiveness, but from a sense that poetry has succeeded as a separatist movement—a poor country that has achieved a Pyrrhic independence and survives only with the assistance of relief organizations. In a postcolonial era outsiders have learned to adopt an attitude of benign indifference and noninterference.

While poets must openly protest their "marginalization," they have learned to reap the benefits of a cultural ecosystem in which their behavior (what they write) is, officially, invisible, for if no one ever says that a particular book is insipid, or inept, or downright stupid, it may be accounted, in an egalitarian way, as good as any other. And stupid books, like stupid children, must never be berated. If a smart poet has been put in the position of having to speak of such a book publically (as teachers must, when ex-students and former colleagues appear with books in need of an authenticating blurb), there is a language of coded equivocations. Stanley Plumly is a master of this art: "With each new book," he blurbs, "[X] has moved more inward, toward the clarifying dark and its complexities. Her native ... landscapes are now as much a part of her imaginative solitudes and isolations as are the figures of otherness that populate them, whether those figures are personal or historical. Her sense of her subject is like her sense of time: projection, identification, and a complete taking-on of the moment." All that's left out from this magistral persiflage is praise for the author's risk-taking.

"Risk-taking" is my favorite blurb-writing maneuver, since rarely is the risk being taken ever specified. The suggestion is that the poet is somehow a member of that international band of persecuted geniuses on whose behalf PEN sends off protests to the dictatorial regimes of third world countries. Usually, of course, the opposite is true, for the political opinions expressed in the poems of reputedly "risk-taking" poets tend to be such as to make university tenure more likely. Is the risk, then, of exposing their soul's secret wound, or a family skeleton, to the view of a reprobating mob? That's not likely either, for the crimes that poets cop to in their confessional poems are never felonies but rather such matter as one brings to a group therapy session in the hope of enlisting sympathy or, at least, interest. Might the risk then be of a formal nature? Theoretically, yes, but in that case the risk courted would be overt failure, which, like a figure skater taking a nose dive, is easy to pity but hard to praise. Mediocre poets usually have the good sense to write in a style that is flat, plain, and as little "risky" as possible.

> All that's needed
> after all
> is a way of breaking
> the line so as to
> create a slight
> syncopation in
> the underlying flow
> of what is really
> ordinary prose.
> Look at any grocery list
> long enough & a sonic

pattern begins to
emerge. Erase
some of the connecting
lines, throw in
a metaphor or two,
and bake. That's what
we call
taking a risk.

Theoretically, reviewing and blurb-writing are distinct genres, but in practice they can be distinguished chiefly by length. Reviewers employ the same boilerplate praises for the same politic and prudential motives. In any case, most venues that do review poetry accord reviewers only enough time for a handshake of official acknowledgment, as at a presidential banquet. One is apprised of the poet's name, address, race, gender preference, family background, recent travel, hobbies and special interests, if any. Receiving such a perfunctory review is like having one's picture in the school yearbook: it is an honor that is also considered (even by those to whom it is denied) an entitlement. To be reviewed is the poet's right; ask Adrienne Rich if that's not so.

It goes without saying that the review to which every poet is entitled is a good review. A bad review is just another form of censorship—censorship by judgment, by taste, by arbitrary standards of so-called excellence. The least deviation from the unstinting can earn a reviewer flaming vituperation.

For instance, in reviewing Brad Leithauser's second collection of poems, *Cats of the Temple* (see p. 154), I characterized him as "the prom king of American poetry," a reflection less on the quality of his verse than on his then position as the novice Most Likely to Succeed, a position that a longish self-portrait in his first book fairly trumpeted. The epithet so rankled Leithauser that he revenged himself by inventing a character, little Tommy Disch, in his novel *Hence,* who commits suicide by drowning himself in a toilet bowl. The revenger's editor at Knopf felt obliged to ask my permission for Leithauser to parade his wit in this way, which I readily granted, both as a First

Amendment absolutist and as one who values, and collects, curiosities of literature. I understand that a first edition of *Hence,* with my signature, commands a fair price in the rare book market.

I had not thought my review of Leithauser amounted to a pan, much less a provocation to hysteria. But poets are uncommonly sensitive. When I wrote of *Poets for Life,* an anthology of poems on the theme of AIDS, for *The Nation* (November 27, 1989; see p. 158), I explicitly exempted it from being "reviewed." Despite a great many poems that were shrill or bathetic, I remarked that "I can't imagine any critic considering *Poets for Life* as suitable grist for the critical mill," and likened it to the AIDS quilt—another "metaphor for the mass grave the plague is busy filling." This warranted a three-page letter of denunciation from one of the book's contributors that began: "Much like the critic John Simon, whose career is predicated upon self-hatred and self-loathing projected neurotically upon some very worthy, creative people, your recent poetry review smacks of hatred and self-aggrandizement only a prig could muster up and justify.... Secondly, you're a condescending, downright angry critic—perhaps because you're unable to create in your own right?"

If my declining to review the book warranted this one-man ACT UP demonstration, imagine the response an actual pan might provoke. As it happens, the same review was leading up to an actual pan, of Michael Ryan's *God's Hunger* (see p. 159), which led the author to write a letter to the editor protesting that I had misrepresented both the book and the poet. I disagreed, but in this case the poet under review had the last word, for in the course of time Ryan was awarded the Lenore Marshall/Nation Prize for Poetry in the amount of $10,000, an honor for which I like to think I am as directly responsible as any of the three judges, Sydney Lea, Liz Rosenberg, or William Pritchard. Even so, I'm still waiting for a bread-and-butter note.

My favorite *cri de coeur* was that of Marjorie Perloff, whose collection of poetry criticism, *Poetic License,* I reviewed in the *Los Angeles Times Book Review* (May 27, 1990; see p. 162), a review in which I dismissed her championing of the "language poets" as a kind of opportunism, those poets being all that remains of a programmatically obscurantist avant-garde still in need of critical authentification. Perloff wrote in protest to the *Los Angeles Times*: "I find Disch's explanation wonderfully absurd. For, to paraphrase Gertrude Stein (whom Disch calls in a characteristically vulgar phrase, the 'wellspring of [my] aesthetic'), there's a lot of *there* there—a *there* that, after all, includes Disch's own poetry, a poetry that, alas, I have never so much as noticed as being *there*.

"Perhaps that simple little fact has something to do with his venom."

She may never believe this, but I will, even so, protest that until I was asked to review her book, I'd never heard of Marjorie Perloff and so could not take great umbrage that she'd not heard of me.

The world is larger than any of us can quite take in, and even the little world of poetry has thousands of inhabitants, each of them convinced that someone who dislikes or reprehends their work must be motivated by a personal vendetta or a deep-rooted enmity toward what is true and beautiful. On an earlier occasion, in a piece in the *Poetry Project Newsletter* with the portentous title, "An Inclusion of Vectors Inexplicable to Syntax," Perloff speculated that two critics who have spoken ill of her own pet poets must have been motivated by their failure to find employment at a university and their resultant bitterness toward their tenured betters. It escaped her notice that both these critics were enjoying thriving careers outside academia, and so did not need to obey the injunction, "Network or die."

But why, if I am not a failed aspirant to a teaching job, or a poet embittered by Ms. Perloff's inattention, or a self-loathing, priggish, condescending, and downright angry critic on a par with John Simon—why do I take the trouble to write unkind reviews of poets who, after all, are human beings, and whose feelings I must know will be hurt, when I might as easily say nothing at all and let time accomplish its own unfailing work of criticism, covering dull books and dead poets with their allotted portion of dust?

In part the answer to this may be found in other letters that those same reviews have provoked, letters from writers offering applause and agreement, which confirmed my own sense that I've been able to say things that were oft thought but never, or hardly ever, expressed.

The larger value of negative criticism—beyond the sigh of relief that "At last someone has said it"—is that, without it, any expression of delight or enthusiasm is under suspicion of being one more big hug in that special-education classroom where poets minister to each other's need for self-esteem. There are multitudes of mediocre poets, but there are also, among those multitudes, more than a sufficiency of Olympic-class 8s, 9s, and, according to one's lights, even a few 10s.

I have been reading contemporary poetry for most of my adult life, but my sense of "contemporary" in poetry encompasses the past twenty or thirty years. Except for the work of a few favorite poets and close friends I usually felt no urgency to read each season's crop as it reached the bookstores. When I began to review poetry, intermittently, in the late seventies, first in the *TLS,* then in a variety of American venues, I began to learn what I'd been missing—some few excellent poets and, no less awesome in its way, the Great Plains of plain-spoken, well-meaning, mind-numbing mediocrity. Two years of service on the board of the National Book Critics Circle expanded that vista, for board members are expected to read through the entire gamut of potential candidates in at least one award category. And so I actually *read* a significant amount of all the poetry that would ordinarily have flowed by, unnoticed, in the middle distance. In the light of that experience, poetry reviews that had once seemed only innocuous or bromidic came to appear mendacious in a systematic way, like the false bookkeeping records of a well-ensconced embezzler.

When bad poetry is valued at the going rate of good poetry, Gresham's law is bound to kick in. Bad poetry will drive out good. For bad poets are likely to be capable careerists, who will have the good sense, when they act in some related bureaucratic capacity, such as judging a contest or hiring a teaching candidate, to favor those as ill favored as themselves. In effect, Cinderella's stepsisters are in charge of the invitation list to the ball.

As that fairy tale makes clear, in the long run Cinderella—good poetry—will triumph, Gresham's law notwithstanding. Her dainty foot will slip into the glass slipper of valid criticism effortlessly. As for her stepsisters . . .

But let us say no more of them. In the happy ending Cinderella is united with Prince Charming, the Poet with the Ideal Reader, and that's how book reviewing is supposed to work.